D0864170

W/10/2014
R.L.S.

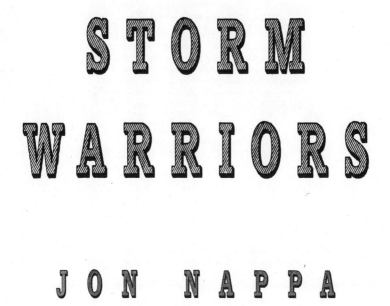

STORM WARRIORS

JON NAPPA

NAVPRESS

OUR GUARANTEE TO YOU

For a free catalog
of NavPress books & Bible studies call
1-800-366-7788 (USA) or 1-800-839-4769 (Canada).

www.navpress.com

NavPress
P.O. Box 35001
Colorado Springs, Colorado 80935

ISBN-13: 978-1-60006-172-1
ISBN-10: 1-60006-172-9

Cover design by studiogearbox.com
Cover images by Arnulf Husmo/Getty, Underwood & Underwood/Corbis, and Veer
Author photo by Julianne

Creative Team: Jeff Gerke, Reagen Reed, Darla Hightower, Arvid Wallen, Kathy Guist

This novel is a work of fiction. Names, characters, places, and incidents are either the product of the author's imagination or are used fictitiously. Any resemblance to actual events, locales, organizations, or persons, living or dead, is entirely coincidental and beyond the intent of either the author or publisher.

Unless otherwise identified, all Scripture quotations in this publication are taken from the HOLY BIBLE: NEW INTERNATIONAL VERSION® (NIV®). Copyright © 1973, 1978, 1984 by International Bible Society. Used by permission of Zondervan Publishing House. All rights reserved.

Containing excerpts from the nonfiction book *Storm Warriors* by Rev. John Gilmore, MA, Macmillan and Co., London, 1875.

Published in association with the literary agency of Leslie H. Stobbe, 300 Doubleday Road, Tryon, NC, 28782.

Library of Congress Cataloging-in-Publication Data
Nappa, Jon, 1958-
  Storm warriors : a novel / Jon Nappa.
    p. cm. -- (Storm warriors series ; bk. 1)
  ISBN 978-1-60006-172-1
  1. Shipwrecks--Fiction. I. Title.
PS3614.A663S76 2008
813'.6--dc22
                        2007033174

Printed in the United States of America

1 2 3 4 5 6 7 8 9 10 / 11 10 09 08

To Joanne Davis

(1954–2007)

A true friend and genuine Storm Warrior

ACKNOWLEDGMENTS

I would like to send many thanks to the fine folks at NavPress for their favor, interest, and commitment to me and *Storm Warriors*. Especial appreciation goes to Kris Wallen for being so kind and supportive. I am indebted to Jeff Gerke, the quintessential editor, and Les Stobbe, my agent, whose wisdom, excellence, and friendship have been invaluable. Deep appreciation goes to Dee Ward, for performing grace while practicing law, and Pat Fiumano, for helping me appreciate great minds from the past.

To Julianne, my Proverbs 31 wife, thank you for your unwavering support and belief. And to my four children, who allowed me to read long passages to them at bedtime and didn't fall asleep, I send bunches of love. Finally, thank you, Mom, for everything.

PART 1

I have acts of daring and determination to relate, done by brave men for which I claim a place amid the records of the bravest, grandest deeds of heroism of the age; a tale to tell which, unless I fail utterly in the telling, must excite sympathy for those in peril. A tale which may well stir, even as a trumpet blast, stout hearts to brave and magnificent deeds.

THE REVEREND JOHN GILMORE

CHAPTER 1

"It's like doing a jig, wouldn't you say?"

Lionel was too startled to answer right away. He and his small family were more focused on maintaining balance than making light.

The captain continued without waiting for a reply, "I call it the salty shuffle!"

A sheet of ocean spray hissed as it blasted over the bow. The ship was bounding down the English Channel to Dover. Lionel's land coach stood lashed upon the main deck, already soaked like a rock on the coast.

His wife, Alicia, and son, Luke, were by his side. The rough action of the sea forced them all to lean and tilt and stutter-step as they watched Captain Horace Beeker whittling a small piece of ivory with a knife that bore his initials. Beeker laughed at his own humor in a voice pitched higher than one would have imagined coming from such a square-shouldered sailor. Although the captain appeared intimidating in size, his voice did much to make him seem friendly.

A few miles away were the headlands of England. They formed a blurred edge upon the horizon as the night advanced. The darkness began to swallow most of the glowing dots of lantern light scattered like flickering stars across the distant land. It was the cloud-streaked moon that provided the light by which the outline of the coast could be seen at all, though a heavy fog was rising and the clouds increasing.

The gusts whipped up the surface waters and spat them over the rail in blasts of frigid ocean spray. As the ship pitched, Lionel nearly slipped, his shiny black boots not at all designed to grip a soaked deck. He was dressed in a fine suit, now drenched, and an outer coat that flapped in the wind like a loose sail. He was thin and fair-skinned and beginning to feel quite cold. His short, neatly trimmed hair was light-colored and fine but well protected under his new derby, which he struggled to keep pressed down upon his head.

He squeezed his wife and son tighter as they clung to the ship's rail. This was the first sailing trip for any of them. He lowered his hand from his hat to grip his wife's shoulder, and his derby blew off. Lionel growled and looked for it but refused to release his protective embrace.

The ship scudded on, crashing through the rough seas with strained bow and then lifting and tilting as the coursing waves lapped it with foam. The captain pointed with his knife in the direction of the distant shoreline. Lionel strained to peer through the thickening fog. He could see nothing but dark shapes within dark shapes. He shouted above the groaning wind and pelting rain, "What is it?"

"The double light!" the captain said. "I know it well!"

Suddenly, a large roller broke over the side and sprayed the small gathering. Lionel's young son wiped his eyes then clung all the harder to his mother's skirt.

"Fear not, Luke," Lionel said with a smile, trying to shield his family with his body. "It's only salt water."

The captain said, "It's my home, it is."

"The sea?" Lionel asked.

"No, I mean the double light. I know its place between the rolls of the land—when you can see it."

"It's where you're from?" Lionel asked, fighting to maintain his balance.

The captain stepped away to peer up at the foremast, then returned to answer. Lionel marveled at how the captain took no assistance from the many rope rails running fore and aft. He somehow maintained his balance just by leaning and stepping.

"It's where I anchor," the captain réplied. "When I can. My house is just below it." He pocketed his knife and cupped his hands around his mouth to shout. "Another reef, lads! Be quick and snappy!" He stepped near to Lionel. "I'm certain me wife and eight urchins are sleeping sound even as we ride the crests."

"We're near a reef?" Lionel asked.

"Eight children!" Alicia said.

"And every one as dear as me eight toes!" the captain said with a laugh. Glancing at some crewmen below, he shouted, "Be mindful the coach!" He turned back to Lionel with a wink. "No worry. She's fixed fine."

"Are we nearing a reef?" Lionel repeated.

"Eight toes?" Luke asked.

"No, no, I meant not that kind of reef," the captain said to Lionel. "We also call it a *reef* when we shorten or trim our sails. The wind has freshened, and too much sail is dangerous. True, there are shifting sand reefs in these parts, but we stay clear."

"Because you know where they are, right?" Lionel asked.

The captain winked again. "I know where they aren't!"

Lionel and his wife laughed at the captain's humor. Lionel looked toward the land coach, only now realizing the danger to his latest achievement. If all worked as planned there would soon be a new line of Lukin coaches traversing not only the city roads but also the country lanes of England.

Luke looked up from the refuge of his mother's skirt. "Eight toes? Don't you have ten?"

The captain laughed and scuffed the boy's hair. "I think you not be wanting to hear that tale, lad."

"But I do," Luke said.

"With your Ma being a nurse and all, you've heard plenty of cutting and mending stories, I'm sure." The captain winked again, more at Lionel and Alicia than their son.

"No! Tell me, sir," Luke pleaded. "Do tell me, please!"

Before the captain could reply, a mountainous wave broke upon the ship, flooding the deck with foam. The wind howled loud and long, suppressing all other sounds. Lionel saw a door on his land coach spring open and slam shut several times. He was certain he could hear the thuds above the storming wind and surf.

A sailor clawed his way along a rope guide to reach the wayward door, every step a struggle to ascend and descend against the pitch and roll of the ship. As he reached the door, a blast of wind blew, and, to Lionel's annoyance, out flew several handbills. One of them plastered itself across the sailor's face. It was a poster depicting the very same coach surrounded by bold black lettering. The word *Lukin* was plainly seen across the bottom. The sailor ripped it off in soaking pieces as more copies swirled about him. He finally reached the land coach and lashed the door shut.

The ship pushed bow first into each wave to bury in the trough then break through with her bowsprit pointing to the stars. The waves washed over her and threatened to carry all away.

The captain appeared to shift into a sober and decisive mind. He yelled commands to sailors, his voice no longer high-pitched but loud and deep. He turned to Lionel and his family and thrust his chin in the direction of the stairs. "It might be best to ride this out below whilst we do what needs doing."

Lionel nodded and lifted his son into his arms. He took Alicia's hand and led them to the main deck below. The wind seemed to be dying down. Lionel felt relieved. He looked aft. Perhaps the captain would ask their return now that the wind had lulled. Lionel made eye contact with him, but Beeker didn't smile. Instead, he looked away to where he had claimed to have seen the double light. When Lionel followed the captain's gaze, for an instant, between the mist and shifting fog, he thought he could see some sort of glow, but then it was gone. Whatever it was, the rising sea blotted it from view.

"Prepare to head up!" the captain shouted to his men.

"No, sir! She'll ride into the Sands then!" James, the first mate, said.

Lionel opened the door to the modified berths below and urged his wife and son to enter. Alicia tugged on his hand but Lionel held back. "I'll be right along." They disappeared below while he stayed at the doorway to observe the captain and mate.

"What are you saying, man? We must head up—*away* from the Sands!"

"Look!" The mate pointed to a light rocking back and forth in the distance.

"A ship?" the captain said. "But how?"

Lionel saw a light he hadn't noticed before. It was near where the captain had been looking and appeared to be a ship a long ways off. It seemed to rock gently and safely.

"In no distress, sir," the mate said. "She must be standing the same course as we intended. The tide has shifted us."

"But I just saw the double light of my home, just there!"

"Sir, did you? Or did you *want* to?"

"Oh, James, you cloud the course." The captain looked again upon the light in motion. "You must be right. Sometimes a man sees only what his heart aches for. All right then, ready to fall off."

James shouted the order, "Prepare to fall off!"

The captain's eyes still searched the mist. "Fall off!"

James repeated the command and headed forward.

The helmsman turned the wheel as others pulled hard on the yards. The ship turned downwind and surged forward, its stern charging through the mounting waves.

Lionel was relieved. He didn't understand sailing, but he knew the captain and mate were in agreement about something important and were taking action. Lionel joined his family below.

⸙

The wind surged, harder than before. The captain held fast to the rail. He strained to peer into the darkness and tilted his head to listen for indications of danger. He looked forward and thought he saw the double light. It flickered in and out of view from the rolling seas in the midst of roving strands of fog and grew fainter in the enveloping dark of night. He rushed to the helmsman. "There!" he pointed. "Do you see it?"

The sailor peered hard. "Aye! But look!"

The captain saw a lone lamp-glow shining to the left of the double light—the same light James had discovered earlier. It motioned to and fro and looked like a masthead light from a vessel rocking atop the sea.

"How can this be?" Beeker shouted. "If that be the double light marking the place near my own home, then only cliffs may stand beside her. What madness is this?"

The wind momentarily halted and allowed him to hear a different sound—the fury of breakers, dead ahead. The captain stepped forward. "Oh, my God."

A voice from the bow shouted, "Breakers ahead! Breakers ahead!"

Suddenly, a dozen men were running everywhere, looking over the sides and shouting reports of what they could determine. The mate rushed to the captain, panic upon his face. "The Goodwin!"

"Down with the helm!" the captain shouted. "Round her to!"

It was too late. The ship lifted on a wave and fell hard upon the Goodwin Sands. The crackling sound of splintering timber pierced the night. A quaking tremor shook the vessel from stem to stern.

Amidst shrieking voices muffled by the blowing gale, green seas suddenly rose to wash over the decks and clear all in their way. From atop the quarterdeck, Captain Beeker watched one of his men wash across the main deck in a flood of ocean foam, followed by the Lukin coach breaking up and losing a wheel. It tumbled behind until both the man and the buggy washed clear over the waist into the churning sea.

"Ship aground! Man overboard!"

A sailor yanked a life ring from off the far side of the deck house and threw it toward his flailing mate. The throw missed. He rushed to the other life ring on the deckhouse but never reached it. Another monster wave washed the crewman overboard.

The belly of the ship flooded fast.

Below deck, Lionel and Luke reached the stairs to stay above the flood. Alicia struggled nearby, clinging to a post. She reached out to her husband.

Broken timbers and bales of cargo floated by as Lionel held

Luke with one arm and reached for his wife's hand with the other. Luke clung to his father's neck but cried for his mother. Lionel could scarcely breathe; Luke was clinging so tightly. He leaned from the steps to reach his wife. He clasped her by the wrist and pulled her to him.

"Thank God, we are safe," Alicia said.

They clambered up the steps and stepped out onto the main deck.

Everything was drenched and dark, rising and falling hard. Timber snapped and the ship shuddered. A turbulent wave broke across the ship, shattered an onboard boat, and carried it away.

Lionel and his family clung to each other and the rope rails. The deck was tilted so sharply that Lionel was terrified his wife and son might slip and fall into the sea. He searched for the captain. Beeker would know what to do.

Lionel found him clinging to the stairway rail leading from the stern to the main deck, not far away. He was struggling to stand, this time making much use of the rails and safety lines.

"Tar barrels!" the captain shouted. "With a will, men! Tar barrels!"

Two sailors lashed a barrel to the main mast and stuffed it with rags and grease. James, the mate, set a torch to it, and up went a fiery blaze.

"Up the masts," the captain cried. "The ship's boat is stove and awash!"

"Captain, what do we do?" Lionel yelled, clinging to his frightened family. They clutched the rope rails near the stairs.

The captain's eyes widened. "Climb! Climb fast!"

Lionel set Luke down and helped his wife climb the stairs.

"No!" Beeker said. "Not the ladder!"

Lionel stopped, suddenly feeling sweaty despite the cold. "Where, then?"

"The mast!"

Lionel looked around. Everything was upset. Ropes ran in mazes, waters rushed with frenzy, and the captain's directions were not specific. *Which mast? How do you climb one?*

He looked at Alicia. She held Luke close as they both clung to Lionel. She lifted her head to look at her husband. Lionel knew she needed him to fix this. He felt ashamed that he had picked this trip to bring them along.

Captain Beeker reappeared. "Quickly! Come with me." Using the safety lines, he helped them scale the steep deck to the ship's far side. He led them to the standing rigging that ran from the ship's side to the high parts of the mainmast. "It's like climbing a ladder," he shouted. "Hand over hand, foot over foot. Each square of rigging is like a step. Hurry!"

The weight and bulk of Alicia's soaked skirts and her obsession with holding Luke made the climb difficult.

Lionel pried his son loose from her and held him. "I've got him. I promise."

The captain climbed up the rigging and reached down for Alicia's hand.

"Go on," Lionel said. "Take it."

Alicia took the captain's hand and ascended.

Lionel lifted Luke overhead. "Hold the rigging. Hold tight, son."

"I've got it," Luke said, his voice quivering.

"Don't let go."

A massive wave slammed against Lionel's left side. He felt his breath rush from him, and the rigging scraped his palms as it ripped from his grasp.

Captain Beeker was aghast. The gargantuan wave had washed his passenger away.

"*Daddy!* Where are you?" The boy dangled from the rigging, his tiny hands gripping hard.

"Luke!" the woman cried, halting her climb and turning back.

"Hold tight!" the captain instructed. "Do not let go."

He climbed down and seized the boy by the wrist. Luke cried for his father, but no answer came except the howling wind. The captain brought the boy to his mother. "Hold on for your lives!"

"Daddy's gone," the boy whimpered.

"Lionel!" Alicia shouted. "Lionel! My love!"

Captain Beeker urged them up the rigging, despite their frantic wails for the missing man.

The storm winds strengthened and the frigid seas leapt upon them. Soaked and weeping, the woman struggled to heave her skirts as she climbed. The boy shivered and sobbed. They climbed as high as they could on the narrow rigging.

The captain looked at the crying lad and thought of his own children. He imagined them laughing as they rushed to the pier to see him coming home. It was a pleasant scene, one that had played out many times before but was unlikely to happen again.

He studied the woman as she pressed tight to the ropes, her eyes red and her lips trembling. She had seemed like an intelligent woman and loving person. All three of his passengers had been kind and courteous. He wondered if his own wife sensed the terrible circumstances he was in.

Timber cracked and lines snapped. Iron clanged. The mast creaked. The ship shifted, and waves attacked from every side. His once-beautiful vessel buckled before his eyes.

Below them, the tar barrel burned brilliantly. He thought it might alert any nearby ships. He doubted any would venture near, but the barrel represented some hope.

The gale increased force and dark clouds settled low. The barrel washed out.

Rain squalls fell harder. Air and sea thickened into one mass of flying, chilling foam. The howling wind spat freezing waters into fits that rose and slapped and dunked the tottering masts. The decks squealed from the pressure.

The boat was half tilted over, its keel battered by fierce waves. The masts tipped sideways until they were only a few feet above the torrent in the midst of high-flying spray. The mighty grip of the sea squeezed and beat the ship against the reef, building tremendous pressure in the hold. The decks ripped at the seams and burst open in random places. Air pockets screeched their escape.

Scattered about the rigging upon the two tottering masts, like fish in a net, were the dark shapes of frightened souls. His crew. They were motionless, chilled to the bone and waiting. Their minds feared, he was sure, while their hands and legs clutched and their hearts beat with desperate hope.

With a thunderous roar, the foremast snapped and fell swiftly over the starboard side into a wilderness of waves and tide. His fine crew, who had been clinging to it, fell into the sea and were buried with a mad rush of waves.

James momentarily retained his hold to some broken parts. The captain struggled to keep his grip while he watched James rush along the angled deck and alongside the deckhouse.

"James!" he cried, knowing he could not help. He watched his friend slide past the deckhouse and into the churning sea. "James!"

It was then that the captain spotted the other passenger, the man named Lionel Lukin. He crouched under the deckhouse, looking right at them, his topcoat flapping crazily.

From his place of temporary shelter, Lionel saw the first mate rush by upon a stew of wreckage as if riding rapids.

"James!" the captain cried.

"Help!" James shouted.

Without thinking, Lionel grabbed a rope hanging from above. He followed its length into the rushing sea to swing out to the drowning man. He failed the attempt, swung backwards, and watched the man wash away.

"Daddy!" Luke cried.

Lionel looked up to see his son drop from his hold on the rigging in a hopeless attempt to reach him.

"No, Luke!"

Alicia cried out and dropped from her hold to go after Luke.

"No!" the captain yelled.

It was too late. Alicia and Luke dropped into the angry seas. The freak action of the waves tossed Alicia to land atop her son. She groped for him.

The sea tossed both of them onto the deck and toward Lionel, and he reached for them, but they were quickly caught in a receding wave that pulled them off the deck and into the sea.

Luke screamed, "Daddy, help me!"

"Alicia! Luke!"

Lionel kicked his feet to swing out toward them, but the line was too short and the wind too strong. The rope spun him in circles. As he twirled, he noticed the remaining life ring on the side of the deckhouse. He exerted every ounce of his strength to swing toward it. He managed to grab hold of it with his feet while keeping an eye on his wife and son.

They were being repeatedly submerged. Each time they rose, first separated then united, they drifted farther away.

"Help us!"

Lionel held the rope with one arm and used his free hand to claw at the ring. He released his leg lock and swung back over the wild seas. He looked for his family but saw nothing except for the dark outlines of waves in wild motion.

He frantically searched the dark ocean swells. In a flash of lightning, he saw them clinging to each other. They rode high atop the crest of a mighty wave several yards away.

"I'm coming!" Lionel shouted.

He released his hold from the rope and dropped into the sea, the life ring around one arm. He removed his topcoat and waistcoat, careful to keep the ring. Another thunderous crack pierced the night and the mizzenmast snapped and fell upon him.

It grazed his shoulder and forced him under. He lost the life ring.

From beneath the turbulent surface, he saw his topcoat floating like a rag doll with broken arms waving to him.

He saw thrashing legs and realized the captain had fallen with the crashing mainmast. Lionel kicked and lunged.

He blasted through the surface of the spastic seas into a tangled mass of rigging complicated by shredded strips of sail. Nearby, the captain was being bullied by waves. They were both encumbered by lines and cables.

"Alicia! Luke!"

Captain Beeker tried to help untangle Lionel, but they both remained in a confusion of wreckage. The lightning flashed again, revealing Alicia and Luke far above, higher than the masts had ever stood, atop an enormous wave. Lionel thrashed to free himself but became increasingly entangled.

"They're in the stream-reach!" the captain yelled.

"What?"

"The stream-reach. No hope. Too powerful—carries everything away. You mustn't try!"

"I must!" Lionel said. He tried to get free but his movement was limited. He saw the life ring and grabbed it.

In the next flash of lightning, he could see his wife and child much farther away. Alicia waved and shouted, but Lionel couldn't understand her.

In desperation, he pushed through the tangled rigging, planted his feet on the slanted deck, and tossed the ring toward them with all his might. It disappeared into the night. "My heart! My heart!"

A wave pummeled Lionel and threw him down, away from the deck. The waves were his enemy: chaotic battle formations intent on thwarting his will. When one swell of water retreated to permit a view, it was quickly replaced with another rising up from behind. The sea would not allow him an unblocked line of sight.

Spray and sleet stung his eyes. He struggled vainly to be rid of the lines that entangled him. He fought to see into the storm and find his wife and son. He could not.

The temperature had begun to drop. The freezing rain now became snow. Lionel wailed as he was beaten by the pounding waves. His shirt caught on splintered timber and ripped like strips of paper ribbons.

He flailed, trying to escape the restricting lines. With each kick, his trousers felt like heavy canvas wrapping around his legs. The water felt like ice. His leg muscles started to cramp—wet knots pulling tight — until he was certain they would tear apart. The cramps spread to his arms, his back, and neck. It felt like dozens of knots, then hundreds, then thousands. His body felt like it was ripping. He howled with rage.

"Alicia! Luke! Where are you?"

There was no answer but howling winds and hostile waters.

The swirling snow mixed with icy foam and stinging spray. Finally, his heart began to feel as though it were cramping, too. There was no strength left in his body. It had no capacity to answer the commands of his brain or the wishes of his heart. Despite his will, he could summon no strength. Ropes snaked around him, coiling around his neck and arms and ribs. The depths sought to swallow him. His precious wife and innocent son had been stolen.

Lionel Lukin closed his eyes and surrendered to the will of the sea.

Captain Beeker struggled to cut himself free with his knife. He looked in the direction of the shore and saw, in the great distance, between the rising and falling of frigid seas, the double light marking his home. He was sure he could see it. This was no trick of his mind.

He fixed his eyes upon the fierce waves around him. Would he truly perish within sight of his home? He remembered his family. The double light marked the place near where they dwelled. They were there, awaiting him.

He hacked at the cords with renewed vigor. He was almost free when another huge wave sent a large crate to smash against his head. He fell back and sank below the surface.

He could feel the blackness pressing him to sleep. He fought it, trying hard to think, to take action, to stay awake. It was so hard. He sank deeper.

He remembered his knife, heavy in his hand. He squeezed the handle. He could feel his legs. He knew where his feet were. Things were starting to make sense again.

With a desperate act of will, the captain kicked his feet and approached the surface. As he rose, he looked up and saw the limp body of the man named Lionel hanging from a length of broken mast, floating just above him. If he could just plant his knife into the mast, he could pull himself up—and maybe this man, too. His knife-wielding hand broke the surface of the sea, and he frantically jammed it into something.

The captain attempted to pull himself up but only barely managed to get his blood- and brine-soaked head from out of the water before his strength emptied; he let go of his knife and fell back into the sea.

As he sank deep into the ocean he looked for the flickering double light of his home but could not find it.

The next morning, the tide had ebbed, and the Goodwin Sands, some four miles away from shore, protruded from the English Channel like a sandy beach. Gentle lapping sounds of peaceful waters replaced the angry war dance from the night before. Except for the lone spar that stuck out like a dead tree, there was no sign of the deadly struggle.

An old man and his horse tramped along the shore of the mainland. Much of the wreckage had washed up there, aided by the southwesterly winds and direction of the tide. Bales of cargo were strewn about. A wagon wheel thudded quietly amidst some rocks, and a twine-fastened bundle of handbills floated in the surf.

Some bottles had found their way to shore, and it was these the old man first attended to. He uncorked one and took a nip. He spat it out and threw the bottle back to sea.

He knelt next to a bale and ripped it open with a dagger. Inside he found women's clothes, including a dark blue dress with ruffles and sash. He stuffed the dress into a sack hanging from his horse. He gathered booty into his sacks, rigged crates upon his horse's back, and continued to search the shore.

He saw something that arrested his attention. The body of a man, his hand knifed to a mast, lay awash in the surf. Its only motion came from the action of the waves. The old man looked to see if anyone was near and then pulled the man farther up onto dry sand behind an obstructing boulder so he could rifle through the pockets. He found a pocket watch, coins, and a wallet filled with money. He took them. Then he saw the man's shiny boots. The old man chuckled and yanked them off.

CHAPTER 2

"Gawkers!" Edward said. "Worse than gulls fighting over fish scraps."

Edward Perkins saw what he expected to see as he stood at the bow aboard the lugger *Seahorse*. He and his mates had been working since dawn to discover what might be salvaged from the wreckage from last night's travail.

As the *Seahorse* glided past the lighthouse and through the narrow entrance of the outer harbor walls, he shook his head. Edward could see that the piers and the streets beyond the snug harbor were crowded with throngs hoping to see whatever disabled vessels they might be towing in. But since they didn't have one this time, the crowd was already beginning to disperse.

The *Seahorse* rocked up to one section of a floating dock rigged beside the eastern pier. Two stocky old men bent over to catch the first two lines tossed by Edward and the crew. The two men grunted and sighed but managed to tie the lugger up and pull it close.

Venus and Iris Hogger moved nearer to the docking ship. The thirtyish twin sisters, openly displaying their assets and affections, waved their hankies to the five-man crew.

Edward's forty-four-year-old brother, Arthur, tied the tiller secure. He was a large man with wide shoulders, a broad belly, and a fat, winter white face lashed with a thick mustache. He glanced at the Hogger twins once, then attended to his work.

Edward tossed a third line to one of the old codgers along the pier, then crossed to kick a buoy over the side.

Arthur grimaced. "I'd sooner be kickin' you, I see you do that again."

"Sorry," Edward replied with a smile. He bent down to tip the next buoy off the side by hand.

"That's better," Arthur said.

"Yes, Arthur."

"What did ya find, Eddie?" Venus asked.

"Haw! Haw! Wouldn't you like to know, Venus?" Another of the crewmen, fifty-nine-year-old Tom Hardwell, said while coiling a line near the stern. He was stocky and white haired and wore greasy overalls, deck boots, and a dark cap.

Edward jumped from the boat to the pier and stooped to help one of the older men pull the lugger still closer. "A few bales, ladies. Nothing much."

"Look what the sea done washed up for me," Iris said. She opened her heavy cloak and twirled around in a crumpled dress. It was blue with ruffles and a sash.

Edward smiled politely as he helped make the boat secure.

Arthur clambered out of the boat and approached the girls, his eyes fixed on the dress. "Anybody else bring in a haul?"

"Daddy said there's a wash-up at the west beach," Venus said, stepping in front of her sister. "He's scoured it, though."

"What?" Arthur asked. "No sense in a landsman outscoring a true hoveller. What'd he get?"

Iris stepped forward again, modeling her dress. "What's it look like?"

Arthur gave her a head-to-toe. "Like nothing."

"Humph," she said with a pout.

Tom and the other members of the crew — sixty-two-year-old Henry Hawkins, thirty-six-year-old Jeffery Burton, and his fifty-six-year-old father, John — gathered around Arthur.

"Some kind of wreck washed up at the west beach," Arthur told them. "Hogger's combed it already."

"Hogger?" Henry asked, annoyed. "How is it he always finds the wash-ups so quick?"

"How does any locust find his grub?" John asked.

"Comes natural," Arthur said.

Edward listened from his crouched position as he finished coiling a line around the stumpy bollard along the edge of the floating dock. He stood up to add a comment but saw something in the distance, off in the direction of the Old Military Road along the edge of the harbor. "What the — ?" He walked around his mates to get a better look.

"C'mon, Eddie, tell me!" Iris said, twirling in her dress. "What do ya think? Really. Do I look pretty?"

Edward glanced at her and allowed a faint smile. "It's a fine dress, Iris." He stepped away and returned his attention to the distant sight: a man all but staggering into town.

Arthur stepped beside his brother. "What are you spying?" He followed Edward's gaze, and his face twisted with disgust. "Oh, sea-scud, to be sure!"

"Have some heart," Edward said. "That could be you."

"Heart? Heh-heh! Why waste good muscle on vagabonds? That's *not* me; that's certain," he said with a half-grin. He turned to his men. "What say we eat?"

Iris threw back her cloak and bared her shoulders. She pranced in front of Arthur. "Admit it," she said, "it becomes me!"

"I don't have to admit anything!" Arthur and his crew headed down the pier toward Cannon's, the pub alongside the quay. "You coming, Edward?"

Edward scurried up the steps to the stone pier but turned left onto Old Military Road. His eyes were fixed on the man in the distance.

Down the small embankment between the western cliffs that tapered near the harbor and the western leg of the pier, the shirtless man stumbled. He looked confused.

Edward hurried through the belligerent hawkers, indifferent vendors, working seamen, and ignorant drunks and warily approached the man. "Sir, uh, excuse me, sir? Are you looking for someone?"

"My hand," the man said. His eyes were distant and dry. He held up his hand to display a caked-over and disturbing wound.

Edward winced and helped the man lean against a hitching post. He removed his coat and wrapped it around the stranger's shoulders. "I'll take you to Gilmore. He's a Reverend. Doctor's away."

Edward guided the stranger down Old Military Road and through the crowd of grubby, seafaring laborers going about their business. Some stared, but most paid no attention. They turned left and trudged up Harbour Street to the center of town, where King and Queen Streets joined.

At the intersection, merchants hawked produce, fresh fish, and assorted wares from the open market stalls underneath the town hall. Streams of people flowed in all directions as Edward and the man slogged along.

After a hundred slow steps, the journey became too much and the man collapsed. Edward caught him but had no choice but to lay him down in the middle of the street. "Make way! Give some room, mates. Move around!"

Folks offered no quarter.

Edward stood up, his face hot. He extended his arms. "Make room!"

"Edward?" a man's voice asked. "What is it?"

Edward recognized the Reverend John Gilmore emerging from the crowd.

Rev. Gilmore was a tall man in his early sixties. He stood about six foot four and had a large frame that was just starting to settle in the middle parts. His face was old and kind, his hands strong, and his step sure. This day he wore overalls over a shirt and a cleric's collar. He held a package of wrapped meats under his arm.

"Reverend, just the man I was hoping to see. I was heading to your place when this man collapsed. He's a shipwreck survivor, I suppose, or maybe a man who has been done in by robbers. I'm not sure, but he obviously needs some help."

"Yes, quite," Rev. Gilmore said. He squatted down beside the man and set his meats aside. He lifted the injured man's head. "He's in bad shape, he is. Let's carry him to the buggy."

A few minutes later they were riding the buggy east up King Street toward the countryside. They passed Gilmore's church, Holy Trinity, and traveled to the countryside and cornfields beyond, known as Albion Place. It offered a grand view of both the town and the neighboring English Channel.

Down a country lane, cradled in a section of a sloping hill, stood the yellow-block rectory of the Reverend and Mrs. Gilmore. Beside the adjacent stables and some broken walls, the rolling land was covered with green grass, small crop fields, and scattered windbreaks of trees. Round stone steps rested deep in the grass to line the path from the gate to the front door of the cozy home. From this vantage, on a clear day, the Downs and the Goodwin Sands could be easily seen. The blue-green waters of the English Channel were visible to the east and south, and farther to the north, the gray-blue waters of the North Sea shimmered and gleamed.

The Reverend stopped the buggy in front of his home. He and Edward carefully lifted the man and carried him through the front door.

⎯⎯⎯ ✎ ⎯⎯⎯

The day wore on and the weather again changed as the clouds rolled in. People went indoors and the streets darkened to mirror the nearby ocean waves. Dusk deepened into night.

The lantern lights from Cannon's Pub glowed brighter. Squeezebox music filled the night air, and the hoots and hollers of rum-filled sailors mixed with the beat of stomping boots. Inside, the crew of the *Seahorse* was still at play, and Edward had since joined them.

Arthur Perkins mopped beer foam from his mouth with his sleeve and slammed his mug on the bar. "Cannon, I'll have me another."

Alfred Cannon, the fat and bearded tavern owner, grabbed the mug and filled it from the tapped keg behind the counter. "Here's to sheets belly full, Arthur."

"Aye, belly full." Arthur said. He slapped his money down then tipped his mug to slurp the drink down quick.

"Hey, Eddie!" Henry Hawkins called.

Henry was dressed like most of the other men in the place: a thick, dark sweater covered by a short coat that matched dark trousers, and heavy black shoes or boots, usually topped with a cap or hat. Venus and Iris, the twin sisters, sat on the laps of two sailors at the other end of the bar, sharing drinks.

Henry approached Edward, who was playing darts with Jeffery.

"What's this I hear about you nursing a wash-up today?"

"Isn't much to tell," Edward said, taking careful aim. "Wrecked last night, I suppose." He tossed his dart and hit a triple eighteen. He threw his last one to score a center bull's-eye. "Cricket!"

"I lose again," Jeffery said. He was tall and had a skinny, comical face and large nose. "A wash-up, Eddie? You didn't tell me."

"Tell you what?" Edward asked. "Just a poor soul, that's all." Edward pulled out the darts and held them up to Henry. "You ready?"

Arthur took the darts from Edward. "Henry and me against you and little Burton here."

"Don't call me that!" Jeffery said.

John Burton stepped forward. "Don't let him get your feet wet, son."

"But, Dad," Jeffery protested.

"Just out-toss him," the elder Burton said. "He'll blow over."

The men laughed, and Jeffery sighed.

"What do you say?" Arthur asked Edward.

"Suit yourself, big brother," Edward said. "Just don't be running home crying when you lose."

Jeffery laughed harder than the joke deserved until Arthur stepped to the line and bumped him aside with his shoulder. "Excuse me, but we'll toss first." He turned to Edward. "Be smart, little brother, or you'll be over my knee in no time."

"That's a frightful thought," Edward said.

"Really, Eddie, what about this wash-up you found?" Henry asked. "Who is he?"

"Don't know. I left him at the Gilmores'. What else could I do?"

John leaned against the bar. "But where'd he come from? A wreck?"

"Likely so," Edward said.

"Sea-scud, that's what he was!" Arthur said. "Probably part of the wreck Hogger scavenged below the cliff." He tossed his last dart and scored. "Land ho! Beat that! Triple fifteen and double sixteen to start!"

"Too easy," Edward said. He held out his hand for the darts.

Arthur looked at his brother's hand and chuckled. He crossed to the bar. Edward retrieved the darts and stepped to the line.

"We heard Hogger came up with quite a fill," Cannon said from behind the bar. "You think the Sands had supper last night?"

"In this weather?" Arthur asked. He returned to the dart game with a full mug. "The Goodwin never goes hungry this time of year."

"For sure," Jeffery said.

Others nodded. Edward finished his throws without a score and retrieved the darts for Henry.

"We skirted the hulk," Henry said, stepping to the line to throw. "Wasn't nothing there but some spar saying, 'Here we was, mate, but we're not no more!'"

"Wonder what she was carrying," Cannon said from across the room.

John whispered, "Look what the gale blew in."

"Wonder no more!" Darrin Hogger said in his raspy voice as he entered the pub. All heads turned toward him as he slapped a heavy canvas bag down on a table near the center of the room. He carried a wagon wheel over one arm as if it were a coil of rope.

"You did say 'sea-scud,' didn't you?" Henry asked Arthur in a whisper.

"Venus, Iris, home now!" Hogger said. He jerked his head to one side as he motioned to the door. "No lollygagging!"

Venus complained at once, "Oh, Poppa. It's too early."

"Yes, Poppa," Iris said, cuddling her sailor. "We want to stay."

"Don't utter another word or you'll taste me whip, I tell ya," Hogger said. He pulled back his coat to reveal a coiled whip dangling from his belt.

The daughters were slow to obey but made their way toward the door. Hogger urged them along by raising his hand as if he might strike them. The women quickly departed. Arthur and the others gathered closer to inspect Hogger's merchandise.

"And what useless bait might we have here, Hogger?" Arthur asked.

"Darrin, my good friend," Hogger said, smiling slyly. "Call me Darrin, if you please."

"Don't push it, Hogger," Arthur said, reaching for the sack. "I heard you found a wash-up. What'd you find?"

Hogger tugged the sack away and insisted on pulling things out personally. The first item he displayed was a bundle of posters depicting a land coach. The posters were advertisements promoting a Lukin coach manufactured in London.

"A Lukin coach," Henry said as he carefully took the bundle apart. "I heard of those."

Hogger held up the wheel. "Guess they don't float too good, huh?"

Edward shook his head and returned to the dartboard.

"Wait!" Hogger said, pulling out a knife. "See it all before you decide. I know you haven't seen a finer blade than this one — not in a long time."

"Horace Beeker?" Arthur said in surprise.

Hogger stuttered. "N-no, it's not his. C-can't be!"

Arthur snatched the knife from Hogger and examined the raised initials. He ran his thumb over the *HB*. "Yep," he said, "I know it for certain. Anyone know what Horace's run was lately?"

"Yeah, sure," Cannon said, moving from behind the bar to get a closer look. "He was running from Shields to Dover."

"He could've been abreast the Sands last night. But he knows 'em well enough," Jeffery said.

"Nobody knows the Sands," Arthur said.

"It was going to pay him real well, too!" Cannon said. "I can't believe it! Horace Beeker in the locker."

"I'll be doused," John said. "And all those kids running around. They don't even know they got no daddy."

Arthur shook his head and spoke more quietly than usual, "Aw, Horace." He set the knife down.

Hogger snatched it and hid it away.

Some sailors took a seat to better absorb the shock of the news. Edward crossed to the sack and searched to see if it contained any more clues that linked to Captain Beeker. He found nothing but clothes and a pair of fancy boots, which he placed on the table. He stared down at Darrin Hogger, who appeared to be vacillating between nervousness and defiance.

"Hey, if it is Horace's," Hogger said, "then the prices won't be high. Out of honor to the man. He was a fine captain. But the sea, she'll have her own way, you know. We all know that." He stretched his arms out wide.

"He could've lost his knife accidental like," Tom said. "Maybe dropped it over the side."

"If that was so there would have been no other stuff washed up," Henry said.

"Aye," Arthur agreed sadly. "It is a shame. Beeker was a good sailor. Taught me some things. Some, aye." Arthur grew quiet.

"Well," Hogger said, his voice more sure, "what better way to remember him than to hold dear what was his?"

"The sea rules, mates," Arthur said. "One thing Hogger

says—and only one thing—is true: the sea rules. There isn't anything we can do about that."

"Aye, you sail late season, you know the score!" Hogger said, beginning to grin. "It is the way of things."

"I suppose," Henry said. "If you can't expect a soldier to complain about cannonballs over his head, I guess you can't expect a sailor to not finish at the bottom."

All the men nodded and drank a toast to the memory of Captain Beeker.

Except for Edward. He stepped through the door for fresh air. On the front walk, he could still hear the others inside the pub.

"How much for the boots, Hogger?" he heard his brother ask. "Those weren't Beeker's."

"I think the wheel ought to hang over there, on the wall," Cannon said.

"Buy the wheel, and I'll throw in a poster," Hogger said. "You don't want no wheel without a story to tell."

"I'll take the knife," John said.

"For a price, you will."

"No price. I'll be taking it to his wife."

"Law of the sea, John Burton. It's mine now. For a price it can be yours. Then you do what you want. But it's going to cost ya!"

"You're a squid, Hogger. How much?"

CHAPTER 3

The Reverend John Gilmore walked out of his stable carrying an empty bucket. He set the pail in an empty trough, inhaled a deep breath of morning air, and scanned the broad view.

His vantage atop Albion Place offered a panorama of natural and man-made beauty. The threat of imminent storm had passed for now. The day had begun sunny and the sea was bright. A healthy southwesterly breeze gusted along. Scores of ships bound for home sliced through the seas, their sails full and white like flocks of coasting seagulls.

The outward-bound ships needed a different slant of wind, so they gathered within the Downs, a narrow passageway of sea between the coast of England and the Goodwin Sands, and waited. In a few hours, upwards of a hundred sails would be visible within the first two miles from the coast.

Rev. Gilmore headed for the house. Piano music reached his ears as he neared the rectory.

Joyce, his wife, played a soft melody. She was a large, gray-headed woman with a round, happy face. She wore thick spectacles and a faded dress printed with a dull blue and gray pattern. She looked up and smiled at her husband.

The Reverend spotted the unfortunate man Edward had brought to them yesterday. He was seated in one of the large wingback chairs. The man had been cleaned up and dressed in fresh clothes. Beside him a cup of untouched tea steamed from its place next to a small vase of dried flowers atop a side table. His wounded hand was wrapped in a large mitten of bandages, and his eyes were open, though fixed in a distant stare. His head leaned forward and to the side. His mouth hung partially open.

The music stopped. "I hope that was pleasant for you," Mrs. Gilmore said softly. "May I do anything else for you?"

The man didn't move or talk. He only stared as if lost to some faraway place.

"You haven't touched your tea," Mrs. Gilmore said. "Is there something different you'd like?"

The man remained frozen in silence.

Mrs. Gilmore patted him on the shoulder. "Just say so if you need anything." She looked at her husband, shook her head slightly, and left the room.

Rev. Gilmore crossed the room with a cup of tea in hand. He sat in a matching wingback chair opposite their mysterious guest. "Good morning again," he said, his spoon clanking his teacup.

The man directed his eyes to the cup. The Reverend saw this and deliberately clanked it again. "Kind of sounds like a ship's bell in the distance. Doesn't it?"

The man did not stir.

"I have always thought so," Rev. Gilmore continued. "Have you ever heard a ship's bell?"

The man's eyes moved to look straight at Gilmore.

The Reverend smiled gently.

A tear rolled down one side of the man's face.

Rev. Gilmore sipped his tea then set it down and waited. The man stared back at him then lowered his eyes. The Reverend wondered what was now seizing his attention. He thought it might be the clerical collar. "Would you like to tell me about it?"

"No," the man said in hushed tone.

Rev. Gilmore picked up his tea and sipped again. This time he held it to his mouth, looked over the top of the cup, and offered a friendly wink. He wanted the man to know he was in a safe place. The man looked back with alarm. Rev. Gilmore set the cup down. "What is it?" the Reverend asked.

"The captain liked to wink," the man said.

"To which captain do you refer?"

The man did not answer.

Rev. Gilmore settled back comfortably and lifted one leg to rest his ankle atop his knee. For a long time he sat looking peaceably at the man, available, but with no need to speak.

The man was sitting upright on the edge of his chair, his posture as straight as a pin, though he continued to lean forward with his head tilted slightly to one side. His heavily wrapped right hand rested on his thigh. The man's left hand clasped the inside edge of the vest the Reverend had dressed him in. He was in an awkward but rigid position and looked both weary and anxious, though he said nothing more. The tea grew cold.

Finally, Rev. Gilmore slapped his hands upon his knees and stood before his guest. "I've chores to do. Do you care to remain or attend me? As company, not apprentice."

The man moistened his lips with his tongue. "Are you a preacher or a farmer?"

"Farmer, did you say?" Rev. Gilmore looked at his dirty shoes and grinned. "I do tend a garden."

The man drew a deep breath. "What do you grow?" His every word seemed to require much effort.

"Corn, beans, cabbage, mostly. Though it is God who makes it grow. I'm just His helper."

The man sat back into his chair and closed his eyes. "You're a holy man." He sighed.

Rev. Gilmore laughed and put his hands in his pockets. "I am a minister *and* a farmer. You are in a rectory *and* a farmhouse. It's what it takes in these parts. Perhaps you are from a city. A big city?"

The man didn't take the cue.

The Reverend rubbed his hands together vigorously. "If you accompany me, you can tell me more. If you prefer to rest, that is also fine."

The man seemed to be sleeping now. Rev. Gilmore stood at the entrance to the room for a moment and waited. The man kept his eyes closed.

Lionel awoke to the sound of muffled voices. Through the sheer and frilly curtains that draped the window, he saw the Reverend and his wife standing on the walk before the house.

Mrs. Gilmore, wearing a heavy shawl now, handed a small sack to her husband as he kissed her on the cheek. The Reverend walked down the path of round, grassy-edged stones and exited through the rickety wooden gate to disappear behind the tall thicket and crumbling stone wall. The front gate slammed shut.

Suddenly Lionel was not seeing the gate but the door of his Lukin coach.

It slammed shut, then burst open. He saw Alicia and Luke tumble out of the coach and slide down the slick deck of the ship. A raging wave followed them and forced them through enlargened scuppers. Designed to let water run out of a flooded ship, they instead sealed the fate of his wife and son to drown while he watched.

No! Alicia! Luke! He grabbed the hem of his wife's skirts and tried to hold on. *Alicia!*

"Sir, are you all right? Sir?"

Lionel opened his eyes. He was kneeling in front of the window, draped in fallen curtains and clutching them in his hands. He was soaked in sweat and unable to hold back the tears.

The Reverend's wife knelt beside him and helped remove the sheer fabric. "You are safe," she said. "Whatever horror you've experienced, it's well now."

Slowly, Lionel lifted his head. His lower lip trembled. "It is not well," he said. "I could not save them."

"Who?"

Lionel lowered his gaze and nodded. "My wife. My son. I could do nothing."

"You were at sea?"

"H-he said something about Goodwin," Lionel mumbled. "Something about sand."

"Yes, the Goodwin Sands. They have caused much heartache in these parts. We know them too well."

Lionel spoke as though in a dream. "He said something . . . about a stream-reach. They were in a stream, or something. No hope, he said."

"Who said these things to you?" Mrs. Gilmore asked.

"Captain Beeker."

Mrs. Gilmore raised a hand to her mouth. "Horace Beeker? Captain Horace Beeker?"

Lionel looked directly at her. "Yes, I think so."

Mrs. Gilmore dabbed at her eyes. "What happened to the captain? Do you know?"

Lionel was looking at her but didn't hear. He straightened his arms to inspect them. His eyes fixed upon his bandaged hand, and he raised it closer to his face and turned it as best he could. He looked at Mrs. Gilmore. "Why am I alive? They all drowned and I am . . . Where am I?"

Mrs. Gilmore rested her hand above her bosom and swallowed hard. Her face softened and a certain kindness, such as she was wearing when she had earlier played the piano for him, returned. "You are in Ramsgate, dear friend. A coastal town very near the Goodwin Sands."

"Yes, I know of Ramsgate."

"You are in the home of the Gilmores, I being the missus, and John, my husband, is the rector of Holy Trinity Church. You were found by a local seaman."

"Is your husband a doctor, too?" Lionel asked.

"The doctor is away, and the infirmary, what there is of one, not currently being of a helpful state—well, you were brought to us. We have supposed you to be . . . the lone survivor of a wreck."

Lionel blinked at her, trying to understand. "There was no one else?"

"We have no indications of any," she said. "I'm sorry."

All at once Lionel felt sleepy.

"We have not understood who you are or where you are from. This news of Horace Beeker suggests you were aboard the brigantine *Sanctus*."

Lionel struggled to rise. Mrs. Gilmore tried to help him. He swayed some but managed to place his left hand against the wall for balance. He looked out the window. Through the archway above the gate, he saw the distant sea blending with the sky.

"I told them they were safe."

CHAPTER 4

"Another winter blow for sure," Arthur said. "She's working her dander up."

Arthur Perkins and Henry Hawkins stood bundled up at the end of the eastern pier.

"She ebbs and flows as she pleases," Henry said.

Clouds had appeared in long streaks above the horizon that morning and had slowly advanced across the sky as the day progressed. On the pier and in the harbor, sailors worked despite the increasingly stingy cooperation of the elements. With the sky a palette of gray tones and the wind beginning to moan, all of Ramsgate knew another lashing was near.

It was dusk now and the sea darkened in mood. Some larger vessels continued bowling along as best they could, while others made for sheltering coves to set anchors and wait.

Once again the Downs had become full of ships seeking shelter. Their crews watched the sun grow increasingly obscured by darkening clouds in the west. Local fishermen and sailors beat into the harbor for protection from the rising gale. Some boats were pulled far up the shore, while others were double anchored within port. Captains and crews rowed their dinghies in, and the public houses experienced a good round of business — serving malts, liquors, and stewed beef and onions.

Not far from where Arthur and Henry stood, the *Seahorse* rocked and bucked despite its securely cross-tied moorings beside the eastern pier. She had slack enough to ride the temperamental waters but restraint enough to keep her from being carried away or broken up during the night. Arthur pulled his cap down over his ears. "I hate winter."

"One thing, though," Henry said. "There'd be no hovelling without storms."

"And no fishing with them."

"Everything has a season," Henry said. "Least that's what Gilmore is always saying. Seems true to me. You fish in the sun; you hovel in the storm."

"And then you die," Arthur said, turning to head up the pier.

"You're always so bloody positive, Arthur," Henry said, falling in beside him. "Just more bloody than positive, that's all."

"To everything a season, Henry. Isn't that what you said?"

Henry groaned.

The two of them headed for the same destination as always, a trip through the wet and windy weather to Cannon's Pub at the head of the pier.

The storm finally arrived and beat the coastal village with full hurricane force. Along the pier, the waves pounded and burst into icy spray while the boats rocked wildly in the harbor, threatening to break free of their moorings and crash against the seawall or break upon the rocks. Further out, ships rode the rough waves as the November storms began to roll in. Snow fell.

Between the North and South Forelands and along the Channel, the Goodwin Sands raged with whitecaps and fast-forming quicksand. The wind howled a dreadful dirge, and storm-drenched sailors reefed and prayed.

Light flurries melted upon the fire-warmed windowpanes of the quaint Gilmore rectory. The Reverend sat upon his favorite reclining lounger while Lionel sat straight in the wingback chair near the window. Mrs. Gilmore entertained the two men with her rendition of "O Come, All Ye Faithful." Beside each of them were steaming cups of hot chocolate along with biscuits.

It was mid-November. It had been two weeks since the shipwreck, and though there were still moments when he would suddenly sink into deep depression, Lionel felt safe and warm. For now, despite the storm outside, all was peaceful within the Gilmore home.

Mrs. Gilmore completed her medley and sat still at the keys. "Shall I play one more?"

The only answer from the Reverend was his deep breathing. Lionel nodded.

Mrs. Gilmore looked through the stack of hymnals on the table beside the piano and resumed her playing. This time she sang more quietly in her trembling soprano voice.

> *Brightest and best of the sons of the morning,*
> *Dawn on our darkness, and lend us Thine aid;*
> *Star of the east, the horizon adorning,*
> *Guide where our infant Redeemer is laid.*

As she played the delicate arrangement with bare notes and occasional chords, her voice rose slightly, and she closed her eyes.

> *Cold on His cradle the dewdrops are shining;*
> *Low lies His head with the beasts of the stall;*
> *Angels adore Him in slumber reclining,*
> *Maker and Monarch and Savior of all.*

Lionel looked at the window. Outside, the snow thickened into heavy flakes of frost and multiplied in number until it was too much for the warmth of the window to melt. The sill became layered with a fatness of snow. A coat of condensation fogged over the panes, which trembled as the cold winter wind breathed more heavily than before. A gust of cold air found entrance through the seals and cracks, puffing the lace curtains. It reminded Lionel of how beautiful Alicia had looked in her colorful, flowing dresses.

> *Say, shall we yield Him, in costly devotion,*
> *Odors of Edom, and offerings divine,*
> *Gems of the mountains, and pearls of the ocean,*
> *Myrrh from the forest, or gold from the mine?*

The fire flickered, and Mrs. Gilmore slowed her tempo as she played another verse without singing. Lionel watched her tilt her head back and offer herself and her music. She worshipped with the confidence of one who was alone. Lionel thought it interesting she didn't mind him seeing her do such a thing. She sang the last verse without opening her eyes.

> *Vainly we offer each ample oblation,*
> *Vainly with gifts would his favor secure,*
> *Richer by far is the heart's adoration,*
> *Dearer to God are the prayers of the poor,*
> *Dearer to God are the prayers of the poor,*
> *Dearer to God are the prayers of the poor.*

The wind rattled the window again. The curtains puffed and floated back down. The flames jumped, and Lionel sat up straighter.

Mrs. Gilmore stopped. She closed her hymnal and replaced it

upon the stack, then she stood and smoothed her dress. Retrieving a blanket from the couch, she laid it atop her husband. He snored lightly but otherwise didn't stir. She kissed him on his forehead and bent to pick up another blanket on the floor beside Lionel's chair. She held it and looked at him with a friendly smile.

"A fine recital," Lionel said.

"Thank you, Lionel. Would you care for a blanket?"

"No, I believe I will retire to my room."

"Good. The fire is ablaze there and the blankets much heavier, as you know."

As he headed to his chamber, which was directly above the parlor, he noted the spyglass on the tripod at the base of the stairs. It was tilted upward at a forty-five-degree angle. He spun the metal tube on its axis and then trudged up the stairs to his bed.

He changed into his nightclothes and stared out his bedroom window. He pressed down on the window jamb to make sure it was closed as tightly as possible. Through the glass he saw the chaotic swirling of snow.

Lionel stared into the dizzying pattern of falling and spinning flakes. It captivated him. At times it looked like a funnel beckoning him to fall deep within it. At other times it made no recognizable pattern as it gusted apart and then re-formed. He looked down to the snow-covered yard. It looked serenely beautiful to him, everything so thickly covered with glistening white.

His gaze turned toward the sea. He saw distant squalls gusting down the channel and wondered how they could form such symmetrical shapes. As he peered harder, he recognized the white shapes to be not squalls but sails on a large ship with three or four masts. His eyes watered and he rubbed them. He froze, suddenly afraid.

A ship in a storm. Near the Sands.

He ran downstairs, grabbed the spyglass and tripod, and brought it back to the window. He peered through it but could not find the ship again. Perhaps it had made it safely past. Still breathing heavily, Lionel leaned the instrument aside, opened his window, and slammed the shutters closed. He shut the window and climbed into bed.

He was exhausted. His bed felt soft and cool. He drew the blanket up to his chin and fell fast asleep.

Lionel danced the salty shuffle aboard Beeker's ship.

He slipped and fell and dug his nails into the deck. He saw his land coach on the deck of the *Sanctus*. It was threatening to break free and tumble over the ship's side. The coach door opened, then shut with a loud clatter. Lionel scratched and clawed his way across the deck until he crouched under the shelter of the deckhouse.

He watched as a sailor battled the fierce wind and tried to reach the coach door and secure it. The door became unhinged and flew through the air. It struck the sailor and sent him flying over the gunwale into the sea. Suddenly, other doors on the coach burst open then slammed shut with loud bangs. The battering grew louder and more frantic. Lionel covered his ears as the wind howled and the stage doors opened and shut. He sprang to his feet—but found he was in his bed at the Gilmores', sitting up with his hands over his ears.

Lionel sat still and absorbed the sights of his bedroom. He heard the sounds of a winter hailstorm. The snow had become sleet and was pelting the shutters. One of the shutters he had earlier closed was now banging open and shut.

Lionel went to open the window and pushed wide the shutters.

He reached for the spyglass and this time succeeded in locating the ship he had seen before. He found it, but it looked far different.

The once neatly formed sails were now like the chaos of blustering snow rather than the exquisite symmetry of finely hung canvas. There was an orange glow in the center of the ship like a fire ablaze.

"Oh, no!"

Lionel bounded down the stairs and burst out the front door of the Gilmores' home, still dressed in his nightclothes. He rushed down the walk until he could see the Channel.

"Ship aground! Ship aground!" He yelled in all directions. "Ship aground! Someone help!"

The Gilmores arrived at the doorway behind him.

"Lionel, what is it?" Mrs. Gilmore asked.

"What's wrong, son?" the Reverend asked at nearly the same time.

Lionel whirled around to see them in the doorway dressed in their nightclothes. He pointed to the Channel with his wounded hand. "She's faltering!"

In the misty distance, moonlight streamed through a break in the heavy clouds, and the large vessel was visible to all of them. It could be seen struggling on the near spit of the Sands. The ship had rushed into a desperate strife of waters and was in the thick of the fray.

"Yes," Rev. Gilmore said, nodding grimly. "She is in trouble. You don't often see it clear, if at all. The squalls and fog see to that. But sometimes, sad to say, we do see the worst of it."

Lionel's eyes watered. "We must do something."

"What *can* we do? The winds are cruel, the rocks hard, the seas all too deadly. All ships are frail at such times—men the more so."

"We can't just stand by and let it happen!"

"I'm afraid we must," Rev. Gilmore said.

"We *must*?"

"Lionel," Mrs. Gilmore said, "we have wept a thousand tears, and we will go on weeping—"

"They don't need our pity. They need our help!" Lionel bolted to the stable and swung open the doors. He saw a wagon and buggy and crates and tools. Some horses stirred. Lionel grabbed a bridle off the wall and ran to the nearest stall. He mounted a horse and charged out of the stables.

"Oh, my— my goodness," Mrs. Gilmore said. "What do you think you're going to do?"

"Lionel, you must get down," the Reverend said, running toward him. "God help us."

Lionel yanked hard with his good hand. The horse reared. "Somebody has to do something," he said, his face streaming with tears. "It can't happen again."

"Lionel!" Rev. Gilmore spoke loudly. "Get hold of yourself. It is winter, and the Goodwin will break up ships weekly and daily. There's nothing you can do about it."

"There must be!" Lionel shouted and galloped away.

He rode the horse bareback, clinging to the reins and the animal's mane. He raced down the country lane all the way to King Street. As he charged down the narrow way, he attempted to turn left onto Harbour Street, but the icy brick streets provided no hold for hooves. The horse slipped and crashed into the open market stalls under the town hall. Lionel skidded headlong from his mount.

The animal cried out in pain but managed to right herself and run far enough away from Lionel that he had no chance of remounting her.

He looked down Harbour Street from his sprawled-out position in the market stall. His cheek was scraped and bloody. His nightclothes were torn and his feet bare and cold. He got to his feet and ran down the street toward the quay.

He slipped on the snow-coated road several times but each time got up until he finally reached Harbour Place at the edge of the inner harbor. He searched in all directions, but the town was deserted except for a few street persons tucked here and there under makeshift lean-tos. A sudden rush of laughter caught his attention. He looked up the street to see Cannon's Pub, open and alive with patrons.

Lionel crashed through the doors. He stood in the doorway, soaked from the freezing rain, wearing torn nightclothes and bleeding in various places. He squinted, trying to adjust his eyes to the well-lit tavern.

He saw a handful of patrons. Some sat at a table where they had been playing dominoes. Others were frozen in the midst of their dart throwing. All of them stared at Lionel as he dripped on the floor.

"A ship!" he cried. "She struggles! We need a boat and some hearty men. Who can help?"

The bartender wiped his hands with a rag. "Struggles where?"

Lionel noticed the wagon wheel and the Lukin poster hanging on the wall at the end of the bar. He staggered to it like a man in a dream. He touched it and then turned to the others. His body ached and his head hurt.

"What is it, man?" the barkeep demanded. "Struggles where? In the harbor?"

Lionel spoke softly. "No, at sea. Upon the Goodwin."

"Oh, that's all!" a large man said from the domino table. He resumed his game. "Your turn, Henry."

"We've no time! She'll break up soon!" Lionel pleaded.

"We've all the time 'til the storm breaks," the large man said. He shook his head and rolled his eyes.

"Might as well be upon the welcome mat to hell rather than the Sands," another man said. He motioned to the others for agreement and got some.

"What kind of men are you?" Lionel said. "There are people drowning right now, and you do nothing?"

The large man leaned back in his chair and placed his booted feet upon the table. "We are practical people who know something about the sea. And who might you be, besides some sea-scud looking for handouts?"

Lionel saw his own boots upon the man's feet. He felt dizzy. "Mine," he said weakly.

"See! What did I tell you," the large man said. "This is all about handouts. Be on your way, scud."

Lionel recovered enough to speak. "Never mind. I can see what sort of men you are. I'll find help somewhere else." He looked once more at his boots then rushed outside.

❧

The men looked at each other, and they all laughed hard. Except for Edward. He set his darts down and headed for the door.

"Hey, Eddie, where you going?" Jeffery asked.

"Oh, yes," Arthur said. "Time to play nursemaid again. Be careful, brother. That nut will sting you worse than a jellyfish."

"Is that the man you brought to the Gilmores?" Henry asked.

"The man's confused," Edward said, peering through the door.

"Aye! He's confused for sure," Jeffery agreed, along with everyone else in the pub.

"He's heading for the fishing boats," Edward said.

"What?" John asked, taking a quick gulp then hurrying to Edward's side. "Hey, you!"

Everyone rushed to see what the stranger was doing.

"I hate landsmen," Arthur said.

"You're just bothered your game is upset," Tom said.

Edward followed them out into the rough-weather evening. Beyond the quay, the charges of the waves were so high that the outer harbor itself wasn't much of a refuge. Breaking waves culminated in storm-tossed spray and battered the pier. The increasing surf broke against the bows of the vessels moored there, sending spray flying high. The wind blew strong.

Edward saw the stranger run alongside the large skid ramp used to launch boats into the outer harbor. On either side of the ramp were small boats pulled onto the sandy beach. The man moved among them and suddenly grabbed hold of John Burton's fishing smack. Slipping and struggling, he dragged the small vessel into the shallow waters.

Edward shouted to him, "You mustn't do that, sir!"

John moved to stop the stranger, but Arthur held him back. "What are you doing, Perkins?"

"Hold on, John!" Arthur said. "He's a landsman—a fool. It's worth the laugh. Give it a go."

"But that's my boat!" John protested.

"It'll be fine. You know he can't get her out of here."

The patrons from the pub came out to see the spectacle. They gathered with mugs in hand and agreed with Arthur that it was worth a laugh to watch the fool struggle with the boat and surf.

Edward headed toward the beach.

"Don't even think about it, little brother," Arthur said.

Edward turned to his brother. "The man's a shipwreck survivor, Arthur. God knows what he's lost."

"His mind, I'm certain."

Edward again moved toward the beach, but Arthur grabbed his arm. "Leave him be."

"Yeah, hold on, Eddie," Jeffery said. "We don't have much chance for fun in winter."

The man had managed to push the boat into deeper water, but the surf broke upon him and sent him and the boat back to the shore each time. The men laughed. He was getting banged up pretty good, but he was persistent and tried again to launch the boat. Finally, the boat and the man were pushed close to the edge of the skid ramp, and the boat swaggered dangerously near it.

"She'll be stove she gets any closer," John shouted, running toward his boat.

"Let me handle the fool," Arthur said, holding John back. Arthur stalked the landsman until another wave threw him down and rolled him over in the surf as it broke upon the shore. Arthur towered over him, but the boat caught in a foaming wave and swung around hard, knocking into Arthur and bowling him over into the water.

The crowd roared as Arthur rose wet and mad. The wind howled and the snow squalled. Arthur stepped alongside the man, whose face was rising from the surf.

The man peered at Arthur's boots only inches from his face. "Those are *my* boots!"

"Yeah, well they're on *my* feet." Arthur squatted down and picked the man up by the collar.

The crowd drew closer. Most called for Arthur to teach him a lesson. Some tried to arrest the boat. Only Edward pleaded with his brother to stop the lunacy.

"You stole my boots. I washed up, and you stole them."

Despite the efforts of the men, the boat crashed so hard into one edge of the skid ramp that it cracked the starboard bulwark near the bow.

"The bulwark is stove!" John Burton yelled. "Bring her round! Bring her round!"

Arthur drew back and punched the man in the face, knocking him back into the water. Arthur sloshed close and picked him up again. "You don't ruin a perfectly good boat—a man's livelihood—on an impossible task!"

He slugged him again.

The man struggled to get to his feet, favoring his bandaged hand. His mouth was bloodied from the blows.

"What sort of town is this? People drown, and you do nothing? My wife and son are dead, and you just let them die?"

He took a wild swing at Arthur but missed. Arthur countered with a blow to the chin. The man fell back into the water, and Arthur advanced to dish out more.

"Enough! Enough already!" Reverend Gilmore shouted as he pulled up in his buggy.

"Oh, my, my," Mrs. Gilmore said as she climbed out of the buggy. "Shame on you, Arthur Perkins. You know better."

Arthur looked to the sky. "I'm sorry," he said. "I'm truly sorry. But, with respect, Mrs. Gilmore, it is nighttime, there stands the pub, it's a wee bit stormy, and no lady should be coming down here and not be expecting to find a few waves."

Mrs. Gilmore walked straight up to him and pointed her finger in his face. "Arthur Perkins, I see what's happening here as plain as a mainsail on a windy day. Now you leave this man alone. He has suffered much trouble."

"Aye, and causes the same, ma'am."

The Reverend emerged from the water with an arm around the

man. Edward quickly moved to assist them. "Thank you, Eddie. You're a fine man. Help us to the buggy." Mrs. Gilmore joined them as they lifted the man into the backseat.

"He took our filly," Mrs. Gilmore said to Edward. "Can you locate her and board her until morning, Eddie?"

Edward nodded. "The man did try to launch John Burton's boat—stove it in some, too."

Rev. Gilmore frowned. "I understand." He turned to the crowd and stood high in his buggy to fix their attention. "This man is not from among us," he began.

The small crowd cheered agreement.

"Now, now. He is an unfortunate, shipwrecked here for whatever reason God had in mind. But he has suffered much loss."

"What about me, Reverend?" John Burton asked, his anger growing. "What about the loss of my boat?"

"You're boat isn't lost," Edward said. "Just hurt some."

"Obviously," Rev. Gilmore continued, "there are some things he needs to learn—"

"And pay for," John Burton added.

The man stood up from the buggy and faced them, blood streaming down his face. "I will repair your boat. But I can't say there's any hope to repair any of you."

The men raised their fists and shouted threats.

The Reverend appealed to the man. "Please, don't incite."

The man turned to John. "I will repair your boat."

"I'll believe that when I see it," John said.

"Okay," Rev. Gilmore said. "Everyone back to your homes or to the pub or wherever it is you go. It's all over." He snapped the reins and turned the buggy around to ride back home. "And I expect to see you all on Sunday."

As the buggy headed away, Arthur shouted, "You got it wrong, landsman. We didn't kill your family. The sea rules the coast. The sea decides who lives and who dies. It's the way of things. You're the one who chose to sail at night in November. Be worth your own salt and accept your lot."

The Gilmores' buggy drove up Harbour and turned right onto King Street. Lionel sat in the back. Except for the clip-clop of the horses' hooves, muffled by the layer of slush on the road, the ride was silent. They rode all the way up the hill past the church to the top of Albion Place before Reverend Gilmore slowed the buggy. He turned onto the road at the corner of the cornfield and stopped.

"Lionel," he said calmly, "I'm disappointed by what you did tonight. It wasn't right."

Mrs. Gilmore reached for her husband's arm and whispered, "John."

"Wasn't right?" Lionel shook his head and looked away.

"No. You took a horse without permission. You tried to steal a boat. This is not acceptable. You need to think about this." Rev. Gilmore cracked his whip, and the horses resumed their trot.

When they reached their home, the Reverend dropped Lionel and Mrs. Gilmore at the front gate and then drove the buggy to the stable.

Lionel headed in, but Mrs. Gilmore called to him. "I understand why you did what you did, Lionel. But there has to be a better way. That's all John is trying to say."

Lionel stared at Mrs. Gilmore. "Somewhere out there a ship is breaking up. Men and women and perhaps children are dying in fear. It is happening so close to us that it can be seen under the light of the moon. And what do we do?"

"I know," Mrs. Gilmore said. "I know."

"We sing. Some drink, some eat, and some simply laugh."

"Lionel, people all over this world are suffering right now, and we can't do anything for them but pray and hope. Do you think we should not sing or laugh until the world no longer suffers?"

Lionel stared at her.

"Of course not," she said. "For then we would never laugh and only suffer. We do what we can do. We ache for what we cannot do. We pray to God for what we cannot do. We may still rejoice for those things that we can. We must. It is tragic, but what else is there?"

Lionel turned toward where the ship was foundering, though he could not see it. "Do you know what is rising up from that ship right now?"

Mrs. Gilmore shook her head.

"The prayers of the poor."

"What do you mean?"

"From your song at the piano. If the prayers of the poor are as 'dear to God' as you sang tonight, shouldn't they be dear to us?"

Atop the Goodwin Sands life was drowning away.

The ship that Lionel had seen began to work and writhe. Timbers broke with loud reports. There were now few signs of life as limp bodies washed to and fro, disappearing and reappearing. Planks were wrenched from the sides by the fierce action of the sea. Iron bolts tore from their grips and twisted like women's hair.

Suddenly, the deck itself opened; water rushed down into the hold as the deck broke up and pieces floated away in the wash of the surf. A crash louder than a thunder peal sounded, and the foremast broke off close to the deck.

Clinging to the stump of the foremast were two little girls, alone and afraid. There were no others to be seen. They trembled and tightly clutched each other. They seemed fixed atop the deck as if they might be there for a long time in frozen fear.

It was not to be.

Both screamed—a cry that would never be heard because of the deafening gale force winds and because no one was near to listen. Yet scream they did as they saw an enormous wave tower high above them. It loomed and fell to swamp their fragile place of refuge.

The wave never receded. It simply poured over them and then remained as endless ocean, leaving no sign that two priceless lives were gone.

CHAPTER 5

Before dawn the next morning, Lionel departed from the house to get some fresh air. He bundled warmly and paced back and forth along the road in front of the house. He walked with his forearms resting atop his head, his good hand clinging to the wrist of his bandaged one. He talked to himself. It was only shortly past sunrise when he returned to the house and went upstairs to his room to look through the spyglass.

In such fair weather, there was exceptional viewing from high atop Albion Place. He panned across the Channel and saw the undulating waters rise and fall, chop and spray. The sea looked grayish green with a variety of foamy white veins sprawling and stretching to break apart and re-form in endless patterns. There were ships of many sizes running with and against the wind, which was milder than it had been. The waters looked chilly with edgings of frosty white and swirling masses of rabid foam.

He spotted the northern-most spit of the Goodwin Sands. It protruded as a desolate sandy knoll, not resembling how it had appeared the last time he'd seen it. Nearby, he saw a dark hulk. The remains of the ship he'd seen. How many had drowned?

He lifted his head from the eyepiece and noticed the Reverend returning from town with the horse Lionel had taken from the stable. A rope had been fashioned into a makeshift halter, and

Rev. Gilmore led her home.

Lionel stepped back from the window and placed his arms atop his head as he had done in front of the house. He carelessly brushed against the bruise over his left eye. He pressed it softly. It was swollen and tender. Finally, he walked swiftly down the stairs and stopped in the vestibule to face the front door. He heard stomping feet outside.

Rev. Gilmore entered, hung his hat and scarf, and removed his gloves. "Good day, Lionel."

"Good Reverend," Lionel began, "it is only right and proper that I offer you my deepest regret for any injury or expense I may have caused you last night, both in horse and embarrassment. I am fully able and shall make it my utmost aim to provide restitution soon enough."

The Reverend stared at him, then motioned to the parlor with his hand. Lionel entered and stood in the center of the room.

Mrs. Gilmore walked toward them from the kitchen. "Did Edward have her all right?" She extended her arms to hug her husband; then she saw Lionel, and her color changed. "Oh, I'm sorry. I'll leave the two of you alone."

"No, please!" Lionel said. "It is good that what I have to say is said to the two of you. Please, if I may, please come, sit down."

The Reverend and his wife settled into chairs.

"I was just explaining to Rev. Gilmore that I made a grave mistake to cause you such embarrassment last night," Lionel said, "and I will fulfill my obligation to make it right in short order."

"You are speaking as a new man today, Lionel," the Reverend said. "You are being quite formal."

"Yes, well, it is a style of mine I had previously withheld but find quite suitable in matters such as this."

The Gilmores exchanged glances.

"I had withheld it," Lionel said, "not due to wanting to hide anything but due to not knowing—or better, not understanding—what I was feeling nor what I really wanted to say."

"You are a gentleman, then?" Mrs. Gilmore asked.

Lionel nodded but frowned. "By no evidence seen thus far, I'm certain." He searched for words. "An apology is due, as is recompense, and with a little assistance in the matter of accessing my accounts, I intend to do that very thing with haste."

Rev. Gilmore shook his head. "You've apologized. You appear sincere with your contrition. You don't owe us anything, Lionel. The horse is returned. She is not injured. Amazingly, very little harm has been done."

Lionel's words were shaky. "Mind you, I do not rescind much of what I said, nor do I believe in any substantial way differently than I communicated last evening. But I do acknowledge the inappropriate aspects of my behavior toward your good name and, of course, the private property of the fisherman."

Mrs. Gilmore clasped her hands. "It is helpful to hear your words."

"The matter of the boat is relevant," Rev. Gilmore said, "and any amends that can be made ought to be made. The church has some funds that can be applied to repair John Burton's property, and we can see to it that they are so applied."

"No!" Lionel said with his hands raised. "I am a man of some means and am quite able to rightly deal with this. Unfortunately, my accounts are in London and there are some steps to follow, but I can see to it that they are brought to bear in the very near future."

"London? Wonderful!" Mrs. Gilmore said. "Do you have family there, Lionel?"

Lionel lowered his hands and peered out the window. The rising sun made the snow sparkle. "I'm not ready to return. I'm

not prepared to face a life that was once so rich but is now so . . ."
Lionel looked at the Gilmores. "Friends? Yes. Associates? Yes. But
ready?" He sighed. His ribs still hurt from Arthur's kicking. "I have
no family. Not any more. No, I'm not ready for London."

The Reverend stood and placed a strong hand on Lionel's
shoulder. "There is no hurry as far as we are concerned. The boat,
because it is necessary for some of John's income and food, must be
addressed quickly. The church account can do that. In the future,
when you are ready to return to London, you can settle accounts if
you wish. I already plan to ride back to town today and hire a ship's
carpenter to fix the boat."

Lionel shook his head. "Thank you, but no. If you would speak
some credit on my behalf, I would like to accompany you to town,
purchase the supplies, and see the boat repaired."

"That is a fine gesture," the Reverend said. "However, the supplies are one thing, but the carpenter will not likely do the work
on credit."

"I will do the work," Lionel said, straightening his shoulders.

"You?" Mrs. Gilmore asked.

"Yes. I'm a craftsman."

Rev. Gilmore looked surprised.

"But your hand," Mrs. Gilmore said.

"You have kept it bandaged adequately," Lionel said. "My wife
would have been pleased. She was a nurse. It is healing."

"I'm sure John will gladly help fix his own boat," the Reverend
said.

"Eddie, too," Mrs. Gilmore said. "Ask him; he'll help."

"I take it there is more to learn about you, Lionel." Rev. Gilmore
patted him on the back.

"There is more to learn about many things, I'm afraid," Lionel
said.

"What do you propose, my good man?"

Lionel smiled sadly. "If you might speak for my credit, we may purchase supplies for the repairs and deliver them—being sure to make arrangement with the fisherman, of course. I also have need to telegraph London with the report of my whereabouts, and . ..." Lionel continued with difficulty. "And the tragedy as it has happened."

⌒⌒

"Cast off," Arthur said from the tiller. "Up with the jib."

Arthur and his crew cast off for a day of hovelling. Fitted out in winter rigging, the *Seahorse* was dressed for rough labor at sea.

The boat pushed away from the pier. Henry raised the triangular sail to catch enough wind to give steerage. Arthur pulled the tiller arm to port, causing the bow to swing outward to starboard away from the pier and toward the mouth of the harbor. In a few minutes, they were outside of the stony refuge and into the bay.

Arthur steered her head into the wind, causing the jib to luff. The flapping sail was his cue. "Up with the main," he shouted.

The harsh winter weather forced men to cram larger amounts of work and sweat into shorter lengths of daylight. It demanded they be garbed in heavier clothing but still left them chilled and damp to the marrow.

Arthur watched Edward and Jeffery haul the mainsail while Tom helped trim it. It flapped and snapped with great force until Arthur turned the boat out of the headwind so that it came more from the side. The sails ceased luffing and stretched full with wind.

"Wind abeam," Arthur said while Tom pulled lines snug and fastened them to cleats. "Not so tight, Tom Hardwell. Give it up some."

Tom let out some slack. "Better?"

"It'll do."

Arthur whispered to Henry, who stood beside him. "He's not as sharp as you said. He may be a seaman, but he's not a hoveller."

"He'll catch on. I was told he could handle his own."

Tom approached them.

"With such violent weather last night, there ought to be some fair hovelling to be done," Arthur said to Henry.

"God knows we need it," Tom said.

"God's got nothing to do with it, mate," Arthur said. "'Tis the devil racks this place."

"You know what I mean," Tom said.

"I don't. You haven't been part of this crew long enough for me to know what you mean."

"I only meant it's been scarce work lately. We need a good find, that's all I was saying."

"We don't take to complaining. Not on my ship," Arthur said.

"Who's complaining? I was just saying." Tom's face darkened, and he drifted a few steps away.

"Don't press him, Arthur," Henry said. "He'll be fine."

"He's sloppy."

Henry looked across the waves. "You're right about the devil. The Goodwin is his playground."

"We all know that." Arthur spat perfectly with the wind, his spittle flying off the leeward side.

Tom cautiously returned. "So what's the plan for today?"

"What we always do," Arthur said.

"We skirt around the Sands with a sharp eye for ships in distress," Henry said.

"We sure have plenty supply of extra chain and anchor aboard to sell," Tom said. "Hope somebody needs it. It isn't easy providing for the wife and kids through the bitter cold of off-season."

"It's our lot, mate," Arthur said, not looking at him, "so get used to it. Fish can't run all year. Besides, this time of year, wrecks will be happening nearly each day."

"There haven't been but a few shillings to split amongst ourselves," Tom said. "I hope it gets better."

"You can always stay ashore, mate."

"I was just saying."

Arthur looked at him now. "Your saying sounds like complaining, so why not say nothing?"

Tom opened his mouth to speak. Arthur stared, daring Tom with a penetrating glare. Tom folded his arms, leaned against a rail, and said nothing. Arthur smirked at Henry.

A healthy southwesterly pushed hard on the little lugger. She bounded and leapt over the chops of water at great speed. The weather was holding fair for mid-November, and the distant clouds weren't moving in any hurry.

"Wreck ahead!" John shouted from the bow. "North sand head!"

Tom stood up straight. "There be a fine chance!"

They saw the dark hulk rising above the waves. The brig was all the way over on one side, her keel facing the crashing seas. Her masts and yardarms pointed straight over the northern end of the Sands, just a few feet above it, poking and digging. The spars were forming a pool of sorts. Much of the rigging bobbed and swirled like a badly tangled fishing net within the pool.

"No sign of survivors!" John shouted as he peered through his spyglass.

Arthur knew what had likely happened. The poor souls anchored in the Gull Stream or the Downs to ride out the storm, dragged their anchors without realizing, and soon found themselves struck up against the deadly reef. With such a swirl of snow and wave under cover of dark, and with only a sporadic moon for light, no one on shore would've even known the unlucky sailors were involved in a death struggle until it was too late.

"What went on here was terrible-like," Tom said.

Henry nodded solemnly. "Even knowing, there isn't any say in it."

"Aye," Arthur said. "No one can approach the Sands during weather without the same result."

"They knew they were dead once they struck the reef," Henry said.

"Aye," Arthur said. "Most sailors know they're dead before they're dead."

As the *Seahorse* approached the hulk, the crew waited on Arthur for his next commands. He studied the pounding surf on all sides of the brig. He knew the present action of slamming waves and leaping sprays of white foam were the final fits of a receding tide and that the *Seahorse* had no business getting too near them. In about thirty minutes the sea level would drop sufficiently that the rough action of the waves would lessen and the Sands would begin to slowly emerge as a beach rising from the sea.

"We sheer off to her north and drop anchor," Arthur said to his men. "We ride out the tide then lower the boat."

They anchored and waited. After the tide lowered to a safe level, they let out cable and steered in close.

"Check her grip, Henry," Arthur said. "I want that anchor well-grounded. Along with a tight staysail, we'll have good control."

"Caution here," Tom said. "The waters run from deep to shallow real suddenlike."

"Tell me something I don't know," Arthur said.

They ran out an extended cable so the lugger could safely coast to a plain view of the deck side of the wrecked ship. Because the ship lay on its side, Arthur knew access would be tricky.

"You'll be using hatchets to scale the hull," he said as they lowered the longboat. "Two to a man."

The longboat launched with the crew to beach on the sparkling sands while Arthur and Henry stayed aboard the *Seahorse*. Arthur watched the men through the spyglass, though he was close enough to see without it. Henry stood beside him, ready to assist.

The others scaled the wrecked hull like tree climbers and performed much of their salvaging work in topsy-turvy fashion. Jeffery and Edward, younger and more flexible than the rest, reached the top first, which in their position was really the side or gunwale of the vessel. John and Tom were close behind.

"Get what rigging you can!" Arthur yelled.

Tom waved his reply. He and John readied their hatchets and knives to cut free whatever they could coil and remove. The two younger crewmen looked over the side to explore the sideways deck.

Arthur watched his men through the spyglass like a mother hen counting chicks. He particularly followed his brother, Edward, who peered down over the side to look at the weather rigging still in place. He and Jeffery helped each other climb down. With legs wrapped tightly and hands clinging firmly to the network of ropes, Jeffery and Edward searched the deck and tried to gaze into the hold since the hatches had all been washed away.

"Looks like everything's been washed out," Edward shouted. He swung around on the ropes like a monkey swinging from vine to vine. He approached the captain's cabin, which was tricky to enter, since it was on its side.

"Don't be a hero, Edward," Arthur said to himself as he watched through the spyglass. "Stay out of the cabin."

Edward seemed to be taking care to not lose his grip and fall into the pool beneath him, which still posed a considerable threat of entanglement. He swung forward with his legs and grabbed a rope just above the cabin entrance. He hooked his legs on the rope, then released his handholds. His upper body dropped and rapidly swung toward the cabin door. He struck his head hard on the door and dangled.

"Fool!" Arthur yelled. He lowered the glass and walked briskly along the rail, pointing to Edward. "John! Tom! Jeffery!" he yelled. "See to Edward!"

Tom and John, having just reached the gunwale, poked their heads over the sides to discover what was happening. Jeffery, swinging from ropes at the opposite end, spun around to see Edward some twenty feet away.

"Greetings, mate!" Edward said with a grin, hanging upside down. He waved with one hand and rubbed his sore head with the other.

Jeffery laughed and returned to his search. Tom and John frowned over the interruption and Arthur hissed. Edward reached up and grabbed the rope his feet clung to then dropped his feet to kick open the cabin door.

"Don't do it!" Arthur said, again watching through his spyglass.

Edward disappeared inside.

"I'll break his neck!" Arthur cursed loudly as though he wanted to be heard by many. Then he bit his lip and waited. His eyes squinted as a fresh breeze crossed his face. Arthur cocked his head. "Catch that?"

Henry nodded and looked east. "Not only that," he said. "Look over there."

Arthur looked to where his friend pointed. On the horizon, faint but not so faint that a well-trained eye couldn't discern it, loomed a squall and with it a surrounding darkening of weather. "A turning of wind and an approaching squall. Time to disembark. Speak the men!"

Henry fetched a speaking trumpet. He placed the funnel to his mouth and bellowed Arthur's command into the face of the new direction of wind. "Ahoy! Shove off men! It's time to go!"

"What for?" Tom shouted back. "We've much to cut here!" His voice carried well on the back of the wind.

"Gimme that!" Arthur said, snatching the horn from Henry. "Now hear this! A new wind and approaching weather! Belay and return!"

Tom looked toward the distant weather and tapped John's shoulder. The two men talked among themselves from their places atop the jumbled rigging where they had been working to cut and remove the stronger shrouds. Tom looked back at Arthur. "It's just a spoon drift, Arthur. We'll stop soon enough!"

"Make sure of it!" Arthur replied. He looked up to study the condition of his weather streamers. They were straight out, indicating a stiffening wind. He lowered the horn and mumbled to Henry. "Fools! Tom Hardwell is a hardhead."

Henry nodded. Arthur eyed the approaching gray squall then looked back for Edward, but couldn't find him.

"I'm going to kick his stern side!"

❧

Inside the shipwrecked cabin everything was displaced. Edward had not easily entered it, and now he carefully lowered himself to stand on the starboard wall, which had since become a kind of curved floor.

Seawater sloshed about, making a soup of books and charts and eating utensils. A whiskey flask floated nearby, and a spyglass rolled back and forth in a corner section flanked by a broken writing table and padlocked trunk on its side. Edward kicked at the lock with his foot but was unable to loosen it. He looked around for an object to pry it open and saw several silver tubes floating and several more lying in a partially opened oak box with ornate carvings.

He scooped up one of the tubes and ran it under his nose. He twisted off one end and partially slid out the cigar from within to sniff it again. He replaced it and the cap and stuffed several of the shiny tubes into his inside coat pocket. He closed the box and tucked it under one arm.

He balanced himself with his legs spread wide and bent down to pick up the spyglass with his free hand. Suddenly, the entire vessel shifted. It lifted for a moment then settled back on the Sands. Edward fell backward to sit in a pool of sea water.

He managed to keep hold of his goods, but he was struggling to stand when the ship tipped more severely. He fell onto his side, breaking his fall with his shoulder and keeping his goods dry and unbroken, though at a considerable expense of comfort. He swung his legs around, rolled on his other side, and landed upright on his feet on the curved floor.

He looked up to the horizontal doorway of the sideways cabin. He tucked the spyglass inside his coat through the space between two buttons and used his free hand to pull on the beams and rafters to assist his movement toward it. He struggled to grab the door-frame and was just about to pull himself through when a frigid blast of wind burst in upon him.

He didn't fall, but he was surprised. He peeked out the doorway to see what was transpiring above board. He was shocked to see Jeffery hanging from his arms from the guide ropes just outside the cabin.

"Snow and hail!" Jeffery said. "Scrap the haul and be quick! Need a tug?" He reached out a hand.

"No, but take this!" Edward said. He handed the spyglass to his mate, who quickly tucked it away.

"Let's slip this cable!" Jeffery said. He swung from rope to rope until he reached amidships, then kicked a leg over the side and dropped out of sight.

Edward clambered not far behind. He reached the side and peered over. Down below, he saw Tom and John waiting in the boat, which rocked fiercely upon the agitated sea. They reached up to catch Jeffery as he slid down the side into their arms. He knocked them over like pins. Edward waited for them to reset.

White blasts of spray sprang up from between the boat and the steep hull. Edward looked up toward the open channel and saw a whirlwind of gusting snow and hail that blasted him hard. It felt like a blanket of tiny icicles. He couldn't see a thing but knew he couldn't wait until he did. In just a few moments the longboat would be gone, forced away by the conditions, and he would be lost.

He hung over the side and held the gunwale with one hand, gripping the cigar box with the other. He let go and slid like rock across a sheet of ice. He hoped to find the boat at the end of his fall. He was only half disappointed.

Edward's feet went straight into the water but his belly caught the oarlocks, hitting them hard. The air rushed from his lungs, and the box popped from his grip and splashed into the unseen water in the midst of the swirling squall of ice and snow.

Edward couldn't find any strength to reach out and grab hold. He started to slip back into the water. He knew the boat would be tossed back and forth near the wrecked hull, and he half expected to be crushed between the two. Suddenly, two powerful hands reached from over his head and pulled him into the boat by the back of his coat.

"What's this?" John asked with a grunt. "A marlin?"

"Look sharp!" Tom yelled. "Do you want all of us to drown? Take the oars!"

John made sure Edward was in and then grabbed an oar. Jeffery yanked on the anchor, which seemed to take forever to get loose.

The boat was being battered by waves. There was plenty of high-flying spray and swirling snow. Looming dark clouds were sure to follow. Edward knew whiteouts could become blackouts in short order.

"It won't look like midday for long," Edward said.

"Which way do we go?" Tom asked. "Which way do we go?"

❧

"Cut the cable!"

Arthur watched Henry, knowing that another man might have questioned such a command. Cutting away the anchor could create disaster, but Arthur knew Henry would understand.

"Aye!" Henry answered. He took a hatchet to the anchor line and cut it loose.

The ship slipped away fast to make great distance between her and where her longboat would likely be. Arthur wasn't exactly sure where the boat was. He couldn't see a thing in the blowing snow. "It's their only chance!"

"I know!" Henry shouted back.

With the increasing winds, zero visibility, and the current tide level, it was fast becoming a mad craze of violently confused waters.

"Up with the jib!" Arthur shouted. He pushed the tiller hard to port. The tiller action had to be in perfect timing with the hauled sail.

Henry appeared out of the whiteness to stand beside Arthur. "Go round with her and push hard!" he said. As the *Seahorse* caught the wind, she swung around swiftly. "You think they'll figure what to do?"

"They have to," Arthur said as he manned the tiller and searched the far edge of the sandy hulk. There were moments when he thought he could see the reef, but he wasn't certain.

"Edward will know," Henry said. "He'll understand."

"If he's thinking," Arthur said. "That's more the point."

"John is the coxswain. He'll steer them straight."

Arthur pointed. "There!" He saw the vague outline of the longboat through the swirling gusts of ice and snow and in a rage of sea.

"They thought right!" Henry said with a cheer.

"They've rowed around the edge to emerge on this side."

"They guessed well," Henry said. "There's a lesser surf running."

"Only for a short time," Arthur reminded him. "It will soon be ugly, and there's tough work ahead."

"It's already ugly," Henry said.

"It'll get uglier when I get them aboard!"

❦

"The weather has turned foul again." Rev. Gilmore carefully guided the wagon through the narrow streets away from the telegraph office. He looked across at Lionel. "It's no wonder the telegraph lines are down."

As they turned from Marine Road to Harbour Place and toward

the drydock, Lionel looked out across the swirling snow flurries. Slush slopped up from the wheels. The weather had progressively worsened as the day had worn on, and Lionel felt his own stormy mix of emotions. He touched the bruise above his eye.

"Lionel?" the Reverend asked. "You okay?"

Lionel heard him but found he could not answer at once. He ached to hear his wife's voice, to feel her warm touch, and to squeeze Luke in his arms. He could not imagine another moment without them, yet the moment demanded so much. He was in a strange town with strange people. He had a business to return to, and he was witnessing coastal tragedies that occurred with as much frequency as pockets were picked in London.

"I'm fine."

"It is a miserable sea, today is," Rev. Gilmore said.

"I fear you were right," Lionel said. "The wagon will be challenged to make the return trip with all this material. The day started out so clear."

"Winter weather is moody in Ramsgate," Rev. Gilmore said. "But we could never have done as you wished with anything less. So much timber. And what's the copper for?"

"Bottom sheeting. Makes her sturdy."

The Reverend looked surprised. "It's more than John will expect."

"I believe in excellence."

"May I ask you what you were going to telegraph to your workers? I mean, about your family."

"Not yet certain. I'd let them know I'm alive. And who isn't."

"If the weather persists and the lines stay down, there is a mail packet that runs to London. I take it occasionally," Rev. Gilmore said as they turned into the harbor area. "Did any of your workers know your family personally?"

"They all did. They knew them well. Luke often played around the shop."

Rev. Gilmore pulled the reins and set the wheel-brake. "We'll unload here."

Lionel looked at the harbor. Swirling and gusting snow swarmed the rocking boats. He and the Reverend walked to the rear of the wagon.

"I don't see the *Seahorse*," Rev. Gilmore said. "She may be out, God bless her."

"In this weather?"

"It's what hovellers do."

"What do they properly do?"

"The hovelling luggers perform needful services," Rev. Gilmore said as he unlatched the back of the buggy and he and Lionel began to slide out the timber. "Sometimes they chase ships that have fled their initial anchorage in search of better refuge. They offer help and expertise."

"Seems like honest work," Lionel said.

"Some are, others not. They also place men aboard fleeing vessels, either to act as pilots familiar with the area waters or to assist the weary crews. They mostly salvage."

Lionel stood straight and wrapped his coat tighter. It was blustery cold. He studied the harbor. He didn't see many working sailors, but there were many ships rocking wildly, like horses wanting to break loose. He noticed the vessels had moved into the inner harbor, and there was a much lower level of water in the outer.

"It's the tide," Rev. Gilmore explained. "It's peculiar how it ebbs and flows."

"Looks like nobody's working today," Lionel said, reaching for the copper.

"That's why we need to pray for the *Seahorse*. Typically, she'd be in under such conditions, but today's weather changed quickly. She may be caught. The fisherman whose boat you damaged is likely aboard her, as is the one who first brought you to us: Edward. A good man, Edward is. His brother, Arthur, whom you met so intimately in the harbor last night, owns the *Seahorse* along with Henry Hawkins, his partner."

"Fishermen are hovellers?" Lionel asked, gingerly massaging his ribs. "We ought to cover the copper."

"Not everyone hovels. It's a survival thing. Warmer times of the year, the *Seahorse* takes on a different appearance," Rev. Gilmore said. "What should we cover it with?"

"A tarp would do us well."

The Reverend peered into John Burton's boat, already in the drydock station beside the clock house. "We'll borrow John's."

Lionel helped him spread the heavy cloth over the supplies. "It's a living, I suppose," Lionel said. "Hovelling is." They weighted the tarp with two boxes of tools from the wagon. Lionel's hand ached with the work.

"It is just that," Rev. Gilmore said. "And it is better than smuggling, which some in Ramsgate have been known to do."

"Ah," Lionel said, straightening up and looking at the sea. "Perhaps your prayers are answered." He pointed beyond the harbor to an approaching dark shape.

CHAPTER 6

It had taken nearly forty minutes of fighting wind and tide before Arthur and Henry finally recovered the longboat and crew. Edward took his place on the *Seahorse* and avoided Arthur's eye.

The *Seahorse* ran before the wind on a rollicking sea. The tide ball signal on shore made it clear that there wasn't enough water in the outer portion of the harbor for the lugger to ride in comfortably. She would have to come in under great speed and run her keel straight into the dredged sandbank in the middle, purposely raked there for such conditions as these. From there, they'd ride their long boat to the pier and would have to wait until later to pilot the *Seahorse* off the bank when the tide level was sufficient. Having to leave his vessel like that would only add to Arthur's anger.

They tacked and positioned and coursed in on a swift line and plowed in fast to jar deep into the sand and muck. Everyone stumbled forward.

"Lower sails! Let go to anchor!" Arthur commanded. "Prepare longboat."

As they rowed to the pier, Arthur's expression was darker than the weather that had overrun them at the Goodwin. "Humph!" he said. "Funny we have a longboat to tie up with. I would've thought you'd had enough time to smash it more completely."

The two old salts who usually helped the *Seahorse* tie up weren't there. No doubt gone inside to escape the weather. But to Edward's surprise, he spotted the Reverend John Gilmore waiting to receive the lines—and he had the landsman with him. Jeffery threw a bow line to Rev. Gilmore while Henry tossed one from the stern.

"Pretty shivering weather to be running about," the Reverend called. "Hope you did well!"

"Empty-handed again," Tom said, his bitterness clear.

"You know the way of hovelling," John said. He leapt to the floating dock. He signaled Jeffery to join him. He nodded to the Reverend but ignored the man who had damaged his fishing boat.

Jeffery jumped alongside and reached into his coat. He pulled out the spyglass. "Not completely swamped. This ought to fetch a few shillings to go around."

"Hey!" Edward exclaimed. He reached into his vest to pull out his light cargo. He fanned out the half-dozen cigars in silver cases. "How's this for a catch?"

The crew gushed with praise.

"Oh, that's worth a sunken lugger, isn't it?" Arthur asked, his voice rising quickly as he lumbered out of the boat. He passed the men and headed toward the stone steps. "Maybe even a crew of men would be a fair swap for a good smoke, yeah?" He turned to them from halfway up the stairs. "I expect every one of you in Cannon's as soon as you're in dry gear. None absent, neither! Good day to you, Reverend."

Rev. Gilmore watched Arthur stomp away. He turned to John Burton and his son. "John, there is a surprise waiting at your boat."

"I've had enough surprises, thank you, Reverend. No disrespect to you."

"None taken, but I think it worth your time to note the ready supplies to repair your boat when the weather permits."

"Is that so?" John left the dock and walked over to his boat in drydock. Edward followed. John looked at the timber and copper under his tarp. "Who's paying for this?" He looked at the Reverend. "The church? I'll not take it."

Rev. Gilmore smiled and gestured to the landsman. "My friend, Lionel, here, whom you may recognize, has offered to pay for it and help with the work."

"No friend of mine," John Burton said. "He isn't claiming to pay on credit, I hope."

"That's my concern, John," Rev. Gilmore said. "Lionel may have a few surprises for you."

"Is this copper?" Edward asked.

"It's for sheathing the bottom," the man named Lionel said. "For added durability."

John stared at the stranger, appearing conflicted.

Edward smiled. "I've heard of such uses for copper."

"Like I told you," Rev. Gilmore said, "you may discover a few surprises."

"Yeah, well, we've got some other business to attend to," John said. "Maybe tomorrow or when the weather breaks." He and the others walked in the direction Arthur had gone.

"Thanks, mate," Edward said as he passed Lionel. "Thanks, Reverend."

※

Within the hour, Edward joined the crew of the *Seahorse* in Cannon's public house. They had gathered at a table in the back, hidden away from the main area and tucked around a corner.

Within minutes, Arthur launched into his lecture, with each man having a hard time dismissing his points. Not because he was

85

so belligerent and forceful, which he was, but because he spoke convincingly of what might have happened if it hadn't turned out so favorably lucky.

"A few minutes longer, maybe seconds," he said, standing over the men with a mug in one hand, "and you would've been seeing heavy surf along the back of the Sands."

"It's true and you know it," Henry said to the men.

Arthur drank ale from his mug, then turned to assail them again, his bushy white mustache wet with foam and spittle. "When rollers from the deep water hit the edge of the hulk, they mount up greatlike!"

"Too great for the lugger," Henry said, "and much worse the longboat."

"Aye," Arthur said. "They curl over and fall apart to break up backwards with the next rollers straight behind. Then you're rocked, and there's no getting away cheap. You'd sooner see a rock float than a boat make it through that mess."

"You might as well be hauling a cargo of coal; you'd go down no faster," Henry said.

"We would've been right there in front of you, not more than two or three boat lengths away, and no way to get to you or you to us!" Arthur said, his face reddening.

"Arthur," Edward said. "You're right. You're right. It was my fault—"

Arthur slammed his mug on the table. It foamed up and ran over the sides. "Oh, no! No, you don't! I'll be getting soon enough to blame." He pressed in close to Edward and lowered his voice to a threatening whisper. "Won't nobody doubt how it all came to be." He picked up his mug and gulped down what was left. "Cannon!"

Henry used the reprieve to chime in. "A few seconds more and to be certain there would've been no way for you to get off the Goodwin or for us to come and get ya! Now Tom, you should've come when we first spoke ya!"

Tom shifted in his seat. "It's the way of things, Henry. The sea is an odd sort. You know how quick it can change."

"No!" Arthur shouted.

Cannon arrived with a tray of full mugs and set them down. Arthur fumbled in his pockets to pay, but Cannon waved him off. "We'll settle later. Finish your . . . your, well . . . finish whatever you call it. I'm keeping the score." Cannon walked away chuckling.

Arthur gulped some more ale. "A good sailor respects the sea, and because he knows the way of it, he sees the future of it, 'cause he knows it!"

"C'mon Arthur," Tom said, "no one knows the future. It was unfortunate—we erred in judgment. Next time we cast off sooner."

"There won't be no next time 'less you understand what you failed to understand this time," Arthur said. "A good sailor knows the future 'cause he doesn't look at what is, but opens his eyes"—Arthur pointed to his right eye and then to his head—"and his mind, to see what's about to happen."

"Yes!" Henry snapped, slamming his palm on the table.

"You watch the horizon," Arthur said. "There stirs the future. It isn't what's happening that sinks the sailor; it's what's *about* to happen. And that's why we spoke to you, and that's why you got to listen!" Arthur's arms moved like a frenzied symphony conductor's. Then he paused.

Henry seemed to understand the cue. He nodded but this time made no sound.

Arthur stood there a long time, his eyes narrowed and his lips pressed thin and tight. His gaze roved to each member of his crew until one by one they nodded in return. Finally, Arthur relaxed and sat down.

"I'm sorry, Arthur," John said. "I nearly cost us everything, and you're right."

"Aye," his son said.

"Aye," Tom said, but quietly.

"Aye," Edward said. "Sorry, brother. I was a fool."

"Aye, you were. And now," Arthur said, folding his arms and looking grim, "we shall smoke the fool."

Edward felt his eyes widen. "What?"

Arthur smiled and reached forward with open hand. "Where's my cigar?"

Edward laughed and drew out the silver cases to the delight of all. Each man marveled over the silver tubes and soon enough uncapped and prepared for a smoke. Edward lit them all with some safety matches from the bar. They were soon engulfed in a swirl of gray-blue smoke. "If only I'd not dropped the whole lot of them into the drink! A box full, it was!"

After enjoying their tobacco for some minutes, Tom broke the silence. "So what would you have done, Arthur?"

"About what, Hardwell?"

"If it had been you out there today, what would you have done?" Tom drew a long puff on his cigar. "I mean, of course we all know you wouldn't take the longboat to the Goodwin, but humor us now. What would you have done?"

The men grew quiet. Arthur sat still for a long moment and drew a short puff. He exhaled and smiled. "I thought I made it clear. I would've answered the trumpet by debarking when asked to do so."

"Of course," Henry said. "Now don't this swirl of smoke sure beat the swirl of snow and sea, lads?"

The men voiced their agreement, but Tom pressed. "Of course, but I mean if you were in the longboat. We all know you wouldn't be, I'm quite right, but let's say you were and you found yourself in the predicament along the back of the reef with impassable surf. What would a good sailor do then?"

The table again grew quiet. Henry's face soured, and his mouth inverted to a tight pouting shape.

Edward forced a smile. "Who's in the mood for some cricket? Arthur? Jeffery?"

Arthur raised his hand. "No, not just yet, Edward. It's okay. It's okay."

"Assuming," Tom continued, "we know a good sailor wouldn't get himself in such a spot of trouble, what if somehow he was? What would seamanship beg in such an instance?"

Arthur drew a long puff on his cigar and blew the smoke high. "He'd have no choice but to sail back over the Goodwin. The water would be high enough to afford some navigation for a time, but time would be short, of course."

"Of course," Tom said. "Not to mention she'd be ridging."

"That'd be the only sensible option," Henry said. "Under the circumstances."

"Aye," Arthur said, his voice lowering. He directed his gaze from Tom to the others around the table. "Once there, we'd have a short time for rest with the oars. It'd be good to take it because we would need our strength for what's ahead."

"Ah, ahead, like in the future?" Tom asked innocently, reaching for another mug and gulping it down.

"You could call it that," Arthur said, not smiling. He turned to Edward. "You still aching for some cricket? I'm almost done here."

"Say the word," Edward said.

Arthur looked straight at Tom. "You might go to the wreck for a little protection under her lee, but soon enough you'd have to navigate over the beach itself all the way to the in-sand."

"Trinity Bay?" Tom said. "Impossible!"

"Difficult," Arthur corrected.

"Listen and learn, mate," Henry said to Tom.

"That entire backside stretch along the pool would be surrounded by the edges of the Sands," Tom said. "You couldn't get over them."

"Not easily, but you'd have to," Arthur said. "When the tide becomes high enough, it'd still be choppy but navigable. Then you'd get to the center of Trinity and have a few more minutes to rest."

"Sounds like a lot of napping, this escape does," Tom said.

Arthur studied the glowing end of his cigar.

Henry folded his arms and glared at Tom. "What would you do, then?"

"I'd have us row hard and fast to the crown of the Goodwin," Tom said, grabbing another mug. "It would likely still be dry as a beach."

"The squalling would prevent you from knowing that for sure," Henry said, "and once you got there, you'd find you had guessed wrong. The crown would be underwater and your crew exhausted."

"Likely so," Arthur said. "If you chose better to head for Trinity, you might find, under said conditions, to have upwards of an hour to rest. 'Course, you couldn't wait for anything but certain drowning. So soon enough—hopefully with renewed strength and a stout will—you'd row on, with maybe a little nip of rum to warm you up."

The other men chuckled and seemed to relax.

"You'd still have to clear the next bank of sand on the way out,"

Tom reminded Arthur.

Edward sighed.

"No doubt," Arthur said, taking another long puff of his cigar and blowing the smoke toward Tom. "All around us the sea would be curling up with no kind intent." As Arthur gesticulated, his cigar made wreaths and rings around him.

He stood up dramatically, waving on. "The surf would be gleaming and foaming, and our course over the steep edges of sand would be like no dance upon the waves we've yet known personal. It'd be all pitch and roll and icy cold spray to remind us we're not home. Nothing less than a prayer from whoever knew how best to pray and a little secret weapon that every good sailor knows how to wield, would do. That's what it would take to get us over the final edge and into the Downs. From there, we would either make shelter in Dover or find some happy schooner to tie us up and warm us with some brandy and hot bread."

"What's the secret weapon?" Jeffery asked.

"Why, it's a bailing bowl, to be sure!" Arthur answered with a broad smile and a gleam in his eye. The men laughed with him — save Tom, who offered a mere smirk.

"That's a fine theory," Tom said. "'Course we all know you wouldn't be stepping into a longboat or making a landing on no Goodwin Sands anytime soon, now would ya?"

Edward shot him a warning look, but Tom paid no heed.

"It is one thing to make all these, uh, calculations and, say, imaginations from the safety of the lugger lashed to the sturdy tiller by those mitts of yours," Tom said. "It's quite another to rock in a longboat to cut the rigging off a sorry hulk lying on her beam ends atop the deathtrap. We won't find you doing that anytime soon, am I right? Am I mistaken or do I 'know the future' on that one?"

Everyone grew quiet. Arthur stared at his cigar for a long time.

Slowly the huge man reached over and doused his cigar in Tom's ale. "You best not look too far into the future, mate. You might not like what you see."

"Yeah?" Tom said, his voice bitter. "Is the future so bad to see? Or might it be the past?"

Arthur's bottom lip stuck out and Edward knew what that meant.

"Tom, you sure are the fool tonight," Henry said, as calm as a still sea, his mug inches from his mouth.

Suddenly, Arthur tipped the table over and cleared it out of his way. The mugs fell and Arthur grabbed Tom Hardwell by the collar. He lifted him out of his chair so that his feet dangled several inches above the floor.

"You might be belaying any more drink tonight, Tom," Arthur said. "Something like a stormy cloud has fogged your brain, and that don't bode well for fair-weather sailing. Am I clear, mate?"

"I believe," Tom said, his voice strained but even, "I have had a tad much to drink tonight, Arthur."

"If I'm not mistaken," Arthur said, "your pockets aren't far from empty this time of year, and the *Seahorse* is one of the few working crafts that'll have you."

"That's right," Tom moaned. "It's a good job, it is."

"If it's one you want to keep, you best keep your hatch closed from foolish talk, or you'll be finding yourself with no sea legs worth much but maybe a bag of shells."

"Yes," Tom said, his face pale.

Arthur dropped him to the floor, where Tom clutched at his throat and gasped for air. "Cannon will want you to clean up this mess, Tom," Arthur said. "I heartily recommend you offer him a few alms for his fine service tonight."

Edward cleared his throat loudly. "Cricket? The board is open."

"No, I'm not in the mood." Arthur tipped his cap to Henry, settled with Cannon at the bar, and left the pub.

Henry helped Tom up. "You had no business talking like that. And the bit about not stepping into a longboat was a cheap shot, Tom. You're lucky he didn't break your bones tonight."

"I don't like being told what to do like I'm some cabin boy," Tom said, rubbing his throat.

"You crew the *Seahorse*," John said, "so expect it. It isn't always easy, and we get a lecture or two more than most, but it's our livelihood and he's our captain. Besides, he knows what he says, and you can't find much fault with it."

"I just wish he wasn't such a bully." Tom picked up his cap and dusted himself off.

"Just remember what I said," Henry said. "No more wisecracks like those you let fly tonight. You batten those where they don't see the light of day, or you'll be dealing with more than Arthur. C'mon, Eddie, I'll toss you a game."

"Count me in," Jeffery said.

"Aye, I'm in," John said.

Tom grumbled but stooped to clean up the mess.

CHAPTER 7

Lionel thought the Reverend's wagon rode too rough. It lacked the latest modifications. A specially tempered band of steel fastened between the axles and wagon bed would greatly enhance the ride. He turned right onto Marine Place, having chosen a different route into town from near the eastern cliff.

He resented his ambitions as the wagon bumped along. "I have a chance for a good deal in Dover," he had told Alicia.

"It will be an adventure," she had said. "A great story to tell."

He remembered his foreman in London, Boxley. He would take the loss hard. So would the others.

As Lionel neared the harbor, he worked to regain his composure, not wanting any tears to flow. The wagon was loaded with bolts, caulking rope, and pitch. The Gilmores had arranged for him to meet John Burton to begin repairs on the damaged boat.

Lionel arrived at the quayside and eased his way through the busy location until he spotted the fisherman, the fisherman's son, and the one named Edward, who had taken him to the Gilmores. They were grouped around the drydock along the cross wall that separated the inner from the outer harbor. The men looked up at the approaching wagon. Edward smiled and waved. The fisherman looked stern, and his son nodded.

"Good morning, men," Lionel said, reining back then applying the brake with his left hand.

"Good morning, Lionel," Edward said. "How's the hand?"

"Been better."

"I'm sure. You know John here, and Jeffery, his son."

"Good day, gentlemen," Lionel said.

John studied the wrecked condition of his fishing boat. He shook his head and mumbled something. Edward walked up to the Gilmores' wagon and peered in. "You've brought more?"

John looked up.

Jeffery strode over to the wagon. "Quality stuff," he said. "It'll go a long way."

John looked in the wagon and closely inspected everything by touching and turning it. Lionel hopped out and assisted the unloading. They removed the tarp from the previous delivery.

"Well, where do we get started?" Edward asked, clapping his hands.

John cleared his throat. He didn't seem sure what to make of the items. "Okay, uh, clean out the boat and set up that timber for cutting."

Edward and Jeffery emptied the boat of the little stowed in it. It didn't amount to much but oars and anchor, so the task was quickly accomplished.

"I beg your pardon," Lionel said to John, "for damaging your boat. But I maintain I am able to repair her. If you will, I'd like to suggest how we might proceed."

"You're telling it straight to beg my pardon," John said. "That boat there might not seem much to you, but it's the difference between eating and hungering at times. It belongs to me, and no one embarks another man's boat. Not without permission."

"I was wrong to take your boat," Lionel said.

John stared at Lionel. "You say you're able to repair her?"

Lionel nodded. "Is that an invitation?"

"Might be."

"It's all in the quality of timber," Lionel said. "Most know that, but it's the measuring, too. We start by cutting out the damaged area, then accurately measuring what needs replacing. I can't do much with my right hand, but I can direct, if you permit. I know my trade."

The men followed Lionel's lead and worked for some time measuring and fitting.

"You say this is your trade?" Edward said, admiring the work and eagerly assisting. "No doubt!"

Lionel smiled. This was the good man who had brought him to the Gilmores. He appeared to be in his late twenties or early thirties. He was boyishly handsome with dark, wavy hair. His eyes were as blue as the ocean. Luke had had blue eyes, though his hair had been fine and light.

"You okay?" Edward asked.

Lionel looked up, startled. "Huh?"

"What do we do next?" Edward asked, pointing to the piece he'd just cut.

John examined the work. "That's a mite large, I'm sure of it."

"Better to err on cutting it larger," Lionel said. "This way we grind her to fit seamlessly. Otherwise, you either waste much wood or work piecemeal, which is never good."

John nodded grudgingly and worked the crude file along the edge of the piece. "Seems right," he said, without smiling.

After a number of hours, Lionel declared it was time to work the copper. He showed them how to apply the copper sheathing to the bottom.

"I've seen iron keels," John said. "Never seen copper sheathing. Heard of it, though." He ran his hand along the smooth metal.

With Edward's assistance, Lionel pounded out a few swipes with a mallet. They applied the sheet to the hull only to remove it and pound it again.

"Here," John said, reaching for the mallet, "let me do that."

"Sure," Lionel said, handing it over. "I'm right-handed. Don't have as much power in my left."

John struck the metal hard.

"Let the face of it do the smoothing," Lionel said. "It's not so much brute strength as it is steady strikes."

"How'd you get that?" John asked, motioning to Lionel's hand. "What happened?"

"Captain Beeker knifed my hand to the mast. I don't think on purpose. Most likely it saved my life."

"Beeker?" John stopped swinging the mallet and took a sideways step. "You were on the *Sanctus*?"

Lionel nodded. Everyone looked surprised. "What?"

"What happened to the knife?" Edward asked.

"I don't know. Why?"

The three men exchanged dark glances.

"Hogger's a squid," John said, nodding. "That much we know."

"Who's Hogger?" Lionel asked.

"Nobody worth knowing," John said. He resumed pounding out the copper.

When they had finished, the copper shone smooth. They finished the above-board trimmings, and returned it to the water.

"She looks prettier than when you first found her," Edward said.

"I never figured you for a sailor," John said. "I don't get it."

"I'm no sailor." Lionel wiped the sweat from his forehead, taking care to avoid his bruise. "But I know timber."

"You know more than timber," Edward said, holding a discarded piece of copper.

"I know most metals, but not all," Lionel said.

"I never thought I'd say this," John said, squarely facing Lionel, "but I'd be happy to buy you a pint at Cannon's."

"I don't drink," Lionel said, "but thank you." He gathered up the Reverend's tools. "I am very sorry for my behavior toward your boat. I trust you consider my restitution paid."

"Yes, of course," John said. "You don't drink?"

"How about joining us for some shepherd's pie?" Edward asked.

"Actually," Lionel said, "I'd like to see the Goodwin Sands."

John shrugged. "That can be arranged. It might be a good way to prove out your work."

"When?" Lionel asked.

"Tomorrow maybe," John said. "Weather has the say, you know. But weather or not, unless you join us for some shepherd's pie, it won't happen."

Lionel was puzzled.

"My dad likes your work, mate," Jeffery said.

John smiled. "Well?"

"Shepherd's pie?" Lionel asked.

"It's even fresh sometimes," Edward said, "but it's always weighty!"

Lionel smiled. "As long as it doesn't stick to my ribs. They're still a bit sore."

CHAPTER 8

The next day Lionel watched Edward lower the sail as John steered his repaired fishing boat into the mild wind. Jeffery and Edward took the oars and rowed in close to the Goodwin Sands.

"Ho! All ashore," Jeffery jumped out and held the gunwale. "I'll hold her steady."

The seas were reasonably calm. The sky was clear, and the Goodwin looked like a tropical beach that ran for miles at varying widths. In some places, the rolling sand banked down into the water where the seas streamed over in swift-moving currents.

Lionel marked his distance from the harbor and was surprised to see how close it appeared, though it was four miles away. He noted the headlands of England. He could see from the North Foreland all the way down to what John had explained was the small coastal town of Deal.

"If we had gone out farther," John said, "we would have seen around the jutting part of Deal all the way to the South Foreland heading toward Dover."

Dover. That was where Lionel and his family had been headed. They were supposed to have gone to prospect sales for the land coach. Lionel felt sweaty despite the cool air.

Edward and John jumped out. Jeffery headed up the sandy dune while John held the boat near the bow and Edward held it near the stern.

Lionel stood in the boat and looked in every direction. There was nothing but water and sand. There were distant ships and one fishing smack nearby, but none held his interest. He studied the sandy strip.

"Lionel?" John said.

"Yes, I'm all right." Lionel carefully stepped out one leg at a time, more slowly than the others had. Edward joined John near the bow, and they hauled the craft up the beach.

"The Goodwin Sands," Edward said, "are, say, about nine miles long. They have monster parts and several shallows. There is a large middle pool that appears at low water. It is known as Trinity Bay. We call it the in-sand."

"If we walk a bit, I can show it to you," John said.

Lionel tried to absorb the exact topography.

"If you're trying to see her shape," John said, "don't forget that she shifts. There's plenty of chalk within that's solid enough, but most of her is made up of shifting sand. She's impossible to chart."

Lionel walked toward the highest part near where Jeffery had gone. "Where's the stream-reach?" Lionel asked.

Edward and John exchanged glances.

"It's not always here," Jeffery said. He knelt down and pulled out a knife to dig in the sand.

"It's not to be seen now," John said. "How do you know about it?"

"What is it?" Lionel asked, staring into John's eyes.

John shifted on his feet. "Not many people know about it. Not by that name, anyways. *Stream-reach* is a local term."

"The captain told me they were in the stream-reach. What did he mean?"

"Who was in it?" John asked.

"My wife and son. What did he mean?"

"The stream-reach, or 'stream wreckage' as it is properly called," Edward said, "is where the currents set down on each side of the sand and then flow to a point of convergence. Whatever remains of a wreck can get caught up and carried away in one long line that goes for miles to leeward. There's no chance of escape if you get caught in it. The waves can become massive. Almost like . . ." His voice trailed off.

"Like mountains, some say," John said softly.

"They are like mountains," Lionel said. He was surprised that he felt nothing.

"Dead and busted wreckage is sometimes found by hovellers," Edward said. "They're usually foreign and several miles away. That's what's amazing. The stream is long and powerful."

Jeffery stood with clams in his hands. "This is a good snack, heh?" He headed back to the boat with his catch.

"At times the sand will start to ridge," John said, "like those small ridges you see along the coastal shore. Do you know what I'm talking about?"

Lionel shrugged.

"Along a beach there are those tiny ridges you can walk on," Edward said. "Here it's a different world. The Goodwin ridges can run two and three feet high because of the force of the waves and the strong currents. It can be like getting stuck between the folds of a giant squeezebox."

"Do they compress?" Lionel asked.

"Not exactly," Edward said. "The trouble is there's no way to navigate out. The waves slam your vessel into the ridges. If that's not the end of it, there's always the backwash slamming you against the next ridge on the other side. Either way, it's inescapable."

"Don't forget the Goodwin is quicksand," John said. "That fact as well as the heavy battering from the sea and the foul weather makes it a grave for all who touch her when she's testy."

"Not all," Lionel said sadly. He stared at the edge of the Goodwin where it met the water.

"When the tide rises and water flows over the Sands," Edward said, "the part that gets covered becomes *alive*, as we say. It means it becomes soft and deadly like quicksand. It'll suck up anything that touches it."

"Few graveyards can match her accounts," John said, his voice still low.

Lionel pointed beyond the northern spit. "You should float lights out there." He pointed in the opposite direction. "Off the southern point as well."

John shook his head. "They'd be almost impossible for vessels to see."

"But there would be a chance?"

"Where exactly would you place the lights?" Edward asked. "How would you keep them lit? How would you light them in the first place?"

"Right," John said, "and remember, the borders don't remain fixed."

"Don't forget the waves," Edward said. "The waves in stormy weather are like so many mounds rising and swelling. It would be tough to see, and the lights would likely get swamped and become hazards or wrecks themselves."

"That's why we don't just drive pilings into her," John said. "They'd become wreckers themselves. The tide shoves ships in here, some dragging anchors the whole way."

Lionel walked to the back edge of the sand. He watched the water slapping against it and then rolling upwards. "It looks so peaceful."

"It's like that," John said. "It's a monument to how completely she devours. Hardly a sign that a struggle ever was. Some say, and I believe it true, that the real wicked storms can cause former wrecks to belch out. They appear, like ghosts, and then disappear."

Lionel looked north and south.

"It's time to be headed in," John said. "We don't want to overstay our welcome."

"Aye," Edward said. He gently touched Lionel's elbow. "Come along, mate."

The Reverend and Lionel took a late walk in the cold night. The moon was bright and reflected on the freshly fallen snow. Their boots crunched the frosty surface. They walked to the eastern cliffs and overlooked the English Channel. Their breathing formed small puffs of mist.

"When the morning came," the Reverend said with zeal, "not one of the vessels that had been noted the previous evening—I'm speaking of the ones anchored in that dangerous position I mentioned—not one was to be observed again."

"Not one?"

"It was clear to everyone," Rev. Gilmore said, "that none had gotten away to safe harbor." He shrugged. "That's how the story goes."

"But how could anyone know for certain?" Lionel asked. "Maybe some slipped away and went on to some distant port to complete their business." He looked down at the tumultuous waters beating the shoreline. He couldn't decide if the eastern cliffs were shorter or taller than the western.

"That should be such a nice thought," Rev. Gilmore said, smiling. "But there were fishing smacks lying-to, not too distant from the North Foreland." He pointed. "You can see the outline of the Foreland right out there. Do you see it?"

"Yes, I think so."

"There were fishermen out there who saw the entire fleet of vessels driven from the Margate Roads."

"I don't understand. What do you mean from the 'roads'?"

"That's a term for a swath of sea around the point. After seeing the ships driven, they saw signals of distress flying from each. That's an ill omen."

Lionel looked at him sharply. "What kinds of signals?"

"Several kinds, really. The Union Jack upside down. Flaming barrels of grease or tar. These days a torch or flare, a rocket even. When ships fly such signals, they usually have no chance but for miracles." He gazed at the stars.

"The fishermen didn't help them?"

"They could render no such aid. What might they do but be driven with the fleet and end up the same way? No, no fault lay with them."

"So all perished, then?" Lionel asked. "All but the fishermen, of course."

The Reverend looked at Lionel then back at the stars. "A good deal of wreckage was discovered upon the Goodwin in the morning, and there were reports of wreckage strewn for miles along the stream reach. A masthead of one of the vessels protruded from a sandy knoll—a sight more common than any care to admit."

"From what I've seen," Lionel said, his tone growing harsher, "the fishermen wouldn't have tried to help even if the gale had not been fierce. Although I'm sure they were diligent to hovel soon after."

Rev. Gilmore lowered his gaze from the stars. "You've much to learn, son. There are reasons."

"They don't care. That's the reason."

"I don't argue that men have long had great tendency toward selfishness, but those things can change. They will with time."

"With *time?*" Lionel asked. "Not time, but the whip, more likely." Lionel tried to see the harbor. He could see the western pier, part of the clock house, and several masts.

"With inspiration. With a heart open to God."

"I don't mean to sound irreverent," Lionel said. "I understand you are a man of faith, but such sentiment doesn't get it done. You tell me these old stories as though you describe only the past."

"No—"

"I have seen nothing in this place or in the men who reside here that suggests anything has changed. This is a place full of freethinking sailors who profit from wreckage. You can say they sell anchors and cables to storm-racked ships, but I say they profit from the misfortune of others. They pillage the unfortunate who wash up on shore."

"You judge harshly," Rev. Gilmore said. "I understand why. But you are mistaken to think there have been no gallant men who, now and again, have launched into the thickest of the stormy contests, heedless of the risks. Men have dared to forget themselves with the intention of rescuing the distressed. Many men you do not know, and maybe do know, have in different forms labored through dark night amid the rush of waves and in the grip of hurricane blasts. Think of it! The sleet, the snow, the spray—all of it frightfully cold! Men encountered unimaginable dangers in such times, yet persevered through it, to a point."

"Haven't seen it," Lionel said. "God knows I haven't seen it."

"I am not done, Lionel," Rev. Gilmore said, his face wrinkling. "Please do not interrupt me, or you'll miss my meaning. I said the men did it all to a point!"

"Well, then they lost the point!"

"They *paid* the point!" Rev. Gilmore said, his voice thundering. "They were repaid for all they had tried with swift and terrible deaths to add to the number of those they sought to save."

"I haven't met any such people," Lionel said.

"For obvious reasons!" The Reverend exhaled sharply, thrust his hands into his pockets, and stared out to sea, his brow more wrinkled than before.

The surf rolled up the beach, slurped, and foamed. The wind gusted and hesitated, then gusted more. The seas churned.

"I bet you're a good preacher," Lionel said.

"Come to church. You'll find out."

"I just may."

"And I bet you're a good man despite your efforts to prove yourself a cynical, self-defeating complainer," Rev. Gilmore said, his tone kind and his expression transforming to a smile. He did it all without removing his gaze from the sea.

The gusting wind rocked both of them backwards. They agreed to return home.

"Maybe there is some hope," Lionel said as they walked through the snow.

"There is always hope."

"I mean about something I've been thinking."

The Reverend turned to Lionel, one eyebrow raised. "Which is?"

Lionel tilted his head toward the stars. He didn't answer.

"I'm traveling a mail packet up the Thames to London on Monday," Rev. Gilmore said. "Are you planning to return there?"

"I . . ."

"You are welcome to remain here for as long as needed, of course."

"I'm not sure I have anything I want to return to. I have to return, there is no question, but this is a very hard thing for me to do."

"Your work, your associates, your relatives—life for you must go on, Lionel."

"Yes. I am not ready to return just yet, but there may be something you can do for me upon your arrival."

"What is it?"

The men ceased walking. Behind them the moon gleamed over the English Channel. They stood facing each other, silhouetted by the moonlight. Their coats and scarves blew in the wind. Lionel began to speak, slowly at first and then with excitement. He made his lengthy request known. The Reverend listened and nodded.

The next day Lionel did not attend church, but that evening by the fire he did listen to the Gilmores read from the Holy Scriptures. The Reverend read from the gospel of John and explained there were three other short books near the back of the Bible written by the same John. He declared the books had much to say about love. To Lionel it was only mildly interesting.

And yet later, as he lay in his bed, Lionel found himself thinking about one passage in particular: the one about laying down one's life for another. He could see the value of that. He lay there wondering what would happen if everyone lived that way. Would it result in everyone being dead or everyone remaining alive?

When Monday arrived, Lionel attended Rev. Gilmore on his morning errands and loaded some supplies aboard the wagon. In the harbor, the hovelling ships and fishermen scurried about. Just before noon, after loading the last of the supplies, Lionel climbed up to take the reins and drove the horses to the harbor to see the Reverend off. The *Seahorse* was tying up from an earlier run. Arthur and his crew were unloading. John noticed Lionel and the Reverend and waved.

Lionel handed Rev. Gilmore signed notes and written directions. They shook hands. Lionel's wounded hand was finally able to grip with some strength. The Reverend boarded the mail packet, a large steam-powered vessel, and Lionel watched it pass the outer harbor and lighthouse.

Lionel turned the wagon around. As he did, he saw an old man hawking trinkets to a drunken sailor with his billfold open. Two crudely dressed women leaned close to the staggering seaman, almost upon his shoulders, and nearly knocked him over. One of the women held him upright while the other helped him take his money out in wads. The old man dangled a shiny but worthless piece of metal on a tarnished chain. Lionel snapped the reins and pulled up fast beside them. The horses tossed their heads uneasily. One of the women screamed.

"Whoa!" Lionel cried.

"Hey! What in blazes?" the inebriated sailor said.

"Be careful there!" the old man said.

"That necklace. I want it," Lionel said. "I want to buy it."

"You can't have it," the sailor said. "It's mine!"

"Already sold," the old man said.

"I'll pay you double," Lionel said from atop his high seat.

The old man smiled. "Double?"

"Can't have it, I say!" the sailor said. He grasped for the silver piece.

But the old man snatched it away. "This deal is cancelled," the old man said, crossing to the wagon. The women followed, hands on swaying hips.

"Hey!" the sailor objected. "It's mine, I tell ya! Go find your own!"

"You best put your money in your wallet and move on," Lionel said. "Or it's the beadle I'll be calling to slap you in irons for public indecency. There are laws, you know."

"W-what?" The sailor said, his face reddening.

"You heard me," Lionel said with threatening tone. "Now be off!"

Huffing like a steam motor, the sailor nearly choked on his tongue and stomped off, stuffing his money back into his wallet. When he turned for a last look, Lionel peered so hard at him that he suddenly ran to get lost in the crowd.

"Well, well," the old man said. He extended his hand. "Pleased to meet ya, most kind sir."

Lionel looked at the man's grubby hand, pinched his eyebrows together, and soured as if he had just bitten a rotten lemon. "What do you want?" Lionel asked.

The old man looked into Lionel's eyes, tilting his head. "Do I know you?"

"I'm certain you don't," Lionel said.

The old man held up the grimy chain. "It's a nice piece that's got yer fancy."

"I changed my mind," Lionel said. "Now move on."

"What?" the old man said, his eyes wide and mouth agape.

"Hey!" one of the women said. "You said—"

"Ho!" Lionel barked. He snapped the reins and turned the rig. When he glanced back, he saw the three of them rushing to search for the drunken sailor. Then he turned and saw Edward standing beside the road just ahead. "Whoa!"

Edward took hold of a bridle and steadied the horses. "I see you met the Hoggers."

"Hoggers?"

"Yep. You know they'll just find another drunken sailor and get their greedy results anyways."

"Maybe, maybe not. It seemed good to stall it some."

Edward walked to the side. "Maybe. Maybe not."

"How are you today?" Lionel asked. "Boat holding up?"

"Boat's great. John's been bragging on it. I'm fine, thanks. The Reverend left for London?"

"Yes, he did."

"I'm in for a bite with some mates," Edward said. "Care to join us?"

"Not today, Edward. I don't—"

"Drink, I know. I'd like to buy you some grub. We can arrange for tea. It won't be a problem, I assure you."

"I am grateful for your assurance, but I've supplies here to return to the house."

"Maybe another time," Edward said.

"Perhaps."

"You know, all of us are going to be there—the crew of the *Seahorse*, I mean. Some might want to hear more of your ideas. You know, about lights for the Sands."

"I don't believe any want to hear more of that."

"True," Edward said, stroking his chin. "Likely most wouldn't. But I would." He turned to leave. "See you around."

Lionel looked at the supplies all tied up in the back of the wagon. He laughed, snapped the reins, and caught up to roll beside the young man. "I have obligations presently, but supper might be possible."

"I can do that. Say six o'clock at Cannon's? My treat."

"I'll be there."

CHAPTER 9

Sleighs glided along as Ramsgate grew whiter with fresh snow. Lantern lights and flickering fires dotted the windows along the streets. Cannon's was alive with music and laughter.

"Haul it up, mate," Cannon said.

Lionel was intent on his work and didn't realize the barkeep was addressing him.

"I said, 'Haul it up!' I did!"

Lionel looked up. "What?"

"Your scribbling there," Cannon said. "Haul it up! Lift it up. I'm mopping here."

"Oh, yes, my apologies," Lionel said, picking up the board.

Outside, the weather had thickened with clouds. The gray mist dragged like a heavy blanket across the sky, urged by the chilled wind. The waters had since swelled as countless waves pushed and shoved their way across the Channel. Ships rocked restlessly in the harbor, lines straining and timbers groaning.

Arthur and others were wrapping up a game of dominoes at one table while other locals and several foreign sailors told tales. Lionel noticed the tavern was filled with different languages, clashing like waves colliding in the storm-tossed Channel. Some sang rowdy songs to the ragtag music of a squeezebox. Some stomped their feet, and more than one flirted with women of questionable character, including the Hogger twins.

Lionel turned from the bar to watch Jeffery and John across the room. They were well into a game of cricket with boatmen from a different crew.

"Whatcha drawing?" Cannon asked. "A treasure map, maybe!" He laughed.

Lionel set his board back down, shaking his head. He and Edward were at the far end of the bar. He had been drawing his explanations on a piece of slate with some chalk.

Lionel pointed to a mark on his board. "This is a—"

Arthur arrived and leaned close to peer over Lionel's shoulder. "Looks like a chart," he said. "You a mapmaker?"

"No," Lionel said. He tapped his drawing. "I was just saying we can moor headlights at the extreme ends of the Sands. Here and here."

Arthur shook his head. "You're more persistent than a hard rain, landsman. But you don't get it." He looked at Cannon and rolled his eyes. "You need to respect the sea."

"I do respect it," Lionel said. "I just don't fear it."

"Then you're a fool!" Arthur said for all to hear.

Lionel again saw his boots on the man. He stood up, his heart beat rapidly.

Edward stood up, too. "Arthur," he said hastily, "you going to play dominoes or are you ready to try your hand at darts against your baby brother, who can swamp you with one hand tied?"

Arthur eyed Lionel from head to toe, his bottom lip jutting out. "And who might be your partner?"

"Cricket?" Lionel asked Edward.

Edward's eyebrows rose. "Is there any other kind of darts?"

"None worth playing," Lionel said.

Edward looked at Arthur. "You and Henry against my friend and me."

Arthur smiled. "Sweet shepherd's pie! It'll be our pleasure to rake your sides. Henry, we've got ourselves a match!" He laughed and walked away.

"Finally, some good sense!" Edward said to Lionel. "And if you don't mind my saying, sensibility is like a rogue wave with you."

"A rogue wave?" Lionel asked.

"It's a wave with a mind of its own. It comes from a direction nothing else is moving in. It's rogue-like. That's you all over, I'm afraid."

"I suppose."

"Aye!" Edward patted Lionel's shoulder. Lionel set his board and chalk down and followed the young man to the darts.

John and Jeffery reluctantly gave up the dartboard at Arthur's urging.

Lionel was invited to have the honor of the first throws, so he boldly stepped up to the line. He prepared to throw — then froze. He walked up to the dartboard and felt the cork surface.

"Are there many as odd as this one?" Arthur asked Henry in a false whisper.

Henry laughed and cleared his throat. "You can't just stick them in there, mate. You've gotta throw 'em."

Lionel returned to the line and threw his darts. He threw a triple fifteen, a triple sixteen, and a triple seventeen. He pulled out his darts and handed them to Arthur. Then he crossed to the slate board on the wall, wrote the three numbers he had just tagged, and drew circles around them.

"Well, well, isn't that fine?" Edward asked. "Now what were you saying about raking our sides, big brother?"

"That had to be landlubber's luck!" Arthur said, hesitantly approaching the line.

"I assure you, it wasn't," Lionel said. "I am most expert at the game. Would you care to wager?"

Edward and John laughed. Jeffery stood smiling, but Henry and Arthur were neither laughing nor silent.

"Ha! Wager! Right!" Arthur said. "If you were as smart as you were lucky, you might have asked that before you threw. 'Course, if it was luck, then you're surprised to see it yourself, I say!"

"Pride comes before the fall!" Henry said. "Least that's what Gilmore's always saying."

"Very well," Edward said. "For honor alone, take your throws, big brother!"

Arthur snapped his arms out straight, then bent them and snapped them out again. "Don't rush me. I'm concentrating here."

Arthur threw his first dart and hit a single fifteen. He threw the next and hit a double fifteen. "Aha!" he said. "Fifteens are closed for me, too!" He threw his third and final dart and struck the triple sixteen. The dart stuck for a moment, long enough for Henry and Arthur to cheer, but then it fell out.

"He did something to the board!" Arthur said. "He cheated!"

"I did no such thing," Lionel said calmly.

"No way!" Edward said. "Control yourself, Arthur! Nobody cheated. It fell out, you know the rules." He pulled the darts and picked up the one from the floor.

"Who feels a dartboard before playing?" Arthur asked. "He cheated, I say!"

The game continued. In the end, Lionel and Edward won. Henry and Arthur waved them off. "Landlubber's luck, that's all!" Arthur said, retreating to a table with Henry in tow.

"Congratulations!" John said. "The Reverend was right. You're full of surprises."

"Care to toss a game against father and me?" Jeffery asked.

"Thanks but no; one's enough tonight," Lionel said, withdrawing to his corner at the bar. Edward joined him.

They ordered supper and enjoyed a hot meal of steamed vege-
tables, roasted game, boiled onions, and gravy. Edward pried open
a hard roll and used it to mop up the gravy still on his plate. Lionel
sipped his sweet cider.

"So tell me more about these lights," Edward said. "I like the
idea, but it seems impossible to execute."

Before Lionel could answer, the door burst open and a frosty
wind filled the room, pushing in the old man Lionel had seen with
the cheap trinket at the harbor. The old man slammed the weather
doors shut. The windows rattled and the pipes shook. Outside,
something made of wood tumbled down the street, pushed by the
wind.

"Hogger," Edward whispered to Lionel.

"There's a storm a brewin'," Hogger said.

"Sooner the salvage!" blurted one sailor seated in the middle of
the bar. He raised his mug in toast.

"Aye!" another said.

Hogger approached the tall fireplace and warmed his hands.
He looked around at the patrons, nodding to some, ignoring most.
He stepped away and swung off his outer cloak, sending droplets
of melted snow flying in all directions. He draped the cloak on his
arm and headed for the end of the bar where Edward and Lionel
sat. Then he spotted Lionel and stopped in his tracks.

Lionel looked at him from his feet to his face. Hogger wore
tattered breeches and a loose-fitting shirt, everything dark. His
too-tight-to-button vest was brown but soiled black; his waistcoat
was mostly black but cluttered with poorly sewn patches of gray
and tan. His outer cloak was blue and could have at one time been
fancy but was now faded and worn, especially in the elbows, shoulders, and under the arms. A bright gold chain draped from his vest
pocket, a striking contrast to his otherwise ragged assemblage. His

face displayed a nervous discomfort as he met Lionel's gaze.

Hogger's eyes scrunched up so tightly as to seem very difficult to see through. His head angled back, and he looked straight down the barrel of his pointed nose. His upper lip peeled back to reveal unsightly teeth with as many missing as present. Of those that remained, most rested in a sort of lazy sailor lineup atop a bottom lip that curled inward to form something like a platform. The nubs of his prickly beard jutted straight out above his angular chin. With his head in such a twisted pose, he walked toward the middle of the bar and sat beside the man who had raised his mug in tribute.

The wind howled outside the doors, rattling them in their jambs.

"Whoa! Someone wants to introduce her tormented self," one sailor said.

"She'll turn you on your heels, she will," another said.

Tom Hardwell tipped his mug. "A northeaster to be sure."

"There'll be a happy hovelling in the morrow," Hogger said. "Whiskey, Cannon, with a pint of dark to chase."

The sailor next to Hogger whispered loud enough for all nearby to hear. "If rumor be straight, there be a well-laden ship with exactly that most adored cargo supposed to be skirting the Sands this very night. You never know."

"What kind of cargo you inferrin'?" Hogger asked. He gulped down his whiskey, guzzled some beer, and mopped his mouth with his sleeve. "Cannon! Another!"

The sailor motioned with his pinky finger to Hogger's empty shot glass. "Precisely that."

Hogger's eyebrows lifted, and his voice became musical. "Whiskey? Who's been saying?"

Edward spoke only loud enough for Lionel to hear. "It always amazes me how desperate we make ourselves sound. Just utter a word of valuable cargo—just mention it in the same breath as a rising storm—and I swear spit drops from the mouth of some like foam at the bow."

Lionel looked at his plate of half-eaten food and pushed it away. "I noticed."

"I swear," Edward said, "Hogger sometimes seems to have as much ice in his veins as does the snow outside."

The pub talk grew more animated as several imagined what a salvaged load of whiskey could do to ease their pains, line their pockets, and sweeten the season. Hogger entertained them with jokes of wrecks and drowning drunken crews until he had worked his small but vociferous audience into such a frenzied state that several took turns regurgitating their own vain imaginings of successful scavenging outcomes.

Lionel observed it all with distaste. It continued for quite some time in concert with the worsening weather. Finally, a most uncomfortable knot formed in his stomach and he stood up. "It's time for me to go."

At the same moment, Hogger also announced his departure. He said he wanted to be well rested for what could be a major scavenging opportunity in the morning should the weather persist. He insisted his daughters follow him, and out they went with another cold blast of frigid night air.

"I'll walk with you as far as King and Queen Streets," Edward said.

"Not necessary, thank you," Lionel said.

"I insist," Edward said with a smile. "I could use the walk myself."

Outside, the two saw Hogger arguing with his daughters at the base of the western slope. He insisted that his daughters go straight home while he persisted in ascending the hill in order to walk off his ale. The daughters wanted to go with him, but his threats of whipping them finally persuaded them to cease. They drifted to the base of the hill and watched their father disappear into the dark.

Lionel and Edward observed the theatrics with detachment as they headed the other way, up Harbour Street. The force of the wind beat against them, and they buried their hands in their coats and wrapped their scarves high upon their faces. Their hats were pulled low.

When they reached the town hall, Edward tapped Lionel's shoulder. "If you might spare more time, I have something to show you that might interest you."

"What is it?"

"Catacombs," Edward said. "Not far from here. Some think the Romans built them."

"Really? For what purpose?"

"Well, for one, it's warmer in the caves than on the street, and for another, there's no Hogger to upset the evening."

"No, I meant the Romans," Lionel said.

"That I don't know. Personally, I think smugglers built them since they go from some pubs to the shore," Edward said, now bouncing up and down to generate warmth. "What do you think? You up for it?"

"I think so. Yes."

The entrance to the cave wasn't far. It was well hidden within a rocky outcrop behind a smaller pub on the west side of town. Edward secured a torch and a lantern from his home and handed the lantern to Lionel.

The cave was cold but free of the gusting wind. The occasional puffs of heat from the torch made it warmer.

"This is all chalk," Lionel said as he held his lantern up to the wall and ran his hand over it the way he had the cork on the dart board. The wall had been crudely hacked, resulting in an uneven, blocky surface.

"Flint and chalk are all we have around here along the coast," Edward said. "You can't tell right now, but the tunnel travels a long way in this direction, all the way to the western beach, even west of the shipyard."

Lionel held up his lamp. "Lead the way."

"You sure?" Edward asked, his face lit on one side from his flickering torch. "It's a good walk."

"It's out of the wind."

"Until we reach the beach. The tide will be running too, but it won't reach the cave entrance."

Edward led the way and Lionel followed. The tunnel was mostly straight, with enough clearance that a man of average height could walk erect. Every few feet, Lionel examined the walls for markings but saw none. Eventually, he stopped looking. The floor was like finely ground dust, which made the air heavy to breathe. There were remains of broken crates, torn nets, and a pile of broken plates.

"I can guess why the Romans might have built these," Lionel said. "For defenses of some kind. Your smuggling theory also seems like a good explanation. It rings consistent with what I've seen."

"Consistent?" Edward asked, plodding ahead.

"With the occupations of this place."

Edward stopped. "Are you equating smuggling with hovelling?"

"Yes." Lionel looked directly at Edward.

Edward laughed. "They're not actually." Edward pointed at the dull light ahead. "Up there. I think we've reached the shore."

The night shore was sleek and dark and cold. The water moved in as countless rollers in reckless formation. One after another they curled over in an uneven rhythm and broke into a conflict of foam and sand and then pushed onto the shore to soak it deep. The waters withdrew with whatever the beach spewed forth and carried it all away to sea.

They stood with lights in hand at the mouth of the cave. Their shadows danced large on the rocky cliff behind them.

"Plenty of whitecaps," Edward said, raising his voice to be heard. "She's storming for sure. Look!"

Plain to see under the moonlight, though nearly four miles away, a large ship with six masts lit up like a holiday decoration rode uneasily on the waters. It pierced the water well despite large sheets of spray taunting her on every side.

"She's quite big," Lionel said.

"A schooner," Edward said. "She rides roughly but has good bearing. She'll not entertain the Sands. Good for her!"

Lionel stepped out from the protection of the cave. "Are you certain?" Lionel held up his lantern with outstretched arm.

Edward placed a reassuring hand on Lionel's shoulder. "It is all right, Lionel. Just keep your lantern low, we don't want to confuse her."

Lionel lowered his arm. "Confuse her how?"

"Well, we're too low to be trouble. The waves block us well enough, and a good captain knows the difference between a masthead light and a shore light, but it is a courtesy to not make him judge."

"Really?" Lionel said, alarmed. "Then let's snuff them out completely! The moon is bright enough tonight. We don't need them."

"We'll need them in the cave!" Edward said.

"Can't we head back along the shore? Is it possible?"

"You should know the answer to that. This is the direction you came from the morning after a night much like this. We can do it, but it's so cold. Let's stay warm and return the way we came."

Lionel opened his lantern and let the wind blow it out. "No, please. Let's walk back. I want to watch this ship. I need to be certain she is safe."

"Even if she gets in trouble, there's nothing we can do, Lionel. Sometimes it's better not to know. There are countless wrecks this time of year."

"No!" Lionel shouted, louder than necessary to be heard above the blowing wind. "Please, Edward. I must know she is safe."

"We'll not be too warm. But if you must." Edward led the way.

"Wait!" Lionel said, grabbing Edward by the arm. "Snuff the torch, just in case."

"It's fine. I'm keeping it low enough. The rising and swelling of the waves are enough to block us from even being seen, and we are so low on the headland horizon we are little danger. If we were atop the cliff it would be different."

Lionel still held Edward's arm. "Let us be *no* danger. Please."

"Fine," Edward said, snuffing the flame. "C'mon, watch your step. Let's cross out of these rocks and walk the sand."

Lionel stumbled more than once as he kept his eyes more on the schooner than the path before him. The wind blew bitter cold. One gust knocked them both off their feet. Edward caught himself with his hand and fell to a squat. Lionel fell sprawled out across the sand.

"You okay?" Edward asked, extending a hand.

Lionel smiled with embarrassment. "At least it's not snowing."

As he grabbed Edward's hand to pull himself up, a lone flake fell onto Edward's coat sleeve. He laughed. "Shhh! Don't say that again!"

They reached the shipyard.

"Moses," Edward said.

"What?"

"Moses' shipyard."

The structures blocked Lionel's view of the schooner.

"Shall we take Jacob's ladder?" Edward asked. "It'll get us clear of the shipyard and put us on the cliff. We can walk to town from there. It won't be quite as cold."

"Jacob's ladder?" Lionel asked.

Edward pointed. Up ahead, built into the cliff face, was a stairway that cut back twice as it ascended the cliff.

"Can we see the boat from there?" Lionel asked.

"It's a *ship*. A schooner," Edward said, already heading for the stairs. "And yes, we'll be able to see her from there."

Lionel followed him up the stairs. Halfway up, Lionel's sight line to the schooner was restored and he saw the ship continuing to make good way.

"I'd hate to be aboard her this night!" Edward said.

"Why? Is she failing?" Lionel looked closely at the ship then rushed to catch up to Edward.

"No, it's just that working a rig like that in this weather is terrible hard. Cold and wet and numb."

The men reached the top and were preparing to descend the slope into town when Edward spotted a lantern along the cliff. "What fool is anchoring atop the cliff tonight?"

Lionel saw the glow. It moved about sporadically between two dark shapes, one large, the other small. He watched the distant ship. "That could be confusing to the schooner, don't you agree?"

"Maybe," Edward said. "It's not only light but a certain movement of light that can be confusing."

"Well, how does that light rate?"

"Out of courtesy it shouldn't be up there at all in this weather at this time of night," Edward said, sounding agitated. "At least it's steady enough to not be mistaken for a ship. Still, it boggles me why anyone's up there."

"Let's check it out."

"For a landsman, you sure are getting around tonight. You sure you want to walk all the way up there? We still have to walk all the way back, you know."

"Yes, I'm sure." Lionel led the way.

Lionel could hear sounds from the mysterious figures now. The larger shape snorted and the smaller shape spoke. "Easy, gal."

Lionel recognized the voice. It was Hogger, the old man from the pub. He was holding a lantern and leading his horse.

"Hold on, Lionel," Edward whispered into his ear. "Stay put. I want to see what old Hogger does."

Lionel watched Hogger turning in circles as if paranoid someone was watching. "He's behaving like he's nervous."

Edward pointed to some moving shadows under the trees off to the right of Hogger. "He's being followed."

"This man is no good," Lionel said. "No doubt he's connecting with some of his own kind up here." They hunkered down behind some bushes and watched.

Hogger positioned himself and his horse close to the edge of the cliff. He looked in all directions, then carefully took his lantern and affixed it with leather straps to the tail of his horse. He faced the horse inland, its hindquarters toward the sea. Uncomfortable from the heat and weight of the lantern, the horse flit its tail back and forth.

"What is he . . . ?" Edward said, looking from Hogger's horse to the ship.

The shadowy figures that had been advancing on Hogger sprang upon him. Lionel recognized them at once.

"Venus and Iris," Edward said.

"Hey, Poppa!" Iris said. "What are you doing? Fishing for ships?" Her laughing sounded like screeching.

Venus added a delighted squeal of her own. "You owe me a fine dress, you do!"

Hogger yanked back his cloak to remove his whip. He held it high in the air. "I'll skin you alive if you don't run home this instant!"

"She's in chains!" Edward said.

"What do you mean?" Lionel asked, turning away from the Hoggers.

Edward pointed. "The ship!"

Lionel saw the schooner struggling in a choppy torrent of unruly waves.

"She's changing her course," Edward said, his pitch rising, "and turning into the wind. She's luffing. She'll turn through it, and the sails will fill again but with a new heading."

"I don't understand," Lionel said.

Edward looked at Hogger. A dark expression came over his face. "She's being tricked by the lantern! She'll head straight for the Sands! She'll be wrecked!" He burst from the bushes and ran toward Hogger. "You there! Avast!"

Hogger and his daughters whirled around. "Keep away from me," Hogger shouted, "or you'll be sorry!"

"You're a wrecker, Hogger!" Edward said. "Douse that lantern now!"

Hogger snapped his whip and struck Edward above his right eye. Edward staggered, a flow of blood quickly streaming from his face. Hogger snapped the whip again and struck Edward in the stomach, doubling him over.

Lionel stood and rushed toward Edward, but stopped when he heard an explosion. He saw rockets racing upward from the schooner, suddenly aground upon the Goodwin Sands, deadly waters leaping about her.

Edward stood erect now, one hand covering his bloody wound, his other with fist clenched. "You've doomed them. You will regret this night, Darrin Hog—"

A rock struck Edward in the head, and he fell to the ground.

"Nobody threatens my daddy!" Iris yelled. She picked up another rock.

Edward moaned from his crumpled position.

Lionel raced out toward Hogger. "You animal!"

"Help!" Venus screamed, running down the slope toward town. "It's the crazy man! The crazy man!"

"Shut up, Venus!" Hogger yelled. "I'll handle him!"

Venus disappeared into the dark. Iris threw a rock at Lionel but missed.

Hogger hit Lionel with the whip and yanked hard, but the straps failed to wrap up Lionel's legs. Hogger tried to strike again, but Lionel was upon him, filled with rage.

"You murderer!" Lionel flailed at him with kicks and wild punches.

The men grappled and rolled along the ground in a bloody clench atop the cliff. The horse became nervous and reared up. Its hooves landed dangerously close to Lionel's head.

Hogger landed a swift kick to Lionel's ribs, but Lionel seized him by the throat. The old man gasped for air.

Iris screamed and jumped on Lionel's back, clawing at his eyes. "Die!" she yelled. The three of them rolled toward the edge.

Hogger reached for his whip lying nearby, but Lionel tossed it away.

In town, the pub patrons poured into the street to discover what the screaming was all about. Nearby windows lit up as other locals became disturbed enough to want to see what was happening. Venus ran down the street toward the pub. "Help! Somebody help!"

A crowd gathered outside Cannon's. Arthur and his crew were there. John Burton pointed to a flare in the sky.

Tom Hardwell watched it arc and fade. "The Goodwin, no doubt!" he shouted. "Let's run the pier and see what gives!"

"No!" Venus shouted. "To the cliff! The crazy man is there. He's killing my father."

Arthur spat and looked toward the pier.

"And he's hurt your brother, Arthur," she said. "He's hurt Eddie bad."

Arthur spun on the toes of his boots. "What's this?"

"It's true," she said. "He's laying on the ground and bleeding."

"Men!" Arthur yelled. "The west cliff! Now!"

Hogger and Lionel rolled along the edge of the steep cliff. Lionel got both of his hands to Hogger's neck and pushed the man's face over the edge. He had started to squeeze Hogger's throat when he heard the approaching mob. He looked back to see them rushing toward the cliff. Then he saw Iris's feet, inches away.

"I'm going to crush your face!" she screamed.

Lionel saw Iris standing over him with a large rock held high over her head. Then he heard a snapping sound.

"No!" Iris screamed.

Lionel saw a strap of leather wrapped around her arms. He watched her fall backward and drop the rock.

Edward, bloodied and dizzied, yanked the whip back and dragged Iris several feet away. He staggered to her and wrapped her hands and feet with the whip. He looked at Lionel, then dropped to his knees. Arthur and Henry rushed up to him.

Hogger tried to push Lionel off.

"Never!" Lionel said. "This is where it gets finished. Did you murder my family, too?" He focused all of his strength into his grip on Hogger's throat. The old man's breathing became like a rattle.

Suddenly, Lionel's arms were grabbed by two large hands and yanked away from Hogger's neck.

"Let me go!" Lionel shouted.

"Kill him!" Hogger said, clutching at his throat, gasping and coughing.

"I've had enough of you," Arthur said, holding Lionel up by the collar.

The gawking mob grew as pub patrons and other locals pressed in.

Arthur cocked his arm back.

"Hogger lures the ships!" Lionel said. "He tricks them with his lantern." He breathed hard, and his nose flowed with blood. "Like you don't know!"

"I'll send you to the sea myself," Arthur roared. "Right to the bottom!"

"Look!" Henry said, helping Edward to his feet and pointing toward the Goodwin.

The schooner was hard aground. Violent winds raged against the vessel.

The mob grew in number as those wakened by the commotion ventured into the frigid night. They were dressed in nightshirts and cloaks, long stocking caps and scarves, and huddled in woolen blankets. Their foggy breath wafted upwards as they watched the forces of wind and water beat upon the aching schooner.

The constable arrived waving his nightstick. Short and burly, his dark curly hair jutting out in all directions from his towering helmet, he burst through the huddled group, shoving several people aside. "What in heaven's name is going on? Have you all gone raving mad?"

"A wreck has just begun," John said.

Arthur held Lionel by the collar with his right arm still cocked and ready to unload.

"Perkins! Put him down," the constable said. "What is going—?"

"I'm not certain what's happening here." Arthur shoved Lionel away, then looked at the schooner as she began to list to one side. "But no doubt she's in desperate trouble."

"Hogger did it," Lionel said, pointing at the cowering man. "He tied a lantern to his horse's tail, made it appear as a ship on course, and tricked the vessel to run aground!"

"I didn't!" Hogger shouted. "He's a lunatic! A liar!"

"He's likely done this before," Lionel said.

"It is true," Edward said, holding his bloody hand to the side of his head. "I saw him do it."

Hogger's eyes grew wide, and he frantically turned his head from side to side.

"I don't expect you should be bothered," Lionel said to the mob. "After all, there may be whiskey on board."

The crowd stood transfixed as they watched the wild sea foam up on all sides of the struggling ship.

"It's not true!" Hogger said. "I did no such thing." He tried to press back into the crowd but found no quarter.

Arthur marched over to Hogger and belted him hard. He

dropped like an anchor. Arthur stooped to pick him up for more.

"Enough!" the constable shouted, stepping forward and seizing Hogger by the shirt. "I'll handle the snake."

"He's a squid," Arthur said, spitting. He crossed to the edge of the cliff beside Lionel. "We didn't know, landsman," he said. "We didn't. Fate is one thing, but treachery another."

The ship began to wrench and twist.

Tom walked up with the spyglass Edward had salvaged. He held it out to Arthur, who shook his head. Lionel took it. He extended it and peered through.

The seas rushed over the schooner's deck and flew halfway up the masts. Some of the passengers and crew were taking refuge in the rigging while others managed an extraordinary feat.

"They have a boat free!" Lionel cried, hope alive in his voice.

The crowd drew closer to the edge. A few had brought spyglasses.

"It's right rough what they do!" one man said, looking through a larger spyglass.

"A few moments, they might do it!" someone else said.

Lionel felt his throat tighten. "Mostly women and children in the boat!"

"All women and children, I'd say," the other man said.

Lionel panned to those in the rigging. He could see passengers and crew clinging tightly, but one by one they were dropping into the thrashing seas. He remembered Alicia and Luke doing the same. Were they dropping to join others? Were they trying to reach the boat? Or were their grips giving out? Each disappeared into the frightful waters.

Lionel tilted down to the ship's boat, heavily laden with women and children and a sailor at the tiller.

"The small boat is full!" someone shouted. "She's managing clear!"

As Lionel watched, a huge wave mounted up under the stern of the little boat and flung it upward.

"Oh, dear God, no," Lionel said.

The people in the boat were tossed in sprawling forms through the air. Some disappeared into the foamy blasts of churning sea. Some fell headlong into the bow of the boat, crashing hard into those who had tipped backwards in their seated positions. It was a mass of confusion as the boat fell hard and then reared up again.

Another wave flipped the boat sideways into the sea, dumping the people out. Their heads momentarily appeared like floating coconuts, then suddenly disappeared.

The boat heeled over. Only the hull remained visible in the roiling surf. It rushed away from the side of the ship and disappeared into the teeth of a foaming white roller.

Lionel searched for any sign of life but could find neither boat nor passenger.

"They're lost! Lost!" someone with another glass said from the midst of the crowd. "All of them are gone."

Lionel tilted his spyglass higher. "There are some still in the rigging."

"Aye! I see three."

"Five, no, six!" Lionel said.

"Seven! There yet be seven, glory be!"

Some in the crowd cheered, though many of the women sobbed.

"Oh, no! One has fallen!"

"And another!"

One by one, the exhausted sailors dropped from the rigging to perish in the heavy sea.

Before their eyes the vessel was torn to pieces. Within minutes all remains were carried away until nothing was left.

After the last spyglass was slid shut, the crowd stood as if frozen under the light of the bare moon. Many wept. Some uttered prayers.

The constable led Hogger away, the twins pleading their father's case as they stumbled after him.

The crowd broke up in little groups as people went home in somber silence, the mood very much as if they had attended a funeral.

Arthur and his crew, with Lionel and a few others, stared out to sea.

Lionel peered into Arthur's face. "What do you see out there, Perkins?"

"I see the sea," he answered, the wind muffling his reply. "I see death."

"You don't see enough," Lionel said, his voice rising. "I see empty beds. I see desolate homes. How about hearing? Didn't you hear anything? Didn't you? Did you hear anyone calling?"

"A call for what?" Henry asked. He was sorrowful but annoyed. "Your own drowning?"

"No. A call for what we're made of—in the deepest part."

"You weary me, landsman," Arthur said, turning away. "The only deep part is the bottom."

"You know, Perkins," Lionel said, "you're already at the bottom."

"Lionel, don't," Edward said.

Lionel faced all of them. "You're all dead. You're already dead."

"There are things you don't know," Edward said, trying to inch closer.

Lionel clenched his teeth and fists. "There are things I *do* know. That's where you start." He trembled with rage.

Arthur turned to his brother. "Are you hurt, Eddie?

"I am, Arthur," Edward said. "I'm hurt much. There's a ship-load of folks out there, many of them women and kids, all drowned because Hogger wanted to force a wreck. For what? Whiskey!"

"Hogger's a squid," Arthur said. "We don't have nothing to do with him."

"He isn't one of us," Henry said. "We're not like him."

"Yeah?" Edward said. "What are we like?"

CHAPTER 10

The Reverend John Gilmore walked through London with his eyes wide open. The picturesque city was alluring to the eye and romantic to the heart, but only when one glanced superficially. Closer inspection revealed as much heartbreak and squalor densely tucked into the shadows and corners of tenement row houses as there was grime and mold packed between the bricks of the narrow pavements, all of it to be trodden underfoot.

The Reverend traversed the wide streets according to the directions Mr. Lukin had given him, and eventually found himself in the center of a transport and livery district, at the end of an alley wider than most. He grabbed the large ring and knocked.

On the outside, at least, this building was much tidier than the adjacent shops. The windows were clean, the double carriage-like doors recently stained, their metal hinges polished. The sign overhead was professionally lettered: LUKIN SHOPPE — COACHES, WHEELS, AND UPHOLSTERED ASSORTMENTS.

The well-oiled door swung open without a squeak.

"Hello, kind Reverend," a portly man said from the doorway, his face cheerful.

Rev. Gilmore smiled. The short man was as impeccably neat as the exterior of the business. "Good day. A Mr. Boxley, please. Reverend John Gilmore of Ramsgate calling on behalf of the owner, Mr. Lukin."

"Lionel!" the man said, his face brightening even more. "What of him? We've heard no word, and he's now several days past due from Dover." He spoke with such excitement that he nearly ran out of breath before finishing his words. "He is well?"

"He is," Rev. Gilmore said.

The man exhaled long and slow. "Thank the heavens. I am Boxley. Please, come in."

Richard Boxley, the foreman and accountant left in charge by Lionel, was an elderly man, short and squat with wisps of white hair atop his age-spotted head. Bushy sideburns hung like two smoking pipes made of snow on either side to frame his puffy face, making it seem very pink. His mouth was full of tiny teeth, mostly white or brownish white, all in a row and no less even than a good accountant's bottom line.

As they walked, the Reverend was impressed with the interior of the modest but well-kept facilities. He noted the modifications tooled especially to build the Lukin coaches. "Are there many who work here?"

"Not as many as Mr. Lukin would choose had he infinite resources," Boxley said, leading the way down a narrow corridor past smiling office clerks on both sides.

He ushered the Reverend into a larger office with a packed bookcase. Miniature coaches adorned some of the shelves and a few tables. One miniature coach was particularly ornate, golden and encased in glass upon an oak base. A drafting board stood in the corner of the large office with a dozen drawings plastered around it.

"Mr. Lukin's office, this is."

They continued down the corridor, finally arriving at an open area where several craftsmen were busily carving and machining various woods and metals.

"Watch your step." Boxley pointed to a stack of metal rings as they crossed the work area to a glass-enclosed office space in the rear. He led the Reverend to a large table within the office and seated him at the end. "May I offer you some water or tea? We sent out for more cider today, hoping it might be a good omen, being Mr. Lukin's favorite refreshment. It seems it was! At last, some news. A drink?"

"No, thank you. I'm quite refreshed for the time being."

Through the glass partitions, Rev. Gilmore saw the craftsmen looking up from their work at him. All of them smiled and nodded.

"Do tell," Boxley said, "what is the report? Has Dover commissioned us? Do you know? And how are Mrs. Lukin and Master Luke? I daresay we miss them as much as our benefactor."

"Yes," the Reverend said, clearing his throat.

"Hmm?" Boxley asked, his face pink and smiling.

"I'm afraid there has been a tragedy. Not all is well."

He began to relate the story of the shipwreck. As his words continued, he remained aware of what he was saying and knew his mouth to be forming the correct words. He was confident his pastoral manner was in proper play; however, he felt very much outside of himself.

Boxley trembled as the news came forth. Rev. Gilmore again noticed the craftsmen watching through the panes of glass. They no longer smiled at their posts but gathered at the window and seemed to surmise the ill news as they beheld their foreman sobbing.

"I have relief that he is well," Boxley said, removing his spectacles and wiping them dry with a knotted hanky from his trouser pocket. "But there is nothing sadder you could have told me."

Boxley replaced his glasses and looked at the Reverend. "Is he coming back?" He sounded like an earnest child.

The workers slowly entered through the doorway. They were each dressed in heavy shirts, overalls, and work shoes. They were middle-aged men but all brawn and all of them heavily mustached. One of them had long hair that hung out from under his cap to rest on his shoulders.

"What of him?" asked a short man in front.

"Reverend," Boxley said, his voice weak, "meet some of many who love the Lukins as I do. He is Martin."

"Has evil news come today?" Martin asked.

"Mr. Lukin is alive and well," Boxley said. "He is in Ramsgate."

Rev. Gilmore was not prepared for the chorus of sighs and bodies going limp. One man fell to his knees and uttered a grateful prayer. Another hollered so loudly that the clerks down the hall must have heard.

"But," Boxley said, regaining their attention, "our lovely Alicia and brave Luke have perished at sea."

Again the Reverend was not prepared for their reaction. The men cried out in anguish. And Boxley turned once more into a broken heap. He buried his face into his hankie and sobbed.

The Reverend wept with them, feeling their loss, and Lionel's, for perhaps the first time.

He soon learned that had it not been for Lukin's vision and leadership many of these men would have been in workhouses or debtor's prison. Each had attended the Lukin home and come to love the happy family. More than one of them related recollections of bouncing Master Luke upon a knee and of being on the receiving end of gracious attention from the missus.

It was a long time before Rev. Gilmore finally presented the instructions written by Lionel's own hand and bearing his signature. Boxley examined them through his smudged eyeglasses, tugging on one of his woolly sideburns. "Yes, it is possible, I dare say. Not recommended, but possible. He's astute, he is."

"And the tools?" the Reverend asked. "I noticed he mentions tools."

"Longley and Anderson will fetch them. Load them up for you nicelike. Are you sure there isn't more?"

"This is all he asked for, except to tell you to complete the present orders without delay. A certain Mr. Pennington—was that it?"

"Yes, yes, Pennington, what of him? Ho!" Boxley blew his nose in his handkerchief, and new tears streaked from his eyes.

"I'm sorry," the Reverend said. "I can wait. Take all the time you need."

"Ho! Ah, no, it is fine. I'll be fine. Young Luke was a joy to have visit the shop, he was. But Pennington—what of him? He is in sales, a representative really, he sells many things. Not just for us. A good man, Pennington. What of him? Oh!" Boxley reached again for his handkerchief. "And Alicia, how does he go on without her?"

"He is having difficulty, of course, but he will recover. He wants you to have Pennington try to get a coach overland to Dover, and make the sales effort, if possible, without him. He will wire you soon."

Boxley replaced his glasses and looked at the Reverend with sad eyes. "Should we all keep going?"

Rev. Gilmore smiled. He leaned across the table toward Boxley and spoke in a soft, kind tone. "I believe that's what these arrangements are for. I believe he will return. I believe he must, when he's ready. In the meantime, it seems he has much confidence that you have your hands full and you will be well suited to manage his affairs until such time."

"Yes, of course, of course. He can count on me," Boxley said, looking reassured and then suddenly alarmed again. "But what of these items on the list? The tools? The materials? What does he plan to do?"

The Reverend sighed and stood up. "I don't know. I was hoping you'd tell me. Do you think he can build a coach all on his own?"

"No, not possible, not even for Lionel. Repair one maybe, but not build, no, no. And another thing: These materials are not right for a coach." Boxley stood up and walked out of the room, leaving Rev. Gilmore wondering what to do.

In a moment, two square-shouldered men returned. One squeezed the Reverend's hand in a strong handshake.

"I'm Noah Anderson, at your pleasure, Reverend. Stewart here and meself will get you Mr. Lukin's tools. Some of the others are arranging for the materials. I'd say it'll fill two good-sized trunks. We'll load 'em for you."

"Thank you," Rev. Gilmore said.

Boxley arrived to stand between the two movers. "Whatever Lionel wants. Come, I'll show you more of the place. It is good to see."

"Very well," the Reverend said.

"Interesting he sent you, Reverend," Boxley said as they walked. "Alicia, yes, I could see that, but Lionel . . . well, he never really had much to say about such things as God, though he's a good man, mind you, better than a lot of holy types I've known, begging your pardon. Now, myself, I know there's a God for certain, but Lionel sending a Reverend to do his bidding . . . ? It's a surprise."

Boxley stopped. He twisted his sideburn in his fingers for several seconds, then looked up with a tiny-toothed smile. "Oh, I get it! On the account of Alicia and Luke, it is. Am I right? He found God in this terrible thing. Ho!" Boxley started to sob again and pulled out his hankie.

"I do not know the answer to that," Rev. Gilmore said. "But I assure you it constitutes much of my prayers these days."

The two walked down the hallway. "Pray for me, Reverend. Pray for all of us."

Two days later, Rev. Gilmore rounded the North Foreland aboard the packet ship and came upon Ramsgate with his heart filled with anticipation. He looked forward to a time of refreshment with his wife and Lionel, but also enjoyed the thought of a short nap before conducting his midweek service.

The Reverend scanned the quay and spotted his wife waiting in the buggy. He was disappointed Lionel wasn't beside her.

When the boat docked and he and his wife had shared an affectionate greeting, he quickly expressed his excitement. "A right good shop he has built," the Reverend said. "Many men are able to provide for their loved ones because of Lionel."

"I am happy to hear it," Mrs. Gilmore said, her countenance not matching her words.

Other than a few updates concerning church matters, she had little to say as they drove toward Albion Place.

"Where is Lionel?" the Reverend asked at length. "I want to give him his things before they are on my person too long." He laughed and patted his bulky pocket and nodded toward the trunks.

Mrs. Gilmore sat silent. Her lips were pressed tight and her chin trembled.

"What of Lionel?" the Reverend asked. "Is everything aright?"

She shook her head.

"What is it? Has he fallen into depression again?"

"He has not come out of his room, not even to eat."

"That is to be expected, dear. I am not surprised."

"There is something more to say. There was a tragedy upon the Goodwin, one witnessed by many."

"When? Did any survive?"

She sighed. "Darrin Hogger lured a ship to wreck in hopes of securing whiskey."

"Lured? What do you mean?"

"With a lantern. We think he's done this sort of thing before."

"Treachery? It's unimaginable!"

They arrived home. The front door opened and Lionel walked out. Under his arm he carried a rolled-up paper.

"Reverend . . . Ma'am," he said with a nod. "Do you have my things?"

"I do." Rev. Gilmore reached into his pocket and pulled out a stack of currency and handed it to Lionel, who stuffed it into his own pocket.

"It's good to see you about," Mrs. Gilmore said.

"Thank you," Lionel said formally. He looked at the Reverend. "There was a tragic incident while you were away."

"Yes, I only just now heard of it. It's terrible. I'm sorry."

"I'm not sure whether this town is courageous enough for the idea I've had," Lionel said, his face like stone. "I'm afraid that you might have wasted your trip of errand for me." He pursed his lips and stared at the ground.

"I've done no such thing. It was fruitful. Your Mr. Boxley and all your workers send their deepest condolences. They were quite beside themselves with grief when they heard the news, though they are glad you are all right."

Lionel sighed, his face softening. "They are good men." He fell into silence, his eyes unfocused. He sighed again. Finally he squared his shoulders and looked up at the Reverend. "I am not certain, but

I may try to share my idea tonight, to see if there are any men who might be inclined to help me. I shall need your assistance."

"You wish to address the people at church? A fine plan, Lionel," Mrs. Gilmore said. "What is your idea?"

"No, not church," Lionel said.

"But we will be at church this evening," Mrs. Gilmore said.

"What is it you are saying, Lionel?" the Reverend asked. "Be clear."

"I have little hope it will turn out as I wish, but I do indeed ask your assistance, the both of you." Lionel glanced at Mrs. Gilmore.

She looked skeptical. "How?"

"Please join me while I make a presentation of sorts in Cannon's public house tonight."

Mrs. Gilmore's hand rose to her neck. "Oh my, no, Lionel. We do not frequent such places. We cannot."

"Must it be done at the pub?" the Reverend asked.

"It must," Lionel said.

"I'm sorry, Lionel," Mrs. Gilmore said. "We have service tonight."

"After service. Please."

"What is it you wish to say in such an environment that we must be present?" the Reverend asked.

"Your endorsement may be that something extra to win over some. This one time is all I'm asking."

"Endorsement of what?" Mrs. Gilmore asked.

The Reverend, still seated next to Mrs. Gilmore atop the buggy, turned to his wife. "My love, forgive me."

"What? What do you mean, John?" she asked.

"I will make you a deal, Mr. Lukin."

"A deal?" Mrs. Gilmore asked. "John Gilmore, what are you talking about?"

"Yes?" Lionel said.

"You attend us to service tonight, the first since you've known the good graces of our home and fellowship, and I'll attend you to the pub this evening after service."

"John Gilmore, what in heaven's name are you saying?" Mrs. Gilmore asked.

"I cannot speak for my wife, but such is my deal. However, I reserve the right to immediately depart your presence should I determine you or the event itself to be in any way disreputable. Is it a deal?"

"It most certainly is not a deal!" Mrs. Gilmore said.

"Deal!" Lionel said, extending his hand.

The Reverend shook it vigorously.

"Dear," Rev. Gilmore said to his wife, "Mr. Lukin will be attending us to church this evening and I, him, to the pub. I hope you will do the same."

He stepped out of the buggy and marched into his home. He heard a slight peep behind him as he closed the door.

CHAPTER 11

Outside Holy Trinity Church, people arrived in buggies, on horses, or on foot, gathering along the short stone wall that encircled the gothic meeting place. The parishioners came from all directions—down lanes, across fields, from in town—and along well-worn paths.

Most of them were farmers, though sailors and merchants were among them, breathing misty vapors into the cold winter night. Henry was in their number, as were John, Jeffery, and Edward. Arthur was not.

There were gentlemen with ladies on their arms, walking sticks in their hands, and servants beside their coaches. There were widows, old and young, feeble men and strong, youths and children, all of them bundled warmly. With flurries falling, there was already a light dusting of snow covering the many trees.

The arriving congregants entered the narrow front gate at the southwest corner of the churchyard, across the way from the small park. A few paces away stood the double doors under the massive stained glass window. A line of folks clogged the stairwell. They conversed where they stood. Others entered from the side gate leading to the large single door that jutted out from the vestibule. A jam of people shook hands and shared news. Men cracked jokes. Women embraced, and children played tag.

Inside, the church was cold. There was no fire or any form of heat except what would be produced by the closely gathered bodies. There were dozens of lanterns and hundreds of candles, but people did not remove their cloaks, nor did anyone complain about close quarters in the pews. The locals shuffled through the vestibule and down aisles, eventually filling the many pew benches.

Lionel watched them through the parted curtains hanging in the doorway of the tiny room at the front of the sanctuary. Inside this room were hung the copes and other priestly garments.

Behind him was the Reverend in formal attire. The cope he was wearing was wine colored with black, gold, and white accents. He broke from his silent praying. "Go find a seat now."

Lionel walked through the chancel and took a seat beside Mrs. Gilmore. She was dressed in a silk dress of blue and gold gathered at the back and flowing loosely to lightly touch the floor, completely hiding her feet.

The church filled and, except for the pair of modest but neatly dressed men who stood in the altar area as if at attention, all sat in the pews. Mrs. Gilmore crossed to the organ where, Lionel thought, she took a considerable amount of time to situate herself comfortably and arrange her dress just so.

She bared her ankles and feet enough to have free access to the organ pedals but no more. As she prepared to play, the mood immediately changed. Silence ensued. Even the coughing stopped as Mrs. Gilmore raised her hands to play. She momentarily froze them in midair before thrusting them down. The most unexpectedly loud chord filled the room, blasting forth from the harmonic pipes. The chord resonated and then transformed into a medley of notes that seemed to swirl in as many directions as a gusting squall of snow.

The music surged and swelled, clamored and fought until the

very air of the place seemed to pulse with deep bass notes and melodic fireflies buzzing about. Even the holy plate upon which rested the flagon and chalices seemed to vibrate in a sort of harmonic percussion as Mrs. Gilmore attacked the keyboard with the same ferocity Lionel had seen in the seas that lashed against straining bulwarks. The effect was all-encompassing. Then suddenly, like a rushing wave that had crashed upon the shore and was fast retreating back to sea, the music hushed.

Mrs. Gilmore lifted her feet from the pedals and slowed her hands to glide and dance upon the keys until the music fell like the flurries outside, light and soft and swiftly melting on contact. Lionel felt light-headed. He realized he hadn't been to church in a long, long time.

When the song concluded, Mrs. Gilmore returned to her seat beside him.

The Reverend John Gilmore entered from the small room and stepped to the altar with his back to the congregation. The back of his cope displayed a pattern of colors in mostly circular shapes with fanciful accents. At length he turned, his voice booming like thunder at sea.

"In the name of the Father and of the Son and of the Holy Spirit."

Nearly everyone responded with a hearty *Amen.*

The Reverend continued with short exhortations, and the people replied in kind. He prayed aloud concerning the propensity of all toward sin. As the prayer continued, Lionel felt sleepy.

Next, the Reverend told a story about a man beaten and robbed and left at the side of the road while many passed by. Some spoke blessings and moved on, but only one offered what was really needed—food and shelter. Lionel perked up.

The Reverend addressed sin as not only pertaining to things

done but also undone, things neglected or ignored.

"We are truly sorry," the Rev. Gilmore continued, "and repent of all our sins. For the sake of Your Son, Jesus Christ, who died for us, forgive us all that is past and grant that we may serve You in newness of life, to the glory of Your name. Amen."

There were other things he said and other replies by the assembly and even a series of priest and parishioner exchanges concerning mercy, but it was words declaring sin to be possible in an unwillingness to act that seemed to have a life of their own. Lionel agreed with those words. He had felt them.

Good deeds undone. Lionel had always thought of these as *distasteful* but never as sin. He wondered if it were true. The words hung in the air like so much fog. He looked around. The attention of most seemed rapt.

He stretched so that it seemed normal to turn his head to one side, and then stretched again, permitting his head to turn in the opposite direction, allowing him a full sweep of the assembly.

The *Seahorse* crew sat in one row. Henry seemed attentive, though he often pursed his lips in such a way that they puckered. Other times, his eyebrows bunched together. John Burton bore no pained expression and sometimes mouthed the last words spoken by Rev. Gilmore. Jeffery seemed to tune in and out, if the positions of his eyelids were any kind of measure. Edward's eyes looked watery. He nodded with agreement, listened intently, and never took his eyes off of the Reverend.

Lionel looked up to see Rev. Gilmore now standing behind a lectern carved in the shape of an eagle. It was a tall lectern and might have blocked the face of most men, but the Reverend peered over the top, hardly glancing down at his text.

His words were a mix of prepared text and what seemed like extemporaneous utterance. He spoke of love and forgiveness to be best expressed in action. He spoke of brotherhood and family, patience and grace.

"This is the word of the Lord."

"Thanks be to God," the congregation replied.

Lionel wondered how so many knew what to say in return. He yawned. He was beginning to feel overwhelmed. He hoped it was ending. His senses were overloaded.

To his surprise, Mrs. Gilmore returned to the organ. Another hymn was played and sung, followed by another reading from the Gospels, a reciting of a creed, and several prayers of intercession. Then Communion was served. After a closing hymn, the Reverend stood in the center of the chancel and extended his arms.

"The peace of God," he said, "which passes all understanding, keep your hearts and minds in the knowledge and love of God, and of his Son Jesus Christ our Lord; and the blessing of God almighty, the Father, the Son, and the Holy Spirit, be among you and remain with you always. Go in the peace of Christ. Amen."

"Thanks be to God," the assembly replied.

Lionel rejoiced. It was ending. His end of the bargain was satisfied.

The people arose and milled about, meandering and conversing in exit as they had upon entrance.

Lionel was thinking about what he would say when they got to the pub. That's when it hit him. All along he had thought it was his idea and the others were simply too blind or too indifferent to see. Now he wondered if it was an idea that had existed long before he had ever thought of it. Had he found it, or had it found him?

⚭

An hour later, the Gilmore buggy stood outside Cannon's public house. The flurries were falling heavier, and the breeze from the harbor was blowing stiffer. The Reverend stood on the street reaching outstretched arms to Mrs. Gilmore, who was still seated in the buggy. Lionel waited at the entrance, the rolled paper under his arm.

"Dear," the Reverend said kindly, "I'm waiting."

"I cannot do it, John. It is most inappropriate." She wrapped her coat more tightly as the wind gusted and nearly blew off her feathered hat.

"I've my word to keep, dear. Please, it won't take long."

"Your word, John, not mine. I never spoke such a deal."

Lionel stepped forward and took off his hat. "If I may be so bold, did I not hear in that sacred place atop Albion Place this night the very words of His gospel spoken to the people?"

"You most certainly did, and I am glad for it," Mrs. Gilmore said. "Much good can come out of that for you, Lionel. But entering such a den where men are prone to stumble and entertain spirits not holy"—she hesitated, as though searching for the perfect words—"is *not* likely to produce much good."

"But Mrs. Gilmore, within those sacred walls and contained in the sacred readings, am I erring in my remembrance, or do I recall words declaring that our Lord went into the homes and gathering places of thieves?"

"Dear Lionel, He most certainly did. But it was not to drink or thieve among them. He was on a mission."

"As am I, Mrs. Gilmore." Lionel glanced down at the rolled paper under his arm. "I hold under my arm a plan with a mission. A mission to save lives. It is a plan that, I believe, ought to be heard by those inside."

The Reverend tilted his head, his eyebrows lifting as he looked at his wife. She took a deep breath and seemed about to speak. But as she opened her mouth, a gust of wind blew her hat off. It flipped in the air and would have fallen to the ground if not for Lionel's attempt to catch it. As he bumped the hat with his hand, it flew across the walkway and, with the help of the wind, pinned itself against the front doors of the pub. The rolled paper, having dropped from under his arm, also rolled to become pinned alongside the hat. Both items appeared to be attempting to get inside the pub.

"Now," Lionel said, "if that is not divine invitation, then there is no convincing you, I'm afraid." He retrieved her hat, offered it to her, and tucked his paper back under his arm.

Mrs. Gilmore smiled briefly, then covered her mouth. Her cheek quivered. She stepped out of the buggy with the aid of her husband and replaced her hat atop her head.

"I'll have you both know I'll be praying under my breath the whole time," she said.

Lionel and the Reverend opened the doors, and Mrs. Gilmore led them in.

They stood inside the doorway. The squeezebox music ceased. All conversation hushed. The patrons froze and stared. Some had mugs pressed to their lips, others stood with glasses held high, and a man stood on one leg in an unfinished jig. The whole world had gone still.

Lionel crossed to the center table, flanked by the Gilmores, amazed at how loud their footsteps and the rustling of their clothes sounded. He noticed Arthur seated at the table with his crew, including those who had earlier been to church. Their eyes followed the Gilmores' every move.

The patrons slowly became conscious of their positions. Mugs were lowered, bottles of hard liquor were corked and slid away, and gaping mouths were closed. One sailor pushed a woman off his lap so hard she fell to the floor. The dancing sailor lowered his leg and sat meekly upon a stool.

"I have something I want to tell all of you," Lionel said.

Everyone looked at him, still very much in shock. Some of the sailors recovered enough to tip their caps to Mrs. Gilmore, and a few offered their hands to the Reverend. Henry hastily put a cork back into the bottle of rum in front of him, and stepped around to the other side of the table.

"Wait!" John Burton said. He stood up. "I have something I want to say to you first." All eyes went to him. "Please."

Lionel found a chair and sat. The Reverend and Mrs. Gilmore did the same.

"You're not a bad mate," John said. "For a landsman, I mean. You did a fine job on my boat, and I thank you for that. 'Course it was you who stove it, but you did the right thing. And, well, you've done a few right things, and we haven't been so good to you."

John's face softened. "The other night on the cliff was ugly. I really wish we could've done something. But that's the rub, mate: We can't. But we would if we could, I mean. It's true, Hogger is a squid, and we'd like to kill him if we see him—" He seemed to startle himself and paused, quickly looking at the Gilmores. "Truly, we didn't know he was that sort. We had no part in that treachery. None." He sat down.

Jeffery stood up, fidgeting with his cap. "What Dad is saying is that going out in a mad boil of waves is certain death. It's not about being brave or cowardly. If there was the faintest hope for . . . well, the faintest hope at all, we'd be rushing to the oars. It breaks our hearts—it does!—to see women and kids perish, almost in the shadows of our own houses." He sat down next to his father.

The wind rattled the windows. Lionel gathered his feet to stand, but Arthur stood abruptly. Everyone looked surprised, but he didn't speak. He moved halfway across the pub to the bar and turned his back on all of them. He called for a pint, and Cannon served it up.

Lionel smiled gratefully at John and his son and then stood. "I respect the sea," he said to the crowd. "At times, it does command my fear —"

"Hear! Hear!" Arthur said, raising his mug without turning around. "The landsman is beginning to learn."

"But," Lionel said, not even glancing at Arthur, "I'll not let it drown life out of me while I'm yet dry."

"Then you're still a fool," Arthur said, his back to all.

Lionel turned in Arthur's direction. "No, Arthur, you are the fool."

Gasps went up across the pub. Arthur whirled around. Mrs. Gilmore prayed loudly enough that her *S*s were heard.

Lionel stood with his feet squarely planted. "You couldn't be more worthless to those who cry for help if you were already drowned and had taken up your place at the bottom of the sea."

Arthur slowly stepped closer to Lionel. "Worthless? Try hopeless. There's a reason we men of Ramsgate hold the tack as we do. Show me a boat that'll stand the storms and the conditions we know all too well. Some of us, by bad luck or by rotten chance, have slipped the depths closely enough to know there is a wild sea that's not to be bested by man or boat or beast. If we knew different, there isn't a man here who wouldn't give it a try." His face softened for an instant. "Some of us have tried with less."

"I will make such a boat." Lionel approached the center table. "Make room here, please."

Henry snatched the rum off the table. Lionel unrolled the paper he carried and pulled out two large wads of money to place on the top corners to keep the paper from rolling up.

"This money here — my money — will cover most of what is needed: lumber and rope and materials. But it can't buy courage. I'm wondering if such can be found here."

Arthur moved to the opposite side of the table. He glanced at the money and the paper. "What are you saying?"

"I'm looking to recruit men to help me."

"Help you do what?" Arthur asked indignantly.

Lionel beamed. "Build her and sail her."

"What is it?" Tom asked.

"A boat to rescue with!" Lionel said. "A storm boat that can ride rough seas!"

The paper contained drawings as detailed as an engineer might produce. It displayed multiple views of a small boat with strange features.

"You? A landsman?" Arthur said. "Do us all a favor, will you? Waste no more of our time and go back to wherever you came from and whatever trade was yours. Start a new family and let rest your troubled past."

Lionel stomped forward. Arthur raised his fists, but Lionel crossed to the far end of the bar and pointed to the Lukin poster and the carriage wheel hanging there.

"Do you see these?" He ripped the poster off the wall. "Can you see this?"

"Hey, I paid good money for that!" Cannon said.

"I paid more!" Lionel said fiercely. He brought the poster back to the center of the room and tossed it on the table. "My name is Lukin. Lionel Lukin." He pointed to the bold letters on the handbill.

The men stared at the poster. Some looked at the wagon wheel on the wall.

"I build coaches for land," Lionel said. "I will build one for the sea."

Edward looked at Lionel. A smile formed and grew until he broke into uproarious laughter. John laughed too, and Jeffery kept repeating, "I can't believe it." Henry smiled. Tom scratched his head and stared at the handbill.

Arthur, his face red and eyes like glass, smacked his lips. "Impossible."

"Reverend?" Lionel asked, turning to the Gilmores.

"It's true," the Reverend said. "He is the same Lukin. I know it to be fact. I traveled to London on behalf of Mr. Lukin here, conducted some business for him at his sizable shop, and have just returned today. He is indeed the builder of the Lukin coaches and, obviously, a man of some means."

Arthur spat and returned to the bar.

"Oh my," Mrs. Gilmore said.

"Begging your pardon," Arthur said, without turning around.

Edward picked up the handbill. "Magnificent! Amazing!"

"How do you know it can work?" Tom asked.

"Well," Lionel said, "it must be tried and tested until it does."

The men gathered around the table then, taking turns looking at the diagrams of the strange boat.

"You'll note the bow and stern are enclosed," Lionel said. "They're actually airtight. That will make the boat quite buoyant and impossible to plunge under."

"Haw!" Arthur scoffed from the bar.

"A killer storm is an evil thing," Rev. Gilmore said. "This appears to be a good thing, Lionel. I admire you for taking it this far."

"You overcome evil with good, isn't that right, Reverend?" Henry asked. "Least that's what you always say."

Lionel saw Arthur send a disapproving look at Henry, who quickly added, "I'm not saying it can work."

"I don't know," Tom said. "It's interesting to be sure, but plenty doubtful."

"It is an interesting concept," John said.

"Aye!" Edward said. "It is an admirable thing you have here."

"Do you have a plan for such a feat?" John asked, bending over the designs. "Beyond the drawings?"

"I do," Lionel said. "I've been working on it. It will be a lifeboat of a kind never before seen."

"Do you think it really has a chance?" Jeffery asked.

Mrs. Gilmore stood up, and again the room went silent as men resumed nearly frozen postures. "It is a noble work Mr. Lukin proposes. It seems to me an ark of safety in answer to the prayers of the shipwrecked poor. Isn't that right, Lionel?"

"Thank you, Mrs. Gilmore," Lionel said. "It is."

The men loosened, and the small chattering began to grow.

"And the courage you mentioned," the Reverend said. "There is no short supply in Ramsgate; I am most certain of that."

"That is what must become known," Lionel said.

"Reverend," Henry said, "you're always saying nothing's impossible with—"

"Of course it's impossible," Arthur shouted, standing with a mug of ale in his fist. "What does a landsman—a builder of *land* coaches—know of the sea?"

"Now, Arthur," John said, "he does know the feel of wood. My own boat proves me that."

Lionel plucked the bottle of rum from Henry's hand and crossed to Arthur. He yanked the cork out and held it before Arthur's face.

"I know cork, too."

Arthur smirked. "Cork?"

"Aye," Lionel said, dropping the cork to float in Arthur's mug. "Cork."

PART 2

And thinking over the disasters he had seen and known, sorrow-
fully, patiently, and profitably, as great hearts and great minds do
think, did he conceive the idea of a coach warranted against sinking, with airtight compartments. It was designed to brave terrible
seas and maddening storms. He called it a lifeboat, for it was to
save life.

THE REVEREND JOHN GILMORE

CHAPTER 12

"Has any of this been done before?"

Lionel smiled at John's question. John, Jeffery, Edward, Rev. Gilmore, and a few other seamen had just dined upon breakfast sausages, potato meal, and biscuits at the Gilmores' rectory. The plans for the proposed boat were spread across the dining room table, between the plates. Mrs. Gilmore entered from the kitchen with a kettle of hot cider.

"We must test the design, of course," Lionel said, pointing to the forward section of his illustrated vessel. "But it is a design built upon well-established principles." Lionel was in his element, and his passion was high.

"What will you wear?" Mrs. Gilmore asked, filling the Reverend's cup. He leaned against the archway that separated the dining room from the main hall.

"I'm sorry?" Lionel said.

"What will the men in the boat wear?"

"I, uh . . . well, I haven't considered that yet, actually."

"Oh," Mrs. Gilmore said, pouring another cup.

Lionel watched her and smiled. "There are other features as well, all of them equally important and resulting in an increased benefit by fact of them working together. Buoyancy, strength, and navigability are most crucial, I suspect." He looked at Rev. Gilmore.

"Would you care to join us?"

The Reverend stood with journal in hand. "No, you go right ahead. I've some writing to do." He nodded and headed to his study.

"She'll need oars," Lionel said to those around the table, "which will be simple enough, but she'll need at least one sail or maybe two. I'm not strong in this area and will need your minds on this as well as your muscle. So what is it, one or two?"

"One is sufficient if it's added power you want most," John said. "If you want to maneuver rightly, she's better served with two."

"Aye," the men said, almost in unison.

"But there are trade-offs," Edward said.

"What sort?" Lionel asked.

"Ease of operation." Edward placed a finger on the center of the boat Lionel had drawn. "If you place one mast here and know what it takes to keep her standing strong and straight, what with the stays to keep her in place and the running rigging to trim her out, then you'll be edging in on the elbow room for rowing, hauling, and the like. That's understandable. You've got to have some sail. But add another here, and that's much more space to be occupied with such and much less room to row."

"Aye," John agreed. "If you really succeed in recovering some-one from boat or sea there's less room to seat them somewhere out of the way from those of us struggling to get them home. That is, if you have two masts."

"Those are good points," Lionel said. "How critical is it to have the advantages of two sails over one? Is it worth the space?"

The men exchanged glances, scratching their beards and rub-bing their chins.

"Where do you imagine this boat will sail?" John asked slowly. "In the vicinity of the Sands?"

"Quite in the vicinity," Lionel said without hesitation.

"Two," John said.

One by one, the others nodded or grunted their agreement.

Lionel was listening for something more than simply direct answers. He was learning their personalities, temperaments, and perspectives. John Burton seemed a skilled leader, certainly knowledgeable of seas and ships. Edward was something of a visionary. He seemed to see the big picture ahead of the others.

"What about transporting the rescued?" Edward asked. "How many can be gotten with a full crew manning her?"

"That's a good question," Lionel said. "That's something we need to know."

"We can't be running from shore to Channel and back again," John said. "It would take much too long."

"Not to mention we'd be exhausted," Jeffery added.

Lionel straightened up and rubbed his forehead. "Obviously, we do have some challenges."

Jack Davis, a young sailor at the table, folded his arms. "It will be interesting to see who will actually dare ride in her." Everyone looked at him. He shrugged. "Will any of us really enter a gauntlet of stormy seas in an untried vessel?"

"She'll not be untried," Lionel said. "I've already been anticipating the kinds of tests we must run her through, right in the harbor."

"Aye," John said, "plenty of tests, to be sure."

"I hate winter," Arthur said.

"Now what?" Henry asked. "We've had two good days of weather and now a third."

"That's the point. You can't even count on winter to do what winter does."

Arthur and Henry stood in front of Cannon's. The sun glinted off small waves in the outer harbor.

"You're as finicky as a woman," Henry said, sipping his short glass of rum. "It's near December and we're in front of the pub instead of rolling on some breakneck sea, and you're grumbling." He smiled. "You sure it's the weather that's rubbing you wrong? Or is it the sights?"

Arthur slurped his ale, wiped his mouth with his sleeve, and burped.

"Is that your reply?" Henry asked with a smirk. "I swear, sometimes I think that frown clings to your face more than an anchor does a rocky bottom."

Arthur looked at his friend, his eyes narrowing. "You saying I've got a rocky bottom?" He suddenly let go a deep laugh, and Henry laughed too.

"Henry! Arthur!" Tom called from inside the pub. "Dominoes, mates!" He stepped out. "You playing?"

"And miss the show?" Arthur pointed to the edge of the outer harbor where Lionel Lukin and his team of helpers were measuring, marking, and cutting timber. Lionel was surrounded by a dozen old salts, all intrigued by what he was doing. "Do you believe that? He's like a bloody circus."

"I think it's pretty interesting," Henry said.

Tom tapped Arthur's shoulder. "Dominoes?"

Arthur spat. "Come on, Henry. Let's go see the clowns."

"Hey, I'm coming, too," Tom said.

Arthur led his mates, drinks still in hand, to the small section of sloping beach between the boat launch and the clock house where Lionel had tried to launch John Burton's boat. Lionel was again the center of attraction.

He stood in the shallow surf holding an open-ended barrel floating on its side. Gathered in a half circle along the slope were his team of lifeboat builders and the old salts. Behind them stood the unfinished lifeboat they had been working on the past few days—all framed, glued, pegged, and planked. But that was not what was presently fixing Arthur's attention. He watched Lionel move a barrel atop the water.

"A barrel floats well so long as it remains filled with air," Lionel said. "But supplant the air with water and . . ."

He tipped the barrel so that the rollicking surf entered the open end. He released the barrel. It floated for a while but not well. It quickly filled and dropped below the surface. It reappeared in a wave and banged around on the beach but was soon pulled away to sink to the bottom of the harbor.

"It's finished," Lionel said, "gone to the bottom! Now, let me show you another outcome. Edward!"

Edward held another barrel that was capped on both ends. Arthur watched his brother hand it over to Lionel.

"Edward loves to play nursemaid, don't he?" Arthur asked.

"He's a hard worker," Tom said. "You know that."

"I don't know anything if I know that."

Lionel moved the barrel atop the water as he had with the previous one. He addressed the crowd and his crew. "An airtight barrel has the advantage of not being filled with anything but the air already within it." He nodded to Edward for assistance. They forced the barrel under the surface. "So long as the integrity of the seal remains intact, the barrel is able to powerfully resist being submerged. And even if it does submerge—" They let the barrel go. It popped out of the water and into the air to splash down and float again. Lionel smiled. "It rises and floats another day."

The small gathering nodded. Some cheered. John, Jeffery, Jack Davis, and others clapped.

"I wonder if he swallows fire, too," Arthur said to Henry.

"One thing is certain," Henry said slyly, "he knows how to start one in you!"

Arthur stared hard at his friend.

"It was a joke, Arthur."

Lionel and Edward exited the water, soaked and shivering, and joined the crew to encircle their boat-in-progress.

"Maybe he'll catch pneumonia and die," Arthur said.

Lionel tapped the bow of the boat-in-progress. "We are going to enclose this front section and the rear section, the bow and the stern, so that it is as airtight as a sealed barrel. It likely won't prevent the boat from being submerged in all conditions, but it will reduce such action and, in the event submersion occurs, it will always force the boat back to the surface, so long as nothing occurs to compromise the air inside."

He crossed to touch the ribs along the inside bottom. "I had you build the thwarts in such a way so as to provide grips, or holds, as you say. To traverse the seas she's intended to brave is to risk quite a lot of water coming aboard, enough to wash a strong man away. These holds, combined with safety lines and good sailor's knots, will keep the crew in the boat."

Edward walked on the opposite side and thrust his hand into one of the several rectangular cutouts with hinged doors that lined the boat on both sides. "These scuppers," Edward said, "only open with pressure from the inside. Upon rising out of a heavy sea, the grade of the boat's bottom will force the water to rush toward the sides, push open the scuppers and run out. When she dips down into the trough of a wave, the pressure from without will force the scuppers closed."

John draped a cloak on Lionel's shoulders. Lionel let his hand trace an imaginary line down the entire length of the boat. "We will line her with thick cork just below the gunwale to give her added buoyancy."

Arthur rolled his eyes. "It'll never work." He spat and headed back to Cannon's.

"Pretty unlikely, I've got to agree," Henry said.

"That's why I like you so much, Henry. Sometimes you're smart," Arthur said.

Henry stared hard at Arthur.

"It was a joke, Henry."

Tom lingered a bit, gazing at the boat.

"You coming, Hardwell?" Arthur was several steps away. "Or you thinking of joining them?"

Tom laughed harder than the joke merited. "Join them? I'd sooner dive for sponges than get in that boat."

The day aged and the stormy winds returned. The temperature hovered just above freezing. Rain clouds covered the sky until it was dark and gloomy across the region. It soon rained hard and washed away the remaining snow. There were dots of lantern lights and flickering hearth fires sending dancing shadows upon drenched and rattling windows. They pierced the moody darkness with tiny pinpricks of amber glow. In some windows about town, green wreaths with red bows started to appear.

CHAPTER 13

John, Lionel, and Jeffery were in John's fishing boat floating a few feet into the outer harbor, just beyond the seawall separating it from the inner one. Lionel used a speaking trumpet to direct those watching from the shore nearby.

"Embark and launch!" he yelled.

The boatbuilding team lifted their newly completed lifeboat onto a special second launching ramp they had also constructed. The boat was pegged in such a way that it could not slide into the surf until the pegs were removed.

Edward and eight other men climbed into the new vessel. There were four on each side with Edward sitting at the stern as the coxswain and tiller man. Others gathered around it, pulled the pegs, and released it from its restraints. The boat clattered down the wooden ramp and splashed into the mild surf.

From the fishing smack Lionel watched how swiftly the rescue boat entered the water. The launch was something he had considered essential. It would allow a fast response after the need arose. They would not lose previous time trying to get the boat into the water.

"Oars!" Edward called out from the rear.

The men lifted their oars out and fitted them through the oarlocks until all eight oars were extended.

"Put your backs into it, men," Edward said with mock seriousness.

The men laughed and rowed in unison.

As Lionel watched the men participate in lighthearted manner, he considered how fear and adrenaline might one day blend to rattle the savage calm of even the most brutish among his crew, seasoned sailors or not. "Keep focused!"

Edward worked the tiller, and the boat reached a deeper part of the harbor between the launch and the eastern pier, nearer to where Arthur's lugger, the *Seahorse,* was tied.

Lionel saw Arthur, Henry, and Tom aboard the lugger. He wondered how upsetting this might be to Arthur. More than half his crew—John, Jeffery, and his own brother, Edward—were spending a great deal of time with Lionel. Not only that, but the fair weather was hampering the hovelling work. Lionel had noticed the *Seahorse* going out early every day, but it seemed always to come back empty-handed.

Even from across the harbor, Lionel could hear Arthur speaking bitterly, though he couldn't make out all the words. Arthur kicked a buoy over the side of his boat.

On the shore, large numbers of onlookers were gathering at the small beach area behind the clock house. Some of them seemed to be anticipating what might follow, and began to hurry down the eastern pier. Some went all the way to the end at the entrance to the harbor, barely fifty feet from where Lionel and his men were practicing maneuvers.

Lionel shouted to Edward. "On the gunwale, starboard side!"

Edward directed his men to put oars away and to gather along the right side of the boat. They did, and the boat listed heavily. Edward remained seated but placed his foot on the top edge of the boat's side.

"Have them sit on it!" Lionel shouted.

Edward shrugged and instructed his men. They laughed at the unorthodox command, but didn't move.

"What? What's happening?" Lionel asked John.

"These are sailors you're speaking to," John said from beside him. "They are familiar with practical seamanship, which does not include trying to upset a boat."

"Oh, not to worry, they'll stay dry. I'm sure of it."

"You may be, but they're not," Jeffery added.

Lionel repeated the command and, with Edward's urging, the crew moved toward the gunwale.

"This is not a common sight," John said to Lionel.

Lionel glanced to the *Seahorse* and saw Arthur standing with arms crossed and wearing a pronounced smirk. Tom seemed bent over with laughter. Henry was half covering his face with one hand, peeking through his fingers.

With embarrassment upon their faces, the men in the boat hesitantly sat on the top edge of the right side of the boat where the oars usually rested. The boat listed more heavily to that side, but it did not tip so far as to take on any water. Seeing the amazing buoyancy, Edward stood up and placed most of his weight on the starboard gunwale. Even then they could not upset the boat. Some of the other men intentionally bobbed up and down, causing the boat to rock and dip, but still no water breached over the gunwale to collect in the boat.

"It does not upset!" John said.

The crowd of onlookers responded with cheers and scattered applause. Lionel felt their transfixed gazes as he instructed the men to do the same on the port side.

The men joked about how wet they would soon become if they kept it up, but they continued to perform the actions asked of them with a spirit of fun and sport. The men bounced and jumped. The modest vessel demonstrated a remarkable balance, and not a drop of water entered her.

"Okay, take me in," Lionel said to John.

John and Jeffery sailed the fishing boat alongside the *Seahorse* on their way back to shore. Arthur turned away and began coiling a rope that didn't appear to need coiling.

"What do you think?" John asked as he floated by.

Arthur didn't look up. "About what?"

"It looks pretty stout," Henry said. He tilted his head sideways as he gazed at the lifeboat.

"What are you talking about?" Arthur asked as he continued to coil, still refusing to look.

"You know what," John said. "The boat."

"I don't know about any such boat." Arthur finished the coil, set it down, and went below.

Tom smiled. "Irks him some, I suppose."

John laughed and focused on sailing his boat to shore.

Lionel turned back toward the lifeboat and found that the lifeboat men had rowed up beside a small cutter. "What's this?"

"A challenge!" John said.

Edward called to Lionel. "Permission to put up sail?"

"Better wave him off," John said. "No need to spoil a good day."

"Spoil?" Lionel asked, amused. "This will only make it better." He waved to Edward. "Granted!"

"Oh, boy! Here we go," Jeffery said.

John turned the fishing boat for a better view, and he and Lionel watched the lifeboat put up sail and race the small cutter. The lifeboat was surprisingly swift considering the number of men aboard her. It edged past the cutter in the short run. The captivated crowd applauded. Lionel noticed some of the onlookers patting the backs of others as though they were in some way connected to the lifeboat's achievements.

"Now the crane," Lionel said.

"Are you sure?" John asked. "It's peculiar."

"I'm sure," Lionel said. "Take me to them."

The lifeboat crew positioned their boat under an iron crane jutting out from the pier. Lionel climbed into the lifeboat while John ferried the others to shore in his boat. Edward remained with Lionel. The two of them worked with the crane operator alongside the boat. Edward managed to work the crane line under the boat to appear on the opposite side, where Lionel affixed it to the base of the main mast. The crane operator maneuvered the line taut. John returned to pick up Lionel and Edward. They climbed aboard the smack and watched from a few yards away.

The crowd gathered around the crane and watched, whispering excitedly. Lionel imagined he could hear them speculating among themselves about what the activity meant.

Lionel signaled the crane operator, who shortened line until enough pressure was exerted upon the spartan craft that she began to tip. People gasped and wondered aloud how much pressure would be applied. A few predicted the mast would soon snap, but it didn't.

The crane tipped the little boat far enough over that water finally breached her, pouring in over her port side.

⁂

Arthur sulked in his berth. He couldn't decide what he hated more, winter or landsmen. Suddenly, someone banged on the roof of his cabin.

"Arthur!" Henry called. "Come up here. You've got to see this!"

Arthur went topside and saw what the crane was doing to the lifeboat. He shook his head in disgust. "Of all the foolhardy . . . What are they doing?"

"Don't know," Henry said.

The crowd watched as Lionel permitted the crane operator to continue shortening cable. Finally the boat flipped over completely, bottom up, her copper sheeting glistening in the morning sun.

Lionel yelled a command, and the crane released the tension. As if by magic, the boat righted and cleared itself of excess water through the scuppers. The crowd roared.

"Did you see that?" Henry asked.

"I never would've believed it!" Tom said.

"See what? A trick, that's what!" Arthur said.

"I think not." Tom hopped off the *Seahorse* and ran down the pier for a closer view.

Arthur watched him go and then saw Henry looking at him. "What?"

"Nothing," Henry said. "Could be a trick. Might be."

"It's a trick, I tell ya," Arthur said in a huff. He turned to return below deck but Henry halted him.

"They're not done yet. Looks like more."

Arthur watched as Lionel had John ferry him over to the lifeboat, where he and Edward climbed aboard again. This time, after the crane was rightly affixed to the mast, Lionel told Edward to return to John's boat. Arthur could see that Edward wanted to stay, but Lionel insisted.

After Edward and John moved the fishing boat far enough away, Lionel surprised everyone by kneeling down in the center of the lifeboat and grasping the center thwart. He signaled the crane operator to tilt the boat over again. The operator hesitated, but Lionel repeated his instructions with hand motions. The crane operator reluctantly nodded.

Arthur thought this was the craziest sight he'd ever seen. He surveyed the shore to see if everyone was as annoyed as he. He was disappointed that the crowd stood mesmerized. Even the Gilmores had arrived in their buggy and had pulled up in time to see the strange activity. The harbormaster was there. So were the constable and the mayor and a few other officials.

The lifeboat began to tip into the water with Lionel huddled in it. The boat flipped completely over, far quicker than before. Lionel was in it and underwater.

Arthur guffawed. Henry slapped him on the arm with a hearty laugh.

"Fool!" Arthur said. He folded his arms but watched closely.

Aboard John's boat, Edward looked alarmed.

"Something's wrong," Henry said.

"His weight must be acting like a keel and keeping it under." Arthur watched Edward dive off the fishing boat to swim toward the lifeboat. "Did I say 'nursemaid'? I think he's more the mermaid now."

As the crowd witnessed Edward's plunge, the mood darkened considerably. They grew quiet and watched Edward swim toward his friend many yards away.

Arthur watched his brother in the frigid waters. He unfolded his arms and stepped forward. "Something's gone amiss. What do you expect when you purposely keel it over? Fools, I tell you."

"If it is a trick," Henry said, not smiling, "it's a good one."

As Edward swam, John made sail for the lifeboat in his fishing boat. The copper bottom of the lifeboat was just starting to bubble from its sides. It was sinking.

Mrs. Gilmore prayed so loud Arthur heard it. "Oh, dear God, have mercy," she cried.

Tom Hardwell forced his way through a tangle of folks and stepped up to the edge of the pier.

The sinking hull created massive bubbling as air pockets broke up.

Edward strained to reach the boat before it went completely under. He had a few feet to go. John gained on him rapidly as he steered his craft closer.

"I'd say Edward has a mind to catch cold," Arthur said.

"This isn't good," Henry said.

With a jerk and a massive splash, the lifeboat flipped over. Water gushed from the scuppers. The boat bobbed and steadied in right position. Lionel jumped up from his crouched hold in the center, soaking wet. He raised an arm and hooted loud and long.

The crowd erupted with cheers. Some threw their caps.

"I don't like that man," Arthur said. "He's reckless."

"I don't think it's a trick," Henry said. "I think they've got something."

"Nothing worse than false hope," Arthur said. "That's certain. No trick about that."

"You're tough to please, Arthur. You've got to give credit when it's due."

"I don't have to give anything."

❧

Lionel beamed when he saw the crowd's reaction. Young and old, rich and poor, man and woman, sailor and beggar—all of them were cheering. Some embraced. He had done it. They had all done it. They had built an unsinkable boat.

He heard a splash and saw an arm reach over the side of the boat. A drenched head peaked over the edge. It was Edward.

"Ho! It's cold!" Edward said.

Lionel reached out his hand. "Climb aboard, mate!"

Together they waved and shivered before the adoring crowd.

"What were you doing in the water?" Lionel asked.

"I wanted to ask you the same thing," Edward said, grinning.

Lionel stared with wonder.

Edward shivered. "I got concerned."

Lionel smiled and grabbed Edward's shoulders. "You are indeed a lifeboat man."

"Ahoy!" John said, pulling alongside. "I'll be running out of blankets today!" He tossed one to each of the soaking men. "Spectacular!" John said. "That was amazing, Lionel. She doesn't sink!"

Lionel heard variations of that sentiment when he returned to shore. He and Edward were offered more blankets and hot tea. Dozens waited for a chance to touch and congratulate the lifeboat builders. Some inquired to learn more of the purposes and capacities of such a technology. Others simply looked and marveled.

Lionel noticed Arthur watching him. The large man did not look happy.

But Lionel didn't care.

CHAPTER 14

"Well, Arthur, this is a heavy gale," Henry said, looking at his friend.

"It is blowing like a broadside," Arthur replied, staring to sea. "Make no mistake, it's a dreadful night."

The winter squall beat upon Ramsgate. The town was yet awake as several lighted windows—adorned with holiday decoration—attested, but little activity was occurring along the streets. Henry and Arthur stood at the far end of the eastern pier at the entrance to the harbor.

"I'd say there's more than one feast happening tonight," Henry said. "The one at the Gilmores' is one kind, but the Goodwin growls for grub."

"Neither party is one I wish to attend."

"I noticed a slew of vessels out there today," Henry said. "With the wind having changed and moving fast from the north, I fear for them."

"Yep, I noticed them," Arthur said. "They'll be having a bad time of it this very minute. Let's hope their anchors hold. If not, we'll see what we can do tomorrow."

"If any of them touch the Goodwin tonight, it's sudden wreck for sure," Henry said. "I daresay the Goodwin could take a ship at a mouthful with such seas as these."

Suddenly, a flare shot into the night sky from the vicinity of the Goodwin Sands.

"By God!" Henry blurted. "It has happened as we speak of it!"

Arthur's jaw tightened. "I hate winter."

"Ho!" Henry said, aghast. "I don't recall such a season of so many wrecks."

"I do," Arthur said. "So goes winter and the Goodwin Sands."

Another flare shot into the sky.

Henry looked at Arthur. "Do we dare?"

"Dare what?" Arthur asked, immediately irritated.

"Alert the lifeboat men?"

"Not so long as Edward is among them!"

"But they asked if such should—"

"No!" Arthur snapped. He headed down the pier and then stopped and spun around. "Pray if you want, but we'll do nothing until tomorrow, and that's if the weather permits. I'll hear no more about it."

A third flare rocketed into the sky. Henry followed its course, then turned to watch Arthur disappear into the darkness.

❦

"May God prosper the good lifeboat institution and advance its noble object!" The Reverend all but glowed as he spoke.

"Hear! Hear! Noble object!" the men said loudly. Some offered a forkful or leg of meat as a toasting instrument.

Outside, the house was being blanketed with fresh snow, but inside it was warm and festive, lit with candles in every room. The fireplace snapped and crackled with feisty flames. Laughter and good cheer echoed throughout.

Seated around the dining room table were Rev. Gilmore and

his wife, Lionel and Edward, John and Jeffery, and eight others, including Jack Davis. They dined upon roasted goose with cranberry and orange stuffing, raisin-filled bread pudding, baked pies, yellow squash, and fresh breads.

The Reverend stood at the head of the table with his teacup lifted high. "May many a brave fellow be spared to his family and home," he said, "because of the rescues this crew shall someday provide!"

"Hear! Hear!" the men shouted. "Good men spared!"

"May many a man be plucked from death to yet be the joy and support of loved ones!" Rev. Gilmore said.

"Joy of loved ones!" the men shouted. Some whooped.

One gulped down his tea as though it were a nip of rum and reacted to the heat of it, nearly scalding his throat. He coughed hard. Lionel and the others laughed.

The Reverend continued his toast. "And may many a man, unfitted to meet death, be snatched from its jaws to live to repent and to seek that peace which he had formerly disregarded."

"Hear! Hear!" the men said, with much less enthusiasm. "Uh—repent! Yes, uh, repent!"

The jocularity trailed down to a hush until a moment of awkward silence came over the group. Lionel watched everyone. He smiled and stood. He lifted his cup of tea. "Amen!"

"Amen!" the Reverend said.

"Amen!" the men said, not so much in unison as before, but with kindness and approval.

"Amen!" Mrs. Gilmore said all by herself as she stood at the opposite end of the table. "I have a surprise for you," she said to Lionel, then looking around the table. "For all of you."

"A surprise?" Lionel said, sitting down. "Do tell!"

She left the room, leaving the men wondering aloud what was

up. They looked to the Reverend for a clue.

"It is all her doing," he said. "Credited to her alone."

She returned a moment later carrying two unusual vests, one hanging from each hand. She held them up for the men to see. They were vests in every ordinary sense, sleeveless and waist length and made somewhat of fabric. But they were entirely original in one peculiar way.

"Is that what I think it is?" Edward asked.

"Why, Mrs. Gilmore, you astound me!" Lionel said. "Is that—"

"Cork!" she said with pride. "No less inspired by your own use of it upon the hull of your magnificent vessel. I submit that these life vests be made a prerequisite for anyone brave enough to be such a sailor as a lifeboat man."

Lionel took one in his hand. "Magnificent. Ingenious!"

"Hear! Hear!" John Burton said. "A toast to the honorable Mrs. Gilmore, in hopes we may all float to heaven!"

The men laughed and applauded.

"They are ingenious," Lionel gushed.

"Hopefully they will keep you from going to heaven too soon," Mrs. Gilmore said. "They should keep your heads above water. I've made one for each of you."

"These are grand," Lionel said. "One for each of us? I am speechless."

"You must promise to wear them," she said.

"And promise we do," Lionel said, trying one on for all to see.

A knock on the door interrupted his fitting. The Reverend went to answer it.

He returned moments later with a grave look on his face. "Flares! At the Goodwin, just minutes ago."

Into the room stepped Henry. Lionel was shocked to see him

there. What would Arthur think?

Henry fidgeted with his cap in his hands. He nodded respect-fully to Mrs. Gilmore. "It could be a schooner maybe," he said. "There were several large schooners in the Gulls earlier today. Whatever the ship, she's large enough to have brought rockets with her. She's launched three of them, maybe four."

"If it is a schooner," John said, standing up, "it's likely she would have a decent-sized crew aboard, maybe passengers."

"We mustn't waste time," Lionel said. He turned to his crew, some rising to their feet. "This here is a chance, men. If it is such a ship and if she does carry a larger number, we will need a steamer to make way to the point, to drop off survivors in case we can't do it all in one trip."

"The steamer won't go out on a night like this," Henry said.

"She must," Lionel said. "Only as far as the point; no farther."

"I'll ask her captain," Henry said, "but no promises."

Lionel looked to his men. "This is what we've been working for. Are you with me? Are you ready?"

The men said nothing. After a long moment, Jack Davis spoke up. "But it is such a miserable night, Lionel. And, well, some of us have children — or are planning to."

"Of course, it's miserable weather," Lionel said. "Would a ship struggle at the Goodwin when it's fair?" No one met his eye. "Haven't those aboard the ship got wives and children?" The men shifted in their seats or where they stood, but none spoke. Lionel looked at each of them. "Are those aboard the ship not longing for home even as we long for ours?"

The silence was unbearable. Lionel felt the urgency pressing upon him, the familiar desperation rising. He looked at Edward, who rose slowly to his feet.

"Men," Edward said, "shall we all go home now? Was all this

work just a vanity to impress ourselves when all along we intended to turn our backs when the danger came? I'll not do that." He took the other vest from Mrs. Gilmore. "Help me fasten this, Lionel."

John stepped forward. "Nor will I. Where are the other vests?"

"I am with you, Lionel," Jeffery said. His father squeezed his shoulder.

Mrs. Gilmore rushed out to get the other cork vests.

Rev. Gilmore stood at the head of the table. "I don't think it is right to force anyone to go or to make anyone feel guilty for not going. There will be no shame upon anyone who doesn't and no glorifying of those who do. The lifeboat was only tested this very day, and though it did well, it has yet to prove it can accomplish what we all hope it may accomplish on a night like this. So consider well what you do, or don't do. It is a personal choice."

"Shall we abandon the cause before it has begun?" Lionel asked. "Shouldn't we try everything possible?" He looked at the Reverend and remembered something from the message at church. "How much of a difference is there between a Hogger who wrecks ships and a man who doesn't do what he can to save them? I wonder if a ship on the Goodwin isn't the same as a man beaten and bloodied on the side of the road. We must choose whether to pass him by or lend our aid."

Mrs. Gilmore returned with an armful of vests and stood in the archway between the hall and dining room. She looked around, uncertain what to do next.

One of the men stood up. "Some of you do have wives and little ones and should go home. As for myself, I cannot leave those out there to perish thinking of their own families, not after what we've seen these recent days. What with the wreck Hogger caused and the like and for certain not while knowing we've a boat that just might could do it." He reached out his arm. "Give me a vest, ma'am."

Another stood. "Let it not be said of me that I would seek to stay dry while my fellow lifeboat men get to play in the water." He took a vest and slung it on.

"Nor will it be said of me."

"Nor I."

Others did the same and donned the jackets.

"If your heart prevents it," the Reverend said, "stay ashore. We each have different things to consider. Whatever we need to do must be done quickly. Those who are going can go in the wagon."

"I cannot go," Jack Davis said, trembling. "With me and the little lady planning on having a baby, maybe two, I can't do it. But you know my father captains the steamer. I will talk to him and do what I can."

"Good man," the Reverend said. He touched the sailor's shoulder. "Take my horse. Godspeed!"

⟨∞⟩

Along the Goodwin a large ship was grounded hard and fast. She was being attacked on all sides with a frenzied rush of crashing breakers. The seas leapt and boiled around her, lusting for her destruction.

At Cannon's Pub, Arthur, Cannon, and other patrons stepped out to see what the commotion of hooves and wagon wheels and loud voices was all about. They saw the Gilmores' wagon rumble past, laden with the lifeboat crew. Each of the men, save for the Reverend, wore bulky vests over their coats.

"What in blue blazes?" Cannon asked.

"Is Edward among them?" Arthur asked, alarmed.

"Who can tell?" Tom said.

Arthur rushed into the street. He heard running footsteps down Harbour Place from the direction of the harbormaster's residence. It was young Jack Davis, followed by his father in nightgown, cap, and overcoat. The elderly man was tall, with a handlebar mustache. He looked extremely grumpy.

The Gilmore wagon braked to a halt. Lionel jumped off and ran to the steamer captain, Davis's father. "Will you help us?"

"My son told me what you have in mind. On a night like this? It's madness!"

"Maybe so, but will you help us?"

"Most definitely not!"

"There are lives at stake!" Lionel said.

"Yes, ours!"

"We need the steamer to pull us out," Lionel said, his voice rising. "We don't have time to discuss this."

"No!"

"How can you decline? Do you realize what you're saying?"

"My answer hasn't changed."

"Fine, then we'll do without the steamer," Lionel said. He ran to the lifeboat.

Arthur arrived just as Lionel left. "What did he want?"

"He wants me to linger at the point in the steamer. On a night as bad as this—can you believe it?"

Arthur watched the lifeboat men gather around the launch. "Is Edward over there?"

"Yes," Jack Davis said. "He's in the boat. Look!" He pointed to the boat atop the launch.

The lifeboat crew was already seated when Lionel climbed in beside Edward in the bow. John was seated as coxswain. Arthur shook with anger. He rushed toward the lifeboat but was too late.

Other men, including the Reverend and the harbor master, helped release the boat to slide down the launch and crash into the turbulent harbor. Arthur reached them just as John barked out commands for oars.

"What does that landsman think he's doing?" Arthur said. "Edward's with him! Reverend, you let him take Edward?"

"They're attempting to save lives, Arthur," Rev. Gilmore said as calmly as he could above the tremendous wind.

"Yeah, well, we know what will become of that, don't we?" Arthur said with a bitter tone. He watched the lifeboat struggling in the wild surf.

Water flowed into the boat as large waves broke over the sides. Suddenly, a larger wave broke over her entire length on her starboard side and completely swamped the boat in a mad rush of roiling foam.

The boat was buried in green seas but rose and shook free. Before Arthur or anyone else could express relief another powerful combination of wind and wave struck it broadside and pushed it sideways, despite frantic efforts of tiller and oars.

The lifeboat struggled but soon rose upright on its keel. It was well positioned with an appearance of willful defiance. The crew rowed it straight into the next wave head on. They plowed into it, rose up, then rolled down into the trough and rose up at the next.

It was incremental at best, but the lifeboat made headway. The men looked gallant in their overcoats, slickers, and strange jackets. A few wore knit caps, already soaked, but most wore large brimmed rain hats and rowed with all of their might.

John barked commands inaudible to those near the launch. Arthur could tell by the way the men leaned toward him that they were barely able to hear him above the wind. Lionel struggled to maintain a good hold while he fastened short lifelines to rings fixed on the thwarts and laid them at the feet of each man.

A mighty breaker came barreling forth and snatched the boat from its present course, lifting it into a frigid, encircling embrace of choppy waters. The ocean appeared to curl all around the tiny vessel until it upset her so severely to one side that everyone washed out of her.

The boat quickly bobbed to her righted position and floated as an only refuge in the swirling mix of foamy sea and gusting snow. Extended out in all directions, like the arms of an octopus, were the lifelines Lionel had just fastened. Each line connected to the inside bottom of the boat with the other ends being separately grasped by the floundering crew. They bobbed in their jackets, and Arthur deduced the vests were made of something buoyant. One by one, each recovered his hold and tugged along the length of line and tumbled over the gunwale back into the boat.

Arthur watched with tremendous consternation as none made any effort to turn back but took to the oars and resumed the fight. They plodded slowly through the restless harbor.

Arthur searched for some kind of answer, some kind of help. He saw the steamer captain watching nearby. He rushed over to him. "Launch the steamer!"

"What?" the captain asked.

"My brother is out there with that fool. If anything happens to him, it'll be your life for his, understand? Now launch!"

"You out-storm the storm itself, Arthur! Now what am I supposed to do?"

"Tow her back in!" Arthur said.

"No," the Reverend said, stepping forward. "But your assistance would be much appreciated if you could tow her in the vicinity of the Sands."

"That's a death wish," the captain said.

"No," the Reverend said, "it isn't. You can't enter the fracas as that little beauty can, but she'll never get there in time without some assistance. Once you get near the Sands but still outside the worst of it, cut her loose and she can manage well enough."

The steamer captain thought hard and then ripped off his night cap and threw it down. "Jack!"

"I'm right here, Father," the young sailor said.

"Let's ready the *Aid*. We must be snappy."

"She'll live up to her name this night," the Reverend said. He picked up the cap and handed it back to the steamer captain. "Thank you."

"Aye," the captain offered, with no sound of pleasure.

"And if you want to live to see another day," Arthur said, "you'll wait for her somewhere where she can hook up with you for a return tow."

"The point and no farther," the captain said. "Threaten me if you will but no farther!"

"Then do it!" Arthur said, fixing his eyes on the lifeboat.

"You coming with me?" the captain asked Arthur.

Arthur stared back at the man more fiercely than before.

"Yeah, I figured. Sure, send me out."

☙

Lionel hunkered down opposite Edward. The difference between the tests he had orchestrated and their present condition was greater than he had imagined, despite his experience aboard the *Sanctus*. His darling lifeboat was pitching and rolling with violent force. He wondered if his mathematics and theories could hold up against such brutal treatment.

He looked at the faces of his men. They strained with all their might as they tried to steady the boat with their oars. Something more was needed.

"God help us!" John yelled from his coxswain position.

Lionel nodded. He wondered the outcome.

"Prepare for hawser!" a windward voice said.

A steamer appeared, her bow lantern piercing the dark. Jack Davis stood at the bow ready to toss a line.

The lifeboat crew cheered.

Davis tossed the hawser. With the towing line secured, they ventured out of the harbor and into the stormy channel.

The steamer tugged the lifeboat to plunge through the waves. The men put away their oars and bent forward with firm grips. They surged on, running a gauntlet of leaping and tumbling waves. It was a freezing, furious ride as they bounded over the tumultuous waters. The icy sea repeatedly broke over the bow and sprayed the men like a hose. Lionel and Edward held fast at the bow.

It was forty-five minutes of lifting and falling upon storm-tossed waves before the crew could see the stranded ship ahead, her deck lanterns creating a mysterious glow. The seas surged and spanked the schooner, shaking her from stem to stern.

Like great sheets of ice, breaking waves flew over the vessel. Tar barrels were faint with dying orange glows but rich with thick black smoke that swirled and wafted and mixed with the frigid blasts of seawater.

The wind bullied hard and then suddenly followed with a cross gust from an opposite direction. The mix of harsh winds, bitter cold, sheets of icy water, and thick, billowing smoke prompted one of the lifeboat crew to say, "It looks like hell itself."

The crew and passengers aboard the schooner were numerous and appeared in the rigging and atop the decks. Some were trying to light a new tar barrel. The captain and mate launched another rocket. Their ship lifted and fell with each new roll of the sea. With each crash they moved up the Sands. Her hellish ascent continued until she reached the apex, where she slammed down with great force and grounded fast.

The steamer signaled with a lantern flash for the lifeboat to release the hawser. John ordered sail, and the men assumed a tack to head straight alongside the stranded ship. They were seen by the men on the schooner, who cheered with shouts of joy and gratitude.

The lifeboat sailed straight into the tumult and was quickly swamped. It arose and rid itself of much water and surged forward. Lionel saw the captain of the schooner above. He looked aghast. Lionel figured the man had never seen anything like their lifeboat.

John ordered the foresail lowered and an anchor thrown overboard. Using the tiller in skillful fashion, he sheered it toward the wrecked ship, running out cable from the anchor as they went.

Lionel recognized the vessel as an emigrant ship, which meant more passengers than he had been expecting — people with dreams of seeking new lives elsewhere. This night they would be pleased to take whatever life they could get.

The lifeboat reached the end of the anchor cable and jerked to a stop fifty or sixty feet short of the wreck. The schooner passengers became frantic. Lionel looked back at John. His coxswain shrugged.

They had dropped anchor too early and come up short. The lifeboat men had no choice. With quick consultation among the crew, John commanded oars to be taken and they rowed back to where the anchor had first been dropped.

Backtracking to pull up anchor and setting it again was no simple task, since the men were already well worn. But a spirit of

derring-do prevailed among them as they saw the fearful faces of the passengers.

Lionel logged in his mind that a longer cable was needed for next time, or maybe a back-up anchor. If there was a next time.

They rowed away, unable to communicate their intentions to the schooner. Lionel noticed some of those onboard preparing to jump into the sea. He feared they might attempt a swim to the lifeboat. They likely felt the lifeboat would not return. Lionel stood and waved his arms. He pleaded with them to stay put and at last seemed to get his point across.

The sea was wild and the anchor so embedded that it took a full twenty minutes to recover it. Finally, after rowing the boat in a maddening circuit, the anchor was broken from its hold and the men lifted it out of the heavy seas. They made sail and shot in closer, and dropped anchor again. They rode the cable out and worked the tiller until they came alongside the stranded vessel.

They used two heavy ropes, one thrown from the bow and the other from the stern, to tie up in a fair position. Edward and Jeffery manned the two hawsers and alternately hauled and released. They worked hard to keep the boat from banging against the side of the schooner.

The schooner was grounded as solidly as a rock, and the seas tossed the lifeboat like a toy. The crew agreed that if the two vessels collided due to a rogue wave, the result would be the instant shattering of the lifeboat.

Others assisted the same hauling and easing action with the anchor cable. Between the varied efforts of hauling and veering on the three lines, the men struggled to keep close to, but adequately separated from, the big ship.

"How many can you carry?" the captain shouted, peering over the rail high above Lionel's head. "We have more than one hundred aboard — more than sixty women and children."

The lifeboat crew looked at Lionel. He saw more and more heads on the schooner, most of them the tiny faces of children nestled in the arms of adults. All displayed a mix of terror and hope.

The lifeboat bobbed and dunked and lifted. Lionel thought he had done sufficient planning but now realized there was much he hadn't anticipated.

"We have a steamer nearby," Lionel shouted. "We will ferry."

Lionel, Edward, and John conferred briefly and determined it extremely difficult to get the women and children from one vessel to another so they agreed to try a dangerous maneuver.

"The only question is who will go?" John said. "Jeffery and I can do it."

"No," Edward said. "I will do it. You are too skilled on trimming the hawsers. We must be certain to keep the vessels in their needed positions."

"Aye," John said. "You and Jeffery then."

"No," Lionel said. "I am the least suited to assist the sailing. I will join Edward."

"Be smart, mates," John said. "It's right rough."

The lifeboat repeatedly rose and fell while the men hauled and veered on the ropes to keep the vessels in proper attitude toward one another. Lionel and Edward used the rising and falling action to their advantage. As the lifeboat lifted on a high sea, they used the momentum to leap through the air right onto the deck of the schooner.

But neither reached the deck. They clung to the ropes hanging from the side of the larger craft. Urged on by both crews, they scurried up the ropes and swung over onto the bulwarks.

They were wet from spray and more exhausted than they had expected to be, but they found themselves in the center of the crowded main deck.

"Who comes here?" the grateful captain asked.

"Lifeboat men," Lionel said, extending a hand.

"From Ramsgate," Edward added.

"Nay!" the captain said. "You can be nothing less than storm warriors!"

Edward tipped his head. "Suits me."

"Suits us all," the captain said. He turned to the crowd. "Rescuers from Ramsgate! Storm warriors, I say!"

Instantly, Lionel and Edward were thronged. The crowd pleaded for their children to be taken first. Some seized them by the hands, and some attempted to cling to them in full embrace. It took considerable force from the captain, his mate, and other crew members to help make room for the two rescuers to operate.

The captain backed them up and formed groups of ten to twelve, most with children in their arms or clasping to their coat tails. The light from the ship's lamps and the faint moonlight revealed a mass of terror-stricken people. Some looked deadly pale with eyes wide and wild looking. Most trembled, but whether from fear or cold or both, it was too difficult for Lionel to discern. Lionel saw one woman swoon into the arms of her husband. The wind howled incessantly and with great force.

"Bowlines are the way," Edward said to the captain.

"Of course," the captain said and ordered some of his crew to rig the necessary items.

The ship remained fast aground and the seas pummeled her. Timber snapped, canvas fluttered, and chains rattled. The ship suddenly shifted, and many lost their footing. They toppled across the decks but stayed aboard.

"All clear!" the captain yelled to Edward and Lionel.

The two lifeboat men positioned themselves in the rope slings and straddled the ship's rail before nodding to the captain. His crew picked two women from out of the crowd. Each held an infant child. The ship's sailors helped them up to Lionel and Edward, who assisted them to sit in the swings facing the two rescuers, the infant children safely between them. The great ship pitched.

Below, John instructed his men when and upon which lines to haul and which to ease. They worked hard to keep the boats properly sheered, but the rushing tide and fierce weather made it impossible to keep anything still for longer than seconds.

The lifeboat suddenly veered away from the big ship as far as the cables permitted and then swung back in. John ordered the anchor cable to be hauled upon, and the three men did with all of their strength and managed to keep the craft from slamming into the schooner's hull.

The lifeboat rose high on the crest of a swollen sea and momentarily lifted John and his crew to eye level with Edward and Lionel. They were instantly one foot apart. Thinking quickly, Lionel shoved his passenger and her child straight out to John, who just as quickly reached out for her, more out of reflexive action than forethought. He got her as the wave passed and the bottom seemed to drop away. The lifeboat plunged downward like a loose anchor.

The lifeboat dropped with such force that all of the lifeboat men, including John and the two rescued passengers in his arms, fell to the bottom of the boat, sprawled out like dead men after a cannon shot had struck center.

Lionel watched with amazement the gulf of dismal sea between the straining ship and bullied boat. It flowed with beckoning foam.

Another running sea rolled under the lifeboat, lifted it higher than before, and then dropped it deep into the valley trough between two waves. The sea next slammed against the schooner to pour over the side and flood the deck. Water rushed ankle deep across the schooner's deck, foaming white and frigid cold as it rushed past the feet of all. Some slipped and would have slid and slammed against the far side of the ship if not for others grabbing hold of whatever limbs or clothing they could clutch.

Edward still held the woman and child in his arms and looked back toward the lifeboat. John had managed to roll the other woman and child off of him and into the care of Jeffery. John opened up his arms toward Edward and gave an exaggerated nod.

This time the lifeboat rose but not as far and left about eight feet between Edward's feet and John's head. Edward aimed and dropped the woman and child straight down. Just as he had let go, a wave rolled along and the lifeboat dropped further away, outpacing the falling woman and baby. They landed hard at what turned out to be a fifteen-foot drop, but they landed upon the chests of men with outstretched arms.

"Timing!" Lionel shouted to Edward. "Timing!"

"Aye."

The two men signaled again, and the procession continued. Mothers and infants were handled first, and there were many of them.

One woman with an infant was led by the captain and mate to a gangway rigged alongside the place where Lionel and Edward dangled. She pulled back from the edge as soon as she saw what awaited her, but they wasted no time and forced her over the edge where she dangled, her legs kicking and her shouts hysterical. They suspended her over the side like a child in a fit until the lifeboat surged upwards and her feet touched down into the lifeboat. One lifeboat man grabbed her by the waist; another took hold of her child. The captain and mate let go, down the boat dropped, and the woman was transferred in as gentle a form yet delivered.

The men began to get the hang of the timing, and several women and children were moved from schooner to boat without incident.

It was decided there was room for one more. The woman who had earlier swooned was chosen. She was in terror at the prospect but with help from her husband was finally handed off to Lionel. She struggled enough that Edward swung over and assisted. They timed it perfectly and the lifeboat lifted to an even station with the ship. Lionel and Edward let go.

She would have dropped perfectly in place, but she panicked and lunged at Edward to tackle his leg, where she remained clinging for her life. The lifeboat dropped away nearly twenty feet below. Her legs dangled high above the roiling tide.

Edward tried to hold onto her, not wanting her to drop from this distance. Lionel tried to swing over but a sudden gust of wind held him back. The woman couldn't keep her hold on Edward's leg. She screamed and fell into the sea.

The lifeboat surged upward and came up closer. John sheered the boat in so that another lifeboat man could reach out and catch the woman by her clothes. He dragged her over the side from out of the sea. Others helped and pulled her in amidships. The boat dropped and again knocked the men over like pins. They recovered and passed the woman back to the stern where the rescued were gathered.

A passenger aboard the schooner rushed forward and cried, "Here! Here!" He thrust a bundle into the hands of Lionel. Supposing it to be a rolled blanket for the man's wife, who had just fallen, Lionel shouted to Jeffery, "Here, Jeffery, catch!"

Lionel dropped the bundle to Jeffery, who stood up to catch it. He just succeeded in catching it as it almost fell into the sea, and then was rocked by the sound of a baby's cry from the blanket, followed by a scream from the woman in the back.

"My baby! My baby!" She stumbled to Jeffery and recovered her child. Others helped her return to the stern.

One moment the tiny craft was as high as a yardarm on the schooner, and the next it was so low in a deep hollow of the sea that there was hardly any water between the bottom of the lifeboat and the sandy surface of the Goodwin. Lionel and Edward watched from the railing of the schooner.

"Release hawsers!" John yelled.

Two men cast off the hawsers and hauled hard upon the anchor cable. Others rowed to assist the hauling, but it was terrible work and they were exhausted. They progressed to shorter lengths of cable. The boat jerked all the more wildly upon the backs of unruly waves. No sooner was the anchor aboard than they raised sail, felt the reassuring pull of the helm, and beat back past the beached schooner.

The passengers aboard the wrecked ship gave a fainthearted cheer as the lifeboat bounded past their stern. The lifeboat tramped into the fierce breath of the gale. The seas encircled the smaller craft and raged with a mad boil of ice and sleet and spray. Waves slammed the sides of the boat and drenched those within. A mighty cross wave rose up, rushed forth, and crashed atop the clawing craft, filling her to the brim with a pool of cold sea. She listed sideways and more water rushed in over the gunwale.

"She must sink!" a husband of one of the women aboard the lifeboat cried. He leaned over the rail of the schooner and desperately reached out a hand.

"Steady that man!" Lionel shouted as he swayed in his sling.

The lifeboat surged up out of the water, seas streaming through the scuppers, and straightened out. Those on the schooner cheered.

Suddenly a loud snap sounded above their heads. Lionel had heard that noise before. He looked up. A mast was falling.

∞

The lifeboat plunged onward. One moment the stern was precipitously high and angled to the stars, the next moment the stern was bedded deep into the violent embrace of caving waters.

"Port oars, ready! PULL!" John yelled, yanking on the tiller to combine both rowing and rudder with the advantage of the sails to turn the bow headlong into a massive and fast-approaching wave. "Boom!" he yelled. The mainsail swung into new position, sweeping over the heads of some of his crew with a frightening speed, and then suddenly stopping with a bang and rattling of chain.

Though only a slight adjustment, the maneuver worked, and the new course helped avoid a possible upset. With no time to enjoy relief, John watched for every action of the sea he could interpret, doing his best to anticipate the best place to point the bow while still managing a proper course toward where he hoped the steamer would be.

The lifeboat lurched and listed, bounded and scudded, leaped and crashed. The women and children on board were huddled in a frozen heap of saturated bodies. They desperately clung to the thwarts. Some clasped the legs of the lifeboat men, who sat at their stations rowing hard.

"To leeward she waits!" shouted one of the men at the oars.

The instant it took for John to pan his eyes to locate the *Aid* was all it took to miss the narrow window of opportunity to properly position for the arrival of the next cross sea. Before he knew it, a flood of icy water shoved aboard and beat upon the passengers and crew. It flowed past them as a great rushing river, and it seemed endless. "Hold on!"

The level rose across their chests, shoulders, and necks. It was ice cold. The tiny craft suddenly sprang up, and the water drained away.

John shivered, chilled to the marrow. Off to the side and not far ahead John saw the welcome sight of a lantern light. "Ho! The *Aid*!"

The captain had positioned the steamer athwart the seas in such a way to act as a barrier reef, breaking the surf and offering the lifeboat a fair chance.

John understood. He guided the lifeboat alongside the steamer, and the crew accomplished a tenuous alignment side by side. The wind alternately wrenched the two vessels apart and crushed them together. The ships rolled and pitched, bobbed and plunged, in stormy dissonance.

"Alert, John!" the steamer captain shouted. "We'll be stove!"

"We'll not be!" John shouted.

"Alert, I say! Sheer her well!"

John surveyed the situation. He knew they would have to again time the rising and falling of the two vessels, but in reverse. "Be ready men! Little time, there is!"

The lifeboat lifted, and the men fairly tossed the women, who clutched their infants, into the arms of Jack Davis and his father. Many momentarily hung over the side until they were quickly pulled aboard and cast to the deck.

John had no idea how much time it took, but he stood amazed when all were safe. He ordered sail and they veered back toward the Sands. He turned to his men. Their heads hung low and their arms hung loosely over their oars.

"Are you up to it, men? Have you anything left?"

Jack Davis helped the women and children to the cabin, where all of them fell to the floor, weeping and exhausted. They cried to his father, the steamer's captain, for their loved ones who remained stranded upon the Goodwin. Suddenly, the steamer jerked, and everyone toppled to one side.

The captain struggled to his feet and called his son. "We cannot take much more of this, the risk is too great. We must seriously consider leaving."

Back at Ramsgate pier, Arthur whirled like a flag in the wind. He stared out to sea but saw nothing. There was blackness of sky as the partial moon had long ago been obliterated from sight. There was no more sight of rockets or flares and no moving lanterns that he could spot. Henry stood near him, the two of them as still as gravestones.

"It's been almost three hours," Arthur said.

"Aye."

The beat of horse hooves and a carriage brake needing grease broke Arthur's concentration.

"Henry!" the Reverend called.

The two men turned and saw Rev. Gilmore and his wife atop their buggy. Behind them, the harbormaster and a few others approached.

The Reverend got out of his carriage. "Henry. Hello, Arthur. Henry, have you seen any sign of them?"

"Not a glint," Henry said, tense and shivering.

The harbormaster arrived. "I don't like seeing so many grave faces."

The group stood huddled. Puffs of mist wafted from their

mouths around their heads. They stood with their hands stuffed into their pockets, their shoulders hunched, and their feet shifting. They stared into the dark.

"Then we wait," Mrs. Gilmore said.

"And pray," the Reverend said.

"Aye," Henry said. "Jesus walked on water, isn't that what you say, Reverend?"

"That's right," Rev. Gilmore said. He placed his hand on Henry's shoulder.

Arthur growled. "Lukin's boat isn't Jesus."

Everyone stared to sea. Coats flapped and the wind howled.

The Reverend spoke gently, "No, it's not. But it might be an ark like Noah built. I'm sure our Lord would approve of that."

"I'd say," Henry said, his voice rising. "Look!"

"Look!" Mrs. Gilmore said. "A light!"

Arthur grabbed Henry's arm and squeezed it hard. His voice cracked as he spoke, "I don't believe it!"

"Glory to God!" the Reverend shouted.

Word spread quickly that lights had been spotted. Other townspeople arrived at the harbor.

As the lights neared, the sight became increasingly clear. The steamer *Aid* rammed through the choppy water, lit by lanterns all around her rail. She was heavily laden with groups of people: men, women, and children. The people onboard the steamer waved and cheered and received the same in reply. Towed behind them, with lanterns being held up at both ends, was the lifeboat. As the two-vessel fleet clawed into the harbor, the emotions foamed over more profusely than the sea.

It seemed to Arthur like a great military conquest was being celebrated, if judged by the frenzy of the adoring crowd and the strong emotion within his own heart. Flares were lit and waved, gunpowder was shot off, and men hooted while women screamed with joy. Tears of happiness flowed as copiously as the high tide. Men flew flags to match those flying from the masts of the two boats, indicating success and that the work was done.

At final count, there were 120 beaming faces glowing from the deck of the *Aid*. Each of them smiled or laughed and together created such a spirit of goodwill that Arthur later couldn't remember if any of the infants had cried or fussed. It felt like a dream as the vessels pulled up to the pier and were at last made secure.

Henry was among the first to greet the steamer. "You haven't been so heavily freighted since the tourists in summer!" he shouted to her captain.

"Nay, not even then," the captain said, shining with pride.

As the boats debarked, the survivors beamed as if they had stars in their faces though they moved weakly up the steps to the pier. They had obviously been through a horrifying experience and were exhausted, cold, and hungry, but also deeply grateful. Arthur couldn't deny that.

Some were not completely clothed and were wrapped in blankets. All of them shivered. There were young women, pregnant women, women with infants, elderly women, men, boys, and youths.

Arthur watched as Lionel, Edward, John, and the rest of the lifeboat crew debarked. They were showered with hugs and kisses, and hailed as heroes. The rescued made such a ruckus of cheering and singing that many folks who lived close to the harbor were awakened and came to their windows to watch the spectacle in disbelief.

Over the next few days, word of the rescue continued to travel across the coastal communities and neighboring countryside. It became clear that accommodations would have to be made for the shipwreck victims, and Arthur saw locals volunteering their homes and food and blankets and beds and warm fires as the spirit of the hour took hold. Charity abounded in Ramsgate as never before.

In the following days, Arthur sat at the bar thinking. He gnawed his lip and stroked his mustache. Ramsgate had become something different, something new. It was more cheerful and robust. The weather made peace for a brief time and permitted many from the surrounding areas to come and touch the lifeboat, sit in its honorable seats, practice swinging the tiller, and marvel at its unique design. Rumor grew that it was unsinkable. It was being proclaimed as a gift for all mariners who sailed in her realm.

"You're sure taking your time with your mug," Cannon said.

"Huh?" Arthur asked, looking up.

"Your mug, it's still full."

"You pushing me, Cannon?"

"Forget it. I was just saying, that's all."

Arthur picked up his mug but didn't drink. In his mind he saw the lifeboat crew telling and retelling their tale. Of course, as Arthur had suspected he might, Lionel Lukin had beamed through it all. Many lives had been saved; none had been lost. Families that would have otherwise known the most tragic of losses had been spared and reunited.

As Arthur sat brooding, Henry arrived and took a seat beside him.

"Rum?" Cannon asked Henry.

"Beer," Henry replied. He turned to Arthur. "How fares your day, mate?"

"Fine. Yours?"

"It's a sweet holiday this year, don't you think?"

"It's caution I'd advise," Arthur said.

Arthur's mind drifted to something he'd heard concerning the Reverend since the rescue. Apparently, the holy man viewed what had happened as some sort of miracle of faith and an inspiration of God's will in men, or something like that. That thinking was proving pretty popular among the locals and, Arthur had heard, it was a big part of the Reverend's most recent sermon.

"Well?" Henry asked.

"Well what?"

"Are you losing your mind? Didn't you hear anything I've said?"

Arthur stood up and tossed money on the bar. "I'll lose whatever I want to lose."

"What?" Henry asked, his eyebrows pinching together. "What's snagging your bottom?"

"Leave me be," Arthur said, already several steps away.

CHAPTER 15

Lionel and Rev. Gilmore strolled down King Street toward the market. They walked past the cobbler, the sign letterer, and the pamphlet house.

"G'day, Reverend," the constable said, twirling his stick and sauntering up the center of the street. "G'day, Mr. Lukin. We've our rescuing to do, heh?"

"Rescuing only a leg of lamb today," Lionel said cheerily.

The constable laughed. "I'm certain the lamb sees it differently."

A short plump woman emerged from her flower shop. "A good Christmas holiday we're havin', Lionel, not to mention all the others havin' one at all thanks to our noble boat!" She clasped her hands together and rolled her eyes upwards. "God knows it, Reverend."

"True, He does," the Reverend said.

Lionel was enjoying winter and the approaching Christmas holiday in a spirit of friendship quite unlike any he had previously known. It was empty of his wife and son, and they could not be replaced, but it was filled with new friends and the knowledge of having saved so many. Though he still had his dark days, he was having bright ones presently.

"You'd think the whole town had been in the boat with you," the Reverend said.

"It is a healthy pride, I think."

Across the street, the keeper of the hardware store rapped on his display window from inside his shop. He draped the holiday garland over his arm and waved. The men returned the greeting.

"I saw a sign in the lumberyard promoting timber from the same lot you purchased from for the lifeboat," Rev. Gilmore said. "I think folks are buying it more as souvenirs than for repairs."

Lionel smiled.

"You did the impossible, Lionel. You and the crew triumphed over the sea. I'll not forget it. It's worth writing down," the Reverend said.

"You think so, huh? What would you write?"

"Not hard to imagine. I'd write something like, 'Many a good man will now be plucked from death to be yet the joy and support of loved ones.'"

"Impressive," Lionel said.

"I'd write more. I'd say, 'Many a man, unfitted to meet death, will now be snatched from its jaws to live to repent and to seek that peace which he had formerly disregarded.' What do you think?"

"Sounds like it's written by a Ramsgate reverend," Lionel said, laughing.

"And what, pray tell, is the difference between a Ramsgate reverend and a reverend in general?"

"Hmm, good question. Can I have some time to think about it?"

"Take all you need," Rev. Gilmore said, patting his friend on the back.

They reached the market just in time to hear a group of Christmas carolers. People were singing and rejoicing and spreading holiday cheer.

"They're out weeks early this year," the Reverend said. "They don't usually turn out until the week of Christmas. I guess everyone's a little happier these days."

The men crossed the street and milled through the open market stalls. Many of the items were pickled, but the meats were fresh and the breads filled the air with the smell of warm dough.

Lionel lifted up a shank of lamb and smelled it. It was rank. "I think not," he said as he placed it down.

"We can't have everything, can we?" the Reverend said. He crossed to another table and waved Lionel over.

"Calf's livers. The missus sure does know what to do with these."

"Do you think the men will like them?"

"It's a celebration lunch. They'll enjoy anything. Trust me."

"I defer," Lionel said, holding his nose.

"Uh, let's look a little more," Rev. Gilmore said.

They finally settled on chicken, lemon creams, and almond candies and headed home.

Since the rescue, Mrs. Gilmore had been as excited as a farmer with a bumper crop and as grateful as a fisherman with swollen nets. She had been moved to tears by the rescuing episode and inspired to play new songs upon her piano.

"We will feast well tomorrow, we will," she said.

"How may we assist?" Lionel asked.

"Rest for this evening," she replied. "Nothing more."

Lionel noticed that the Reverend had moved down the hall and was already disappearing into his study. Lionel followed him and stood in the entrance to the Reverend's favorite chamber. "Might I be of any further service to you?"

The Reverend whirled around. He held a quill in his hand, and his journal was open on his desk. "Come in! No, I am well attended. I thought I would just jot down what I told you earlier."

"Very well. However, I think I will retire for a nap. I wish to be well rested for tomorrow, and I find I'm still aching some."

"I understand. You're not alone. The others say they are feeling muscles they didn't know they had."

"Quite," Lionel said, excusing himself from the study.

The following afternoon came and the lifeboat crew arrived for a celebration lunch. Mrs. Gilmore, along with some kitchen help, had the meal well prepared in advance. She offered to play the piano to begin their party. She played well, though Lionel did not recognize the song as something he had yet heard her play.

John said, "Your music makes me want not to dance but to run and run well."

"Like your husband's preaching lately," Jeffery said. "There seems to be the force of a hurricane in your melodies, even the warmth of a nip of rum."

A chorus of clearing throats made Lionel smile and the Reverend laugh. Mrs. Gilmore arose and returned with a young lady from the kitchen. Together they distributed punch and cream-topped hot chocolates.

The day continued in a warm spirit, fueled by crispy drumsticks of chicken, buttery potatoes, and jellied breads. One sailor further pressed his point on the subject of rum when prompted by Mrs. Gilmore for an elaboration of a story he had earlier begun to tell regarding their now-famous rescue.

"What did you do then?" Mrs. Gilmore asked.

The man stopped midsentence, his eyes danced a brief jig, and he smiled. "Why, we handed the jar of rum all around, for we were almost beaten to death."

Mrs. Gilmore opened her mouth in surprise, and the man roared with laughter at their secret being told.

"I'm sure that's not true," Mrs. Gilmore said, doubting him well. "With the seas running over the boat and the boat full of water, it would have been saltwater grog very soon."

"Nay, we managed it, ma'am," he said with a wink, and then he looked to the others who had been there. With a vigorous nod, he added, "Whenever a lull came upon us, a man took a nip. Then if there was a cry, 'Look out! A sea!' he would put the jar down between his legs, shove his thumb in the hole, hold onto the thwart with his other arm, and then bend well over the jar to let the sea break on his back!"

The men shouted with laughter. Mrs. Gilmore offered a disbelieving smile and shook her head in playful manner.

Jeffery spoke up. "It was just like a fire engine was playing upon our backs, not in a steady stream, but with a great burst of water at every pump."

"Aye," John said, "at times the boat was so overrun by broken water and surf that we could scarcely breathe."

"Regardless the cold," Edward said, "we were thoroughly warm at our work. We felt like lions, as if nothing could stop us."

"You mean you felt like warriors, don't you?" Lionel asked with a chuckle.

"Warriors?" Mrs. Gilmore asked.

Edward picked up another piece of chicken and bit into it. He smiled broadly as he chewed.

"Yes, storm warriors!" Lionel said. "That's what the captain of the schooner said we were."

The men laughed proudly, and several of them repeated the phrase. "Storm warriors. Yes, that is what to call the brave boatmen of Ramsgate!"

"I like that," Rev. Gilmore said. "It sure beats the *storm pirates* of old."

"For sure!" the men said.

The Reverend stood up with his teacup raised in toast.

"Here comes another sermon!" Jeffery said.

Some clanked their cups and chattered their encouragement for the Reverend's toast.

"No, no sermon tonight, boys. But, as you know, there is some business to attend to." He glanced in Lionel's direction.

The men nodded and settled into silence. The Reverend looked to John, who stood up and raised his teacup. "Aye!"

"Lionel," the Reverend said, "we've something we want to say to you."

"Before we get to the surprise business that all of you know about," John began but then looked at Lionel. "Well, that *most* of you know about. There is some news that none of you yet know that I would like to share."

John reached inside his waistcoat and pulled a letter from his shirt pocket. "I have here a letter dispatched with all haste from the captain of the schooner whose crew and passengers we rescued."

He produced spectacles and rested them on his nose. "The letter reads,

> *'Dear Ramsgate Rescuers,*
> *I do believe your actions in the early morn of that*
> *cold winter day to be unrivaled. Therefore, we beg*
> *to return a vote of thanks to you, dear sirs, who have*
> *everything in such order for the rescue of life. May*

*the Lord bless you all, and look over you, whenever
you again try with uttermost effort to rescue your
fellow seafarers from watery graves. I cannot express
my feelings good enough but will endeavor to do so
in public press after I once again am settled. I con-
clude as your grateful friend, Captain and Master,
William Forman, formerly of the lost schooner,
Tradition.*"

Everyone sat still. Finally, someone started clapping, and the
rest joined in. The men cheered and patted each other on the
backs.

At length the Reverend motioned for their attention. "The
missus and I—"

"Aye! Let's hear it for the missus and those fine cork coats!" said
the man who had started all the jesting about rum.

The men cheered Mrs. Gilmore with so much gusto that the
Reverend could only join in with a laugh. "Hip, hip, hurrah!" they
said, repeating it several times. Mrs. Gilmore blushed and waved
them down with her hanky.

"Mrs. Gilmore and I," the Reverend said, "are pleased to join
with all of you to offer Mr. Lukin a very special gift with our gratitude." He again raised his teacup and looked directly at Lionel.
"God saw fit to wash you upon our shore as a gift of life to us and
others. Therefore, we salute your courage, your wisdom, and your
determination. We are all the better for it. May God bless you, dear
friend of the shipwrecked."

The men stood and cheered for a long time. Lionel absorbed it
all. His felt his eyes well up. He nodded and mouthed his appreciation to the Reverend and the others. Mrs. Gilmore reached under
the table and pulled out a small package that she handed to him.

He was impressed with how well she had hid it up to now. He opened the package.

It was a captain's cap.

"Put it on," Edward said.

The other men egged him on, and Lionel placed the cap squarely atop his head. The men cheered and then shocked Lionel by picking him up, thrusting him upon their shoulders, and marching him outside.

"Aw, come on now, mates! Put me down!" he said, laughing.

They marched him, with the Gilmores following, all the way to the carriage barn. Two of the men swung open the doors to reveal a surprise inside. With the buggy and wagon missing, the barn was filled instead with transport of a different kind.

Positioned in the center of the barn was a brand-new fishing smack. The name LUKIN COACH was painted across its bow.

"What?" Lionel said, incredulous. "Are you kidding?"

"We all pitched in," Jeffery said.

"She's for fishing," John said, "not lifeboating!"

The men set Lionel upon his feet. He took a few careful steps toward his new boat, admiring it. "It's . . . it's grand. I don't know what to say."

"Everyone in Ramsgate has a boat in their family somewhere," Edward said. "This is our way of saying that you're family here, mate. Welcome to Ramsgate, and here's to hoping you'll be planning to stay."

The men surrounded Lionel and patted him on the back. He was speechless as he approached the boat for a closer look. He allowed his tears to fall overboard and roll down his cheeks.

The next day, Lionel and Edward took the boat out—not to scout the Sands or scour the Channel in search of the wrecked—just to scamper about in Lionel's new smack. They began their playful excursion in Pegwell Bay, messing about close enough to shore to see the caves and western cliffs. Edward shared the local history of Roman soldiers, bootleggers, smugglers, fishermen, and farmers.

Lionel was relaxed, spontaneous in his responses, and positive. The two men enjoyed the cold but sunny day and managed the waters well.

At Lionel's urging, they agreed Edward would man the tiller and direct his friend on how to properly trim the sails. There was only one mast, but it carried a mainsail and a jib. Together they did figure eights in the water, tacked against the wind, sailed down-wind, and rode out a stretch with wind abeam.

Later, they put the boat into the headwind so that everything went slack. The sails fluttered and the chains rattled.

"This is called putting the boat in *irons*," Edward explained. "It's usually not done intentionally as it pretty much leaves you helpless. Learning how to get out of it is a good drill."

They practiced their escape from the irons working only with tiller and jib, no oars.

By midafternoon they had sailed clear around the North Foreland to Margate Roads. There they noticed the first signs of approaching weather. The sky was darkening at the edges, and long wisps of cloud were streaking across it. They turned about and headed back to Ramsgate, taking it easy, enjoying a brisk but smooth sail. Handling the boat proved easy enough for one of them to work it alone.

"We wanted to get you something that you could take out by yourself should you want," Edward said.

"It is a magnificent boat. She sails well."

"Would you feel comfortable taking her out alone?"

"I think so, yes."

"Here," Edward said, offering the tiller to Lionel.

Lionel took Edward's place while his friend sat on the starboard side of the mainmast looking ahead. Lionel held the tiller firmly but pushed it forward and back to feel the helm. The small craft responded well, and they bounded toward home. Behind them the weather continued to form and threatened to give chase.

"We're a few hours ahead of the weather and about an hour to harbor," Edward said.

Lionel was glad for the time they were enjoying. He wanted to steer the conversation to some uncharted places. "Do you have a girl?" he asked at last.

Edward spun around. "What's that? The wind."

"A girl? I've never seen you with a girl."

"Oh," Edward said, his smile fading. "No." He turned back to the front.

Lionel had hoped for more but respected the silence. They sped along, the air fresh and salty.

Slowly, Edward turned back. "I was married once."

Lionel tried not to look surprised. "I didn't know." A small wave splashed over the bow. He felt the cool mist on his face.

"She cooked for the Gilmores," Edward said, staring at the bulwarks. "Did they mention it to you?"

"Never," Lionel said. "But I should have known a swell mate like you would've been married. Surely, those wavy locks and blue eyes must have some appeal." He smiled. "I was wondering if there were any women around beyond the Hogger twins."

"Even they're gone, so far as I can tell," Edward said with a laugh.

"Where is your wife now?"

Edward looked at him before answering. "She's gone, mate."

"She left?" Lionel released a little more sail and slightly pushed the tiller to port.

"She died at the Gilmores', actually," Edward said, shaking his head. "In the same room you sleep in. She . . . well, *we* were going to have a baby but—" He stared again at the bulwark. "They both died."

Lionel looked out to sea. "They never told me."

"They're good people, the Gilmores."

"Yes," Lionel said. "I'm sorry if I brought up a sour subject. I guess we both know something about loss."

Edward offered a weak smile. "I don't expect neither of us like it much."

"Not much at all."

The remainder of the trip was quiet except for the splashes, the increasing gusts of wind, and the occasional flapping sail.

As he and Edward tied up to the eastern pier, Lionel was shocked to recognize the meaty hand that reached to catch his bowline. He had seen that hand before. He had felt it slam against his face. He had felt it bury into his stomach. He looked up at Arthur Perkins, who stared at him hard. His massive forearm was extended and his hand open. The large man didn't say a word, didn't even smile, but Lionel held out the line and Arthur made it secure.

"Smart sailing," Arthur said at last. "You managed well ahead of the weather."

Lionel could think of nothing to say. He stood dumbly in the boat.

"Take my word for it," Arthur said, "big storms are coming. I can smell them. Do you smell it?" Arthur breathed deeply.

Lionel shook his head.

"Take my word for it." Arthur nodded to his brother. "Edward."

"Arthur," Edward said, returning the nod.

Arthur walked away without looking back. Lionel looked at Edward, who shrugged.

CHAPTER 16

"The dry spell is over. Finally, she's making her case."

Tom Hardwell spoke to Arthur and the rest of those in the pub.

"Aye," John Burton said. "She'll have her way. She always does."

"She's suffered a black eye and won't take it again!" Tom continued.

Arthur peered through the weather doors toward the harbor. The waters were leaping higher than before, and a deepening shadow crept over the sea. Hardwell's meaning was not lost. The last few days courted a predictable turn of weather.

"Payback for bright skies in winter is always heavy," Arthur said. "The calm has died."

"She'll have her way," John said again.

Arthur and John weren't talking to each other as much as they used to, but Arthur was glad to see him back in the pub. The bad winter weather of late, which Arthur had so accurately foreseen, had stopped most of the lifeboat crew from continuing visits at the Gilmores'. It was too much to trudge up to Albion Place in such deep snow.

Despite the unrelenting storm, now three days old, Cannon's was open for business. There were no wagons or buggies and hardly a horse to be seen. There were no carolers.

"It was a lucky catch," Henry said, referring to the rescue, "like finding a pearl. But it's the tempest now, and who can bear it?"

On these points, Arthur found himself to be in agreement with most of the men — even Tom. "She's come back with her vengeance to let us know the meaning of fate."

The squalls had turned to heavy, constant snowfall about one day in and hadn't stopped for another two days. The temperatures had dropped to near zero and it was too cold, too snowy, and too icy to be moving on land or sea. The harbor looked like a snow-laden forest of masts and lines. If not for the violence of the frosty-edged broken waters, it would have appeared tranquil and sleepy.

"Undeniable," Arthur said, crossing to the bar. "She's undeniable, she is."

"Aye," the men agreed in weary unison. They raised their mugs of ale and glasses of whiskey high into the air and drank their fearful respects to the sea.

The doors banged open. Lionel and Edward stood in the entrance, black slickers flapping but for the parts pressed tight by their cork vests. The brims of their rain hats, like their shoulders, were dusted with freshly fallen snow.

"Rockets," Lionel said.

"From the Goodwin," Edward added.

Arthur stood up so quickly his bar stool fell over. "No," he said firmly. "This storm is too great."

"Too great for whoever is on the Sands," Lionel said, "but not for us."

"Be there storm warriors in this place?" Edward asked.

John stood up. "Aye."

Arthur felt his authority slipping away. His bottom lip slipped forward. He gritted his teeth. Another stool slid back. Arthur looked to see who had stood, and his mouth opened.

"Only two weeks 'til Christmas," Tom Hardwell said. "We ought to get them home in time. If you'll have me, I'm in."

The men rushed out. Arthur heard their muffled shouting from the snow-filled streets. It was only Cannon, Henry, and himself who remained. He crossed to the modified grappling hook on the wall and recovered his winter cloak. He walked outside, still pulling on his hat and mittens.

Men were running from their flats to join others gathered at the launch. Lionel, Edward, John, Jeffery, Tom, and four others from the first rescue boarded the boat.

"Let's help them launch," Henry said, stepping beside Arthur.

"I can't," Arthur said.

"Right, mate. I understand," Henry said, "But I can. I think I should." He crossed the street and jogged toward the launch.

"Where's Henry going?" Cannon asked, joining Arthur.

Arthur watched silently as Henry and others helped launch the boat.

In the harbor, emerging in the midst of swirling snow and flying spray, young Jack Davis and his father piloted the steamer to tow the lifeboat past the point and toward the Sands. They had barely left the harbor entrance when Arthur lost sight of them. Despite Cannon's efforts to get him to come inside, Arthur remained standing in front of the pub. After nearly an hour he returned to the bar and ordered a drink.

"Did you say *rum*?" Cannon asked.

"You heard me," Arthur said. "It's cold out there."

"It's warmer in here," Cannon said, pouring the liquor into a tall glass.

Arthur threw coins on the bar and took his drink outside. He stood at the entrance for some time then headed toward the pier.

He turned right on Old Military Road.

"Arthur!" Henry called out, still hanging around with others near the launch.

Arthur ignored him and trudged to the western pier. The snow was wet and his boots didn't grip as well as he liked. It reminded him that Lionel claimed them as his.

He walked to the end of the pier and stood at the base of the lighthouse, peering into the storm. Seaward, he saw nothing but swirling white and heard nothing but slurping seas. Behind him, a heavy door opened.

"Arthur? Is that you?" the lighthouse keeper asked. "Come in here. It's warmer. You can watch from here."

Arthur took a gulp of rum and entered the lighthouse.

"Edward is in the boat?" the lighthouse keeper asked.

Arthur nodded, his jaw flexing.

"I understand. Sit there. I'll make sure this light stays bright, don't doubt it."

Arthur nursed his rum and stared through the lighthouse window.

"Here's a spyglass. If you want it, I'll set it here."

Arthur ignored the offer and leaned forward, his elbows resting on the edge of the window. He held his glass an inch away from his mouth. He sipped, and sat, and stared. He sipped some more. He stared and shifted. Hours passed, and his eyes grew heavy and his breathing deep. He lowered his face into the crook of his arms and closed his eyes.

"Arthur!" the lighthouse keeper proclaimed, startling him awake. "Behold the sight!"

Arthur's head felt too heavy to lift. He dropped his glass, and it fell to glance off his boot. He was surprised the glass was empty.

"Hoist your head!" the lighthouse keeper said. "Look!"

Arthur rolled his head to the side, peering through the window. He sat up straight.

Emerging from the snowy gale was the steamer and, behind it, Lukin's quirky boat. The lifeboat's crew looked like snowmen at the oars. He quickly counted heads and determined it a full crew. They glided past him as the *Aid* towed them in. Arthur stood up, crushing the empty glass underneath his boot.

"They be lookin' like angels, eh, Arthur?" the lighthouse keeper asked with a smack and a whistle.

Arthur stormed down the lighthouse steps, leapt into the cold, and ran onto the western pier.

"Edward?"

A lifeboat man in the bow of the craft turned and looked at Arthur. He was covered in snow but waved a large gloved hand. "Ahoy, Arthur!" Edward shouted.

Arthur's shoulders dropped and his arms hung loose. He raised his arm and offered a slight wave. Aboard the *Aid* he saw about a dozen sailors he didn't know. They were wrapped in blankets and waving to him. Arthur slowly lowered his hand and barely nodded.

❧

Lionel appreciated the accolades that came when they returned with this new load of shipwreck survivors, but he didn't have time to enjoy them. None of them did.

The weather would calm sufficiently to coax captains to continue their journeys, and then would suddenly turn and hijack them all, slamming many into coasts and rocks and reefs. Though the Reverend emphasized how grateful the mayor and other notables were and how much they wanted to do something formal for Lionel and his crew, they couldn't take any time to bask in the glow of warm praises. The wretched conditions persisted and rescues continued—daily for a full week. The lifeboat men, though admired as bold and gallant, were perpetually exhausted and cold.

A pamphlet was published and wires were sent far and wide, all hailing the historic week. The original letter from the grateful captain of the *Tradition* was published in the local papers. Stories were told of how the lifeboat endured the most grueling experiences at sea. The Reverend wrote in the local flyer,

> And the sea coasts where the Storm Warriors
> gather these days tell a tale of hardihood, of
> courage, and of endurance and skill, no less than
> any older days could boast of. But now courage
> is made clearer to include hardihood and mercy.
> Endurance and skill are quickened into action by
> the noblest of feelings, even a readiness for self-
> sacrifice, which can move the heart of almost any
> man.
>
> And as more guns do fire and rockets flash,
> these warriors of the Storm reply; their flashing
> lights promise of coming rescue, and do not lure
> to destruction; for as the gallant lifeboat men rush
> into all danger, making every effort, battling with
> mad waves and boiling surf, they fight under the
> noble banner of mercy, with a mission to save.

Sailors from neighboring ports came to watch the lifeboat as it launched to sea. They stood in the heaviest of weather giving their fullest attention, trying to follow the path of its storm-tossed lights. The bow and stern lanterns had been added to their equipment list, though rarely was a rescue completed without the lights being washed out. Then darkness added to the peril as they rolled and pitched, since most of the rescues took place at night.

Most significant was the dawning realization in the minds of ordinary people that the hazardous Sands could be replied to. It was no longer a deathtrap impossible to resist. They had long since admitted that ships couldn't simply avoid the Goodwin by knowing its general location, since storm and tide often dragged ships into its deadly grip. After all, over the years, thousands of vessels had been wrecked with no hope. But now, all at once, there was a chance.

Finally an evening came when no rockets fired. Lionel lay atop his bed listening to the crackling fire. He knew he needed to return to London soon. A wire had arrived detailing Pennington's success in making the sale at Dover. The coach had already been delivered, but the shop desperately needed his return. He thought after Christmas to be a good time. He'd start his new life in the New Year, without Alicia and without Luke.

His body ached and his mind was tired. He had focused so intensely during each rescue that, even atop his bed, he felt himself to be within the lifeboat. When he closed his eyes, he would see everything just as it happened, though he wasn't clear anymore about which rescue was which. The Reverend had him repeat the details so often that it never ceased playing in his mind. Gilmore loved writing it all down in his journal, but to Lionel it was all one exhausting blur, wonderful though it was.

He thought of the Goodwin Sands. He had seen its many moods. It foamed along its edge like a rabid animal lusting for battle.

One rescue had involved a brig wedged deeply upon the Sands. Her hull had been in the wash of breakers. The masts had angled sideways and become nearly tangled with the lines of the lifeboat. Snow fell in clumps and the entire scene looked like an ice sculpture doomed to be a monument to the death of them all. Men clamored and cut, hoisted and rowed, shouted and strained — until the rescue was complete and all were saved.

During one rescue, the lifeboat had been swamped. A rogue wave taller than the mainmast of a clipper ship sprang up from an unexpected direction and capsized them. Not one remained in the inverted boat, but to each was fastened a lifeline. When the boat flipped upright, each climbed back in. Miraculously, no one was lost.

In another instance, the lifeboat ran under the lee of a sand-stuck vessel and got too near the toppled ship. This time the ship's yardarms locked horns with the lifeboat's forestay, holding the mainmast in place. The timber of the mast creaked. The ocean hissed and the wind moaned. The shipwrecked vessel started to draw back with the action of the sea and threatened to rip the mast off of the lifeboat. But Edward, quick-thinking as always, cut the entangled lines with a ready hatchet and saved them in the nick of time. The action spared them the loss of their mast and sent them gliding away from the wreck, to come at it again minutes later.

Lionel sat up in his bed. He was proud of his lifeboat men. He found it difficult to remember how he could have doubted them as he had in the beginning. Each day a rocket fired or a flaming tar barrel shone, and never once did the Ramsgate Storm Warriors refuse the call. Day after day they had given no quarter. Everyone had been saved.

They had learned much too. They had grasped how to place multiple anchors in ways that helped them claw back to a wreck. It was monstrously hard, and their muscles froze and strained, yet they did it well. They had learned how to handle the hawsers with precision, sheering and veering in short order.

Lionel crossed to the window and leaned on the sill. He looked toward the Sands—hoping to find them deserted. They were. He looked next toward the harbor, though it couldn't be seen from this vantage, and his smile grew.

He recalled how the quayside had become a regular place for celebration, comfort, and glad tears. Men, women, and children were daily or nightly ferried to shore, weary and wet, to be greeted with applause and welcomed into warm homes. The Ramsgate residents had developed a system for serving hot broths, distributing blankets, and offering beds. Many aspects were still unaddressed, but times were improving, and people hugged and wept and praised the lifeboat men. Some expressed their gratitude with gifts of money, insisting in a manner that made refusing impossible.

The Reverend and Mrs. Gilmore did much to provide organized assistance and comfort. Other ministers and town officials were involved. It was becoming clear to all that it was actually possible to save the lost. What had once been seen as the invincible way of the sea was now being trumped by the light in men.

At least that's what Henry says the Reverend says, Lionel mused, smiling at the thought.

The next day Lionel heard a rooster crow and woke up with a start. He sat up quickly, thinking a rescue was in demand, but there was no alarm. The orange light of morning grew stronger as it streamed through his window. He got up and dressed. He and the Reverend planned to snowshoe to the eastern cliff, weather permitting.

Weather permitted, and they reached the cliff at noon—but not by snowshoe. They rode out to the edge on horseback, and while their horses foraged across wind-bared patches of ground behind them, the two men stared out to sea. They moved lazily, both in a reflective mood. A moderate wind fluttered Lionel's hair and flapped his overcoat collars. The sea beneath them, though choppy, was vast and sparkling. The Sands glistened like a sunny beach welcoming a picnic or a swim.

"Sometimes," Lionel said, slow and relaxed, "I feel like most of my true life has never taken place but for one stretch of time atop that narrow strip of sand when my family was stolen away."

"I can only imagine how painful that memory is," Rev. Gilmore said gently. "But this thing I know, you've helped spare others such pain."

"Yet I am ashamed, and guilt punishes me."

"Ashamed? You have nothing to be ashamed of, only glad and proud of. What are you ashamed about? Not having saved them? You could not."

"No, that's not it. Ashamed that I never thought of saving others until my own family was lost," Lionel sighed. "It makes me wonder. If I had previously been mindful of the trials of others, might my own family have been spared? Must it be that only by suffering personal tragedy will a man at last be moved to answer the cries around him?"

CHAPTER 17

"Hurry, mates!" Edward said, his voice tense.

The weather had changed again. A terrific Christmas storm seized the coast in an icy grip. Edward stood in the lifeboat atop the launch ramp, calling to the crew. Other boatmen arrived in response to the call for a midnight rescue.

John Burton and his son rushed out of their home just a few doors up the street from Cannon's Pub. Edward was relieved to see them. John had proved to be the best tiller man among them, and Edward preferred working at the bow with Lionel. Edward watched the Burtons pull up their oilskin breeches and slip on their cork vests while running to the launch. Tom Hardwell also arrived.

"Get in," Edward said.

The steamer captain and his son, Jack, floated nearby in the *Aid*, ready to tow and ferry.

The horizon was stormblack except for the faint glow of a blazing tar barrel flickering through wisps of fog. The night was bitter cold, the winds prevailing from the northeast, and the snow had been falling heavily for most of the day. Such conditions meant anything could be happening at the Sands, and probably everything was.

"Ready?" Edward asked.

The men were tired but resolute.

"Aye!" John said, climbing into the coxswain position at the rear of the boat.

"Aye!" Lionel answered, slipping in beside Edward.

"Aye!" the others shouted from their seats at the oars.

"Ho!" a voice bellowed from the beach.

Edward turned to see who it was. It was his brother. Arthur came alongside the boat and gripped the gunwale. Henry came up on the other side.

"Not now, Arthur," Edward said. "We've got to go."

"There'll be hell to pay tonight," Arthur said in gritty tone.

"It's a good boat," Edward said. "She'll take it well."

"Aye!" Arthur said. "She'll dish it out herself, she will."

Edward looked at his brother, astonished.

Arthur and Henry pulled out the restraining timbers, and the boat rattled down the ramp and splashed into the harbor.

Edward saluted. "Keep the coffee hot, Arthur."

The *Aid* tossed a hawser and began to tow the lifeboat out to sea. Edward watched his brother along the shore. Arthur hadn't moved from his position near the launch. He was still standing there when the shore lanterns disappeared into the dark and Edward could no longer make out the beach. He faced the bow to watch the lantern lights of the *Aid* as they navigated toward the Sands. Jack Davis waved from the steamer.

The seas broke fiercely over the boat. The men twisted lifelines around their arms and made their cork vests secure. Edward knew what it was to be thrown clear of the boat. It had happened to most of them in every attempt so far. Everyone wished to avoid it because the water was brutally cold. This night would be no exception. Part of the price they would likely pay would be a swift flushing from their ark of safety into a sea determined to feed them to the fish.

"We're not ignorant of your schemes," Edward said.

"Huh?" Lionel asked.

"Talking to the sea."

"Aye."

Edward respected the sea—and feared it, too. His brother would be glad of that. "Not much difference between them, really."

"What?" Lionel asked. "You talking to me or the sea?"

"I think respect is like a healthy fear," Edward said. "What do you think?"

"What do you mean?"

"The sea invents new ways to cheat, and there always seems a new twist of wind to blow. It pays to be mindful."

"Aye," Lionel said. "Be prepared for things we didn't prepare for."

Edward had heard Lionel say that before. The first time he'd said it, no one had gotten it, but, after several experiences, they all understood it too well. There was no telling what would actually happen out there, and the most one could do was not be surprised when it did.

He remembered something the Reverend had said, too. Edward had said that their rescues displayed something *brave* since it was daring to confront the unknown for the good it might accomplish. Lionel had called it courage. But the Reverend had named it love.

"We must love it, or else we wouldn't be doing it," Edward said aloud.

"What's that?" Lionel asked.

Edward shook his head, laughing. "I don't know what it is—fear, respect, or love!"

"What do you mean?"

"Why we do what we do."

Lionel pointed off the starboard quarter. "That's why."

The light of the signal fire lit up the faces of a small crew of desperate men. The vessel was a small schooner with a high stern. She was totally dismasted.

"Release hawser!" Jack Davis yelled from the steamer.

Edward unfastened it. It was time.

"Ready in the bow?" John shouted.

"Aye! Aye!" Edward replied.

"Ready all?"

"All ready," the men answered.

"Up main and mizzen!"

The sails were raised and the lifeboat sped along. It cut through the ravenous waves that leapt upon her. Edward grinned. The brave boat would have none of it. It rose triumphant and sailed on. They plunged forward on a big wave and immediately saw the vessel a few fathoms away.

"Over with the anchor, down with the mainsail," John said. "Keep up the mizzen. Let the boat sheer. Ready oars!"

They saw the fitful blaze of the tar barrel. Edward recognized it to be the Dutch-made, 170-ton galliot that he had watched during the afternoon. "Aye! She was earlier today in a perilous position in the Gull Stream, making very bad weather of it," he informed his fellow rescuers. "She's a coal carrier and should sit heavy here."

Edward surveyed the wreck and caught the gleam of the pale faces of the Dutch crew, who were clinging to the gunwale. As the lifeboat veered in close, Edward could hear their excitement.

"It is a boat—of a sort!" one of the sailors said in English.

"Veer out cable!" John shouted.

Jeffery let many fathoms of cable run out, but just as they expected to be in perfect position, the wreck moved farther from them.

"What's this?" John shouted.

Edward watched the wreck closely. "The tide is much higher than usual. Look at the long lengths of chain-cable dragging over her bows. She's drifting over the top of the Sands. With the gale and the rush of this tide she drifts faster than we're able to veer."

"Very well," John said. "Hold on the cable, men. The wreck is drifting. We must up anchor. To it, my men, as hard and fast as you can."

Wild seas raged over the boat. It was bow to the seas, making it an especially rough ride for Lionel and Edward. They met each wave with full force.

The lifeboat wrenched and jerked at the cable with a power that threatened to tear her to pieces. Several men helped Jeffery lay hold of the cable. They clung to the boat with their legs around the thwarts. They wrapped the hawser a couple of turns around a timber head.

A huge wave passed, and the boat dropped in the trough of the sea. The boat fell and the strain of the cable lessened.

"Haul!" John yelled. "With heart, men, haul!"

They wrapped a fathom or two of cable in when the curling crest of a broken wave fell. It smothered the men and filled the boat. The lifeboat drooped and staggered under the weight of water. The men clung to the thwarts and were again up to their necks. Quickly the boat lifted, the valves in the floor opened, and it emptied itself in a few seconds.

The next wave caught them under the bows and threw the boat high into the night air. The men clung to the hawser for a breathless moment. The wave broke over the boat in a cloud of spray and foam, and then the boat dropped. The men shook their heads free of the water and frantically gasped for air.

John shouted again. "Haul, haul, your hardest, my men! Hand over hand!"

They got in a few more feet of the strong rope, and neared their anchor. They held on with strained muscles for another dread struggle with the next huge sea. There was hardly time for a few quick breaths and the sea came again, gushing and foaming along. It gleamed out of the darkness and leapt upon them.

"She's near, men," Lionel urged. "A few more yanks."

At last the cable was shortened; another pull and the boat moved right over the anchor. She lifted on a sea, and the anchor was torn from its hold. They quickly made in with it and hoisted the sails. John brought the boat around. They again headed for the wreck.

They ran before the wind. The men were exhausted. They took these few minutes to rest. One man pulled up the bottle of rum and passed it around even as he had once described to Mrs. Gilmore.

Edward examined the sailors aboard the wreck. With their shattered vessel shuddering and sinking beneath their feet, the ship-wrecked Dutchmen clung to the rigging as the storm blew from behind. One of them pointed as the lifeboat again came near.

Their captain cupped his hands and shouted to the lifeboat. "Be as quick as you can! We are sinking fast!" As he spoke his ship's deck became almost level with the surface of the water. He climbed atop the chart house with his crew.

The lifeboat ran alongside, and her crew threw grappling irons. They caught in the gunwale of the wreck. The boatmen took turns with the lines around the thwarts and began to haul the boat slowly up to the wreck. It was hazardous work because the small ship was heavily weighted with a cargo of coal and was full of much water.

The lifeboat lifted up on the crest of a towering wave. There was tremendous strain upon the stout grappling lines, and then a moment's lull in the rush of the broken water.

"Haul in hard upon the lines," John commanded. "Get her

alongside, now. Sharp, my men!" Then he yelled to the schooner's crew. "Be ready to jump when we are near enough!"

"Aye!" the captain shouted.

The Dutch crew crouched, ready to spring upon the gunwale and into the lifeboat.

"Be ready, all! Be ready, all!" John cried as he tried to sheer the boat near enough for the men to jump on board. "Now! Now!—Wait!"

A towering breaker swept in fast. It loomed over them like a dark mountain falling onto them. It blotted out the moon.

"Hold on," Edward shouted. "Hold on for all your lives!"

The breaker crashed upon them, deluging the boat with foam and spray.

The grappling lines snapped like threads.

The lifeboat was swept away in the rush of waves.

Behind them, in the glare of the signal fire, Edward saw the despairing Dutchmen aboard the sinking ship. He heard the cries of the poor fellows penetrating the tumult of the storm.

But again the lifeboat righted itself and shed water out the scuppers.

"Have ropes ready!" Lionel yelled with hoarse voice to the Dutch captain.

"Yes! Ropes ready!" Edward shouted.

The swirl of the sea and the force of the gale drove the lifeboat far to leeward. The men hoisted sails again, heaved her to, and tried to stay her. They made in directly for the wreck.

They were exceedingly weary, yet they again ran the boat close under the galliot's port quarter. The sailors were ready with ropes. They threw one on board, and the men in the boat succeeded in throwing two strong lines in return. Once more John gave the order to haul in close alongside.

Another heavy sea came foaming along. It broke across the boat and filled it. It rushed over the ship too, which staggered under its weight. The ropes jerked and wrenched but held. The rescue boat lifted and cleared of water.

"Jump when we near!" Edward cried to the crew. "Jump for it!"

"Jump!" Lionel added. "Do not lose a chance!"

Suddenly, the sea threw the boat closer, and all the Dutchmen fell hard. They scrambled to their feet and jumped onto the lifeboat.

The next rush of sea swept the boat away and buried them all in foam. The sea overran the boat and the crew clung to the Dutch sailors who had sprung on board. Their grip—and only their grip—kept the sailors from being washed out.

"Have we got all?" John asked.

The sailors looked around gratefully, but their looks turned to shock. "No, only four. One is left! The captain!"

"Look out, then, my men," John called. "Up we go again!"

They lifted and neared to make out the figure of a man at the stern of the vessel. Edward yelled to him. "Be ready! It is your chance. You must jump for your life."

The captain lay on the shattered roof of the chart house. "My leg is broken!" he shouted. "I can't make it!"

The lifeboat sank again, tremendously straining the lines. The storm warriors exchanged glances. Edward stood as the boat rose on a sea. "I'll go!"

"No," Lionel said. "I'll go."

Edward smiled at him, unhooking his lifeline. "Not this time, mate."

Using the momentum of the upsurge, he leapt. He sailed over the bulwarks and landed hard on the slippery deck of the doomed wreck.

He hurried toward the crippled captain, dragging him off the shattered roof and across the deck. Waters swirled about the man, choking him and making him cough. Edward shucked off his vest and fastened it to the captain. He dragged him to the rail.

The lifeboat sank down. The lines strained, ready to snap.

Edward lifted the captain over the side, despite the man's screams of pain.

The lifeboat rose, and Edward passed the injured man into the arms of the boatmen. They lowered him to the floor of the lifeboat.

Another tremendous wave crashed into the galliot, and then another, and then several in quick succession. Edward hugged the rail, waiting for his chance.

The lifeboat plunged and rocked wildly in the tumult of the waves. One of the ropes broke. Another gave the next moment. The lifeboat rose on the crest of a wave, and heeled away, the third rope snapping under the strain. The lifeboat was swept under the stern of the Dutch ship.

Edward ran along the rail, his boots sloshing across the deck. The dying tar barrel washed directly in front of him, tripping him onto the dousing flame. He clawed up a rail post and balanced himself on the barely visible gunwale. He crouched.

The lifeboat lifted upon the rolling sea. Lionel reached out from the bow. "Jump!"

It was the right moment. Edward jumped with all his strength.

He hit the bow of the lifeboat and felt Lionel's hand.

Then the hand yanked back and the lifeboat swirled away.

"Man overboard!"

Lionel saw Edward sink low, and a huge wave rolled over him. The lifeboat bore farther away. "I couldn't hold him! Edward!"

He seized a lifebuoy and jumped upon a thwart, but a blast of wind tumbled him down into the bottom of the boat. He peered over the side.

Edward swam hard. He made good progress without his cork vest, but just as he neared them, the lifeboat suddenly drove away faster than he could swim.

Lionel saw him stroking wildly, splashing with his feet and arms. He plunged and groped and grasped at the boat but caught nothing except wave and wind. Edward lifted high on the crest of a wave. He tumbled backwards and disappeared.

"No!" Lionel cried.

He threw the lifebuoy with all his strength to where he had last seen his friend. It sailed into the stormy darkness and vanished.

Lionel stretched forth from the boat, reaching out across the water, nearly falling out.

"Seize him!" John ordered.

Others grabbed Lionel by the waist and pulled him back into the boat.

"Edward!" Lionel shouted. He struggled to be free from their grip, but they held him fast.

Eerily, Edward's figure appeared once more as he sprang up on the top of a wave, clinging to the buoy. All at once Edward was lost to the darkness.

"No!" Lionel screamed. "*Edward!*"

He tried to jump in after the struggling man, but the others forced him to the floor of the boat. John fell atop him. "He's in the stream-reach! There's nothing we can do."

"No, no, no! Edward!"

"Lionel," John yelled, "we'll all be lost. Get ahold of yourself!"

Tears streamed down Lionel's face. The echo of the storm pulsed in his ears like the faintly heard riot of a distant angry mob.

"It can't be," Lionel sobbed. "No."

⁗

At the pier, Arthur and many others waited to welcome the returning storm warriors and assist them with the survivors the flying mast flags declared were aboard.

"That's a happy sight," Henry said.

"Aye," Arthur said, looking at the approaching vessels. "It's getting to become common, it is."

"No, not common at all," Henry said with a chuckle. "I meant your face. You upped anchor on your frown, mate. Dare I call it a smile?"

"Call it what you will," Arthur said.

"How about a miracle?"

Arthur purposely raised his eyebrows and looked at his friend.

"Just a joke," Henry said.

With cheers and smiles of welcome from hundreds of faces, the lifeboat men were well received as they arrived at the pier.

"Ah! Geordie, man," the wounded Dutch captain said to his mate, as several carried him off of the lifeboat. "That was a queer sort of sailing. That boat sailed underwater altogether."

Arthur smiled. It did seem that way. It was a very odd boat.

"Let's help," Arthur said.

Arthur assisted the debarking of the steamer. The Dutch sailors were lighthearted and expressing many thanks. Arthur thought it strange the lifeboat men stood huddled at the lifeboat. He hoped no one was hurt. He crossed over to it.

237

He first saw the downcast face of his old friend, John Burton. He saw Jeffery still seated at the oars, hunched over with his face in his hands. He looked at Lionel, lying in the bottom of the boat.

"What's wrong with him?" Arthur asked.

Tom stepped out of the boat and placed a hand on Arthur's shoulder. "I'm sorry, Arthur. I really am."

"Sorry for what?" He searched the crew. Sudden pain stabbed his chest. "Where's Edward?"

No one met his eye.

Arthur spun around to look down the pier at the group of rescued sailors, then up toward the rail of the steamer, and then back in the lifeboat. "Where's my brother?" he asked, his voice breaking.

"John, where's Edward?" Henry asked.

John's chin quivered and he shook his head. "Gone."

Arthur's eyes stung. "Gone?"

"Storm-reach," John said.

Arthur fell to his knees at the edge of the pier. His body heaved and he wailed into the storm.

CHAPTER 18

Lionel stood alongside his lifeboat, his hand upon the gunwale. It was evening. Three days after the tragedy and two days before Christmas. He was in deep thought. He heard a mild commotion behind him in the direction of the pub, but he didn't react to it.

Suddenly, the wagon wheel that had been hanging in the pub came rolling across the street. It glanced off the launch ramp and rolled crookedly into the harbor waters.

Arthur staggered toward him, bleary-eyed and unsteady. Lionel backed up and squared off. Arthur stood close, face-to-face.

"I'm sorry, Arthur," Lionel said.

Arthur stared back, his face trembling.

"I don't even know what to say," Lionel said, lowering his eyes.

"I do!" Arthur said.

Lionel's belly caved from the punch, bending him over with a grunt. Arthur followed up with a two-handed hammering to his back, knocking him to the ground. *You killed my brother!*" Arthur screamed, swaying over him. "You *and* your grand schemes."

Lionel struggled to all fours, but Arthur kicked him in the jaw. Lionel sprawled backwards onto the sand. Arthur grabbed him by the collar and dragged him to the water's edge.

"I'm going to drown you the way you drowned him."

"I never wanted that," Lionel said. "I never wanted that to happen."

"I raised that boy," Arthur said, dropping him at the water's edge. "He was my brother, but he was like my son. You know why, Mr. Landsman Lukin? Because we lost our parents and a brother when I was but a boy and Edward just a swaddler. You know how we lost them?" Arthur asked through clenched teeth. He towed Lionel to deeper water.

Lionel struggled feebly with the vicelike hands at his throat. He gulped for air. Arthur dunked him and held him under and then yanked him up.

"They drowned! They perished at sea in a winter storm. Many watched it from the end of this very pier. And want as I would," Arthur said, his voice rising, "*I could not save them!*"

He dunked Lionel again and shook him violently while holding him under.

Lionel broke free and rushed up for air. He sloshed away from Arthur and massaged his throat. His breath was raspy.

Arthur stood knee-deep in the surf, looking out at the harbor as if seeing something there.

"My older brother and I watched it all from the end of the pier. I insisted we go out to save them. He was smarter than me and said it was impossible, but I talked him into it. That's right, I talked him into it. Together, he and I went." A sob broke through, but Arthur quickly stifled it. "We were rolled over soon enough. We didn't even make the point. I didn't just lose my parents. I lost my big brother."

Arthur stared at Lionel, his eyes red and his cheeks shaking. He waded closer.

"I promised myself I would take care of my baby brother, and that I would keep him safe—and alive!" Arthur stopped and wailed. "I could not even do that!"

He lunged at Lionel and caught him by the collar, slamming his meaty fist into Lionel's chin.

Lionel fell beneath the surface again. His face throbbed with pain. Arthur dragged him back to shore and slugged him one more time. He fell upon the edge of the beach.

"I'm going to save your worthless, miserable piece of life," Arthur said, seething. "You know why? Because I want you to know what it feels like to drown. Drown in the misery—every day—of knowing you've saved *no one*!"

Arthur kicked him in the ribs and staggered away.

Lionel lay beaten and bruised on the beach. He moaned as he rolled over onto his back and stared at the cloud-streaked sky. He remembered the morning he had washed up from the wreck of the *Sanctus*. He wondered if he had cheated death. He lay there wondering that for a long time.

Then he decided he didn't want to cheat it anymore.

The next morning, Lionel awoke beside the lifeboat. He boarded his fishing smack, headed around the point, and sailed toward the Goodwin Sands. His face was bruised and swollen, and his eyes felt glazed.

It was one of those days when the sandy strip appeared as a beach, and he soon landed his boat. He clambered out and trudged his way to the highest point. There he dropped to his knees and sobbed.

He flopped over to lie upon the sand. With his cheek buried, he squeezed his eyes shut. His body convulsed, and he was glad for it. He felt he should suffer the fate of his days.

He didn't know how long he cried and shook, but it finally subsided. He wanted to sleep.

He looked to his boat. It had grounded on the sand but was now lifting from the rising tide and floating away. So what.

Around him the tide rose, and the circle of safety began to draw tighter as the Sands slowly disappeared under the strengthening current and unceasing rollers.

He didn't care.

⨌

In town the sky was darkening as storm clouds rolled in from the north. There was a smattering of activity on the docks, but most people were turning in, as the weather was about to change for the worse.

On Old Military Road, Reverend Gilmore helped his wife out of the carriage. "I can't find him anywhere."

"You looking for Lionel?" John Burton asked as he approached, his son trailing behind.

"Yes," the Reverend said. "He left the house last night and never returned. Perhaps he's at the cliff. I know he goes there sometimes."

"His smack is gone," John said. "Gone early, too. It wasn't there when Jeff and I went out this morning."

"Did he tell anyone where he was going?" Mrs. Gilmore asked. "You don't think he might have tried to go back to London, do you?"

"In the smack? I think not," John said. "You might ask Henry. Maybe he knows something. Lionel said nothing to me."

"He's taking Edward's loss real bad," Jeffery said.

"I know," Rev. Gilmore said. "We all are. It's a peculiar time."

"Doesn't feel much like Christmastime, does it?" John asked.

The sun quickly darkened as clouds rolled over, casting a shadow upon the group.

"It's definitely wintertime," Rev. Gilmore said. "I hope wherever he is that he knows enough to head in soon."

A gust of wind blasted by, nearly blowing Mrs. Gilmore's hat off.

"We best secure the boat, son," John said.

The noise of galloping hooves drew their attention.

"Is that a coach?" Mrs. Gilmore asked.

"Aye," Jeffery said.

A horse-drawn coach galloped hard into town from the country roads and made a hearty run toward Cannon's.

"It looks like a Lukin coach," the Reverend said.

Jeffery nodded. "It's a fine-looking carriage."

The coach clattered to a rapid stop. The sky was darkening and the day suddenly seemed more like dusk as a light mist of rain began to fall. The Reverend grabbed an umbrella and escorted his wife to the coach. John and Jeffery followed.

※

Arthur and Henry, mugs in hand, led a group out from the pub.

"A Lukin coach," Arthur said for all to hear, noticing the approaching Gilmores and others. "The wheel wasn't enough; now we've got to have the whole blasted carriage." He spat.

The coach driver opened the carriage door and helped a passenger step out. To their wonder, there, dressed in fine clothes and with face beaming, stood Edward.

Arthur dropped his mug, his mouth agape.

"Dear God! Edward!" Mrs. Gilmore exclaimed.

"Praise God, hallelujah, and glory to the heavens!" the Reverend said.

"Eddie!" Jeffery shouted, running to embrace him.

"Lord!" John said. "I don't believe it!"

"No! Not the Lord, but I," an exuberant Edward said. "But, like Him, raised from the dead, that's certain."

A cloudburst opened and a heavy downpour fell, but nobody ran for cover.

Arthur stuttered, "Ed-Ed-ward? Can it be?"

Edward stepped forward and embraced his brother. Arthur sobbed and squeezed him hard. Edward grunted out a laugh, "Believe it, Arthur, but be gentle. I'm not yet ascended."

The Reverend and Mrs. Gilmore laughed and wept.

"But . . . but how?" Arthur asked, still holding his brother firmly.

"By the strong arm of Lionel Lukin," Edward said.

He turned toward the inside of the coach. A woman's arm extended from within and handed him the lifebuoy that Lionel had tossed to him at sea. Edward took hold of it and held up the ring for all to see.

"They wanted to throw this back into the sea as some sort of grateful sacrifice for having snatched and saved my life, but I would have none of it. If not for this ring and the gracious, if superstitious, crew of a certain Belgian hoveller, I'd be in the belly of some fish for sure."

"A hoveller?" Arthur asked, still not altogether following.

"Yes," Edward said. "A hoveller with a ship's log you'll weep to read. Though we've never known, she often stands along the stream-reach, as far out as offshore Calais, some many miles away."

"France?" John asked.

"Oui!" Edward said, laughing. "You've not imagined what she

finds when the storm currents flow! And, glory! What she finds is precious cargo indeed!" He glanced toward the Lukin coach, but then interrupted himself. "Now tell me, where is the man that threw me this ring? The maker of this fine coach that today carries more than his name?"

A foghorn interrupted them. They all turned to see the steamer *Aid* heading into port, the captain and his son at the helm. They were towing Lionel's smack, *LUKIN COACH*.

The captain saw the crowd in front of Cannon's and shouted through cuffed hands, "Adrift alone! No sailor aboard! We seen a lonesome upon the Sands. Too rough for my ship to get near enough. 'Tis the man Lukin, I say!"

The Reverend's heart sank. "Lionel?"

"No, no," Arthur said, stepping toward the harbor. "This is my doing."

"What?" Edward demanded.

Arthur bolted toward the sea. The rain poured down upon his face. "But it will yet be undone." He turned back toward all. "Be there storm warriors here?"

CHAPTER 19

Edward saw Lionel Lukin standing at the highest part of the Goodwin. He was within a small remaining circle of dry sand. Around him the shoal was alive with sucking quicksand. The ridges upon the Goodwin had been shaped to be two and three feet high from the deadly currents that raged in a contest of wind, foam, and torrent.

Edward sat in the first row near the bow of the lifeboat as it rode over the chopping waters near the Sands. Facing the stern, he could see those seated aft. Among them were Tom Hardwell, Jeffery Burton, Jack Davis, and John Gilmore. John Burton sat at the tiller. They were all dressed in oilskins and cork jackets. Edward turned and looked at the two men in front, Arthur and Henry.

Arthur gripped the sides, his knuckles white.

The lifeboat rode in fast. It beached hard at the edge of the Sands thirty feet from where Lionel stood. Tips and ridges of sand stood between them like islands only sometimes visible in the rising tide.

Lionel hadn't seen them. He appeared resigned and unafraid. His head was tilted down toward the waters encircling his feet. It had been raining, but snow flurries were falling now, making Lionel appear as a lone figure within a child's snowglobe.

Lionel raised his arms and tilted high his chin, as if yielding to the fury around him, as if wanting to be swallowed by the thunderous waves.

Edward fired a flare to burst above. Startled, Lionel opened his eyes and saw them. Arthur rose from out of the bow and plodded calf deep through the sea-drenched sand toward him. His boots made a sucking sound as he stepped through the quickening sand.

"I am in hell," Lionel said.

Arthur laughed. He took Lionel by the shoulders and pointed him to the lifeboat bobbing just a few feet away. "You are not in hell," Arthur said. "You are among lifeboat men."

"Storm warriors!" Edward said, standing up. "Of your making!"

Lionel's eyes widened, and his mouth dropped open. "Edward?" He suddenly seemed to need Arthur's help to keep from falling. "I am dreaming, or I have gone mad."

The water was now at their knees.

Edward reached out his hand, swirling snow all around him, the surf thunderous and deafening. "It's me, Lionel. I'm shipshape! But we must go!"

The Reverend rose to appear beside him, and the others all beckoned him to board. "Let us cast off, son," Rev. Gilmore said. "We'll tell you all about it."

"Am I in heaven?" Lionel asked.

"We must hurry, Lukin," Arthur said, working hard to advance another step closer.

Lionel looked at Arthur. "Hell?"

"We'll soon enough find out," Arthur said, "if we're not quick to get in the boat!"

Lionel appeared confused. He tried to back away but was stuck as the waters churned around him. The seas rose to his thighs.

Arthur reached for him, but Lionel pushed him away.

"No! There'll be no more cheating. I am ready." Tears streamed down Lionel's face.

"Arthur!" John Burton yelled. "There is no time!"

"Lionel," Arthur said, "I'm sorry to have to do this again."

He spun Lionel around and belted him in the jaw then caught him as he collapsed in the water. After struggling to lift the groggy man out of the surf and sand, Arthur finally threw Lionel over his shoulder and slogged toward the lifeboat.

"The sand is difficult to walk on! It feels like quicksand gripping my boots."

"A line," Edward yelled. "We need a line."

Henry grabbed a rope from the bottom of the boat and tossed it to Arthur. "She's secure."

It was strenuous work as Arthur pulled along the rope, each step harder than the last as the waters rapidly rose above his waist. He finally reached the boat and handed Lionel to the others, who pulled him in.

"Get in," Edward said.

"I'm stuck," Arthur said. "Go without me."

"Never!"

They rushed the bow and grabbed every part of Arthur that could be grabbed.

"Heave!" John said. "Heave!"

With a giant sucking sound, Arthur's legs broke free from the quicksand, and he fell hard into the boat, his stocking feet pointing high in the air.

"What the—" Arthur said. "I've lost my boots."

The Reverend laughed unexpectedly. "Well, Arthur, they weren't yours anyway."

"Aye," Arthur said with a laugh. "Aye."

"I hate to break up the party," John said, "but she's ridging. We may all be lost."

"We must attempt them," Arthur said, sobering fast.

"No. Impossible," Edward said. "We'll be thumped to pieces. We'll get caught in the squeezebox."

"The gale, she comes in from the sea," Arthur said, in command of himself again. "We'll have no chance in her teeth. We must follow her miserable breath, whatever the route."

"I don't know," Edward said.

Tom pushed forward between them. "I never thought I'd say this, but I agree with Arthur. It's the only chance we've got now. If we have any at all."

"We try for Trinity Bay," Arthur said. "Just like I taught you in the pub, eh, Tom? We'll have time to rest there and, well, you know the tale."

"Aye, Arthur," Tom said. "It is our best chance."

"God help us," Edward said.

The Reverend leaned forward. "He will."

"Anybody bring the secret weapon?" Arthur said, winking.

Jeffery held up a bailing bowl.

"Good, son," Arthur said.

Edward looked at the seas running high. They curled and broke as the crest of each wave was caught by the fierce wind and dispersed into a cloud of spray. "Then let us try."

The lifeboat continually skimmed on steep and numerous ridges, sweeping with the tide from one ridge to the next atop long waves. Lionel moaned in the belly of the boat.

"It's not too bad," Tom yelled.

The lifeboat swung around in a swirl of crossseas and suddenly thumped and jerked heavily, and then grounded between two ridges.

"This is a fix," Edward said.

"Arthur!" John yelled. "Any ideas?"

"Hold tight, that's all."

"Oars? Sail?" John asked.

"Oars as levers. Foresail alone. But only if the bow is head first upon a ridge," Arthur shouted.

"Aye."

The wind raged in concert with the Sands and waters until the peril was almost too much to be borne. The men beat and grubbed their boat over the Sands. They spun around and around, grounding every few yards with a jerk that bruised. No sooner would they wash off one ridge and begin to hope that the boat was clear than she thumped upon another harder than ever. The wash of the surf nearly carried them out of the boat each time.

Edward looked to the Reverend and Lionel. Holding onto Lionel made it impossible for the Reverend to hold fast to the boat. It was good they were in the middle of the boat where it wasn't as rough as at the bow. "Reverend? Are you able to stay put?"

"I am secure," he said.

As if on cue, the boat rolled and the Reverend was thrown off his seat and forced to release Lionel, who fell again to the bottom of the boat. Edward lunged for Lionel. Lionel slammed against the bottom and was jarred awake. Edward fell atop him just as a wave soaked the crew. It receded and flowed through the scuppers. Edward clawed to his hands and knees and looked down at Lionel.

"It's going to be all right, mate," Edward said with a large smile. "Just hold on to something."

"Edward?" Lionel said, his brow furrowed. "How?"

The boat pitched and Edward flew back toward the bow. He landed on his back. He saw the Reverend lying nearby, his head cut and bleeding. "Reverend, can you hear me?"

"I'm well," the Reverend said, touching his head. "Only a little cut."

"We're beating and thumping over the Sands, almost yard by yard," Edward explained. "I don't think it has ever been done, and may yet remain undone."

They were lifted high, swirled to the left, and then swung to the right and slammed down hard.

Something cracked.

Snow twisted like a tornado through the boat, freezing Edward's face. His eyelashes felt like splinters.

"Can we—" The Reverend's mouth continued moving, but Edward couldn't hear him.

"Say again?" Edward shouted above the wind and spray.

"Can we make it?" the Reverend yelled.

"If the boat can take it," Edward shouted. "She's been striking rough. If she holds, we may yet see Ramsgate, supposing we escape any monster rogues."

"What?" the Reverend yelled.

"Rogue waves!"

The boat hurled forward and reversed direction with a terrible yank from a blasting wind. "Ho!" Arthur shouted.

"We ride the tempest tonight!" Henry yelled.

Edward and his mates held on as they beat from sand ridge to sand ridge.

Then came three loud cracks.

"She's breaking up!" Tom cried.

"No!" John said. "She holds together!"

Edward saw the three splintered oars along the port side and was glad that was all that had broken.

"I hope we don't get afoul of any old wrecks," John said.

Edward looked up and thought he saw a huge galleon suddenly towering above them in the swirling snow and about to crush them. Then it was gone. "My mind is tricking now."

"Only now?" Lionel asked shakily, crawling to his friend's side.

"Lionel!" Edward said with another grand smile. "If I've lived only to die rescuing you, it is right with my soul. But live we will! Glad tidings for y——"

The boat suddenly writhed, almost on beam ends, and the waves beat over until the boat was lifted and thrown forward to crash down and ground again.

"I hope if it ends it ends by swift drowning," Jeffery cried.

The lifeboat tipped severely, the bow angling high to the cloud-covered sky. The stern dipped into the mouth of a wave and water rushed in. Suddenly, the stern burst up and the bow drastically tipped down. Edward braced for the thud and fully expected to be flooded or flipped, but it didn't happen. Nothing happened.

He loosened his grip and looked around. The swinging and beating of the boat had ceased. Though they were still in a heavy sea, the boat made way.

"She's clear!" Arthur yelled.

"She's answering her helm and keeping her head straight!" John said.

Edward was too exhausted to cheer but not too tired to breathe and nod. He noticed the others keeping a firm hold upon the boat, expecting each second another terrible lurch and jerk upon the Sands. He waited for the heavy rush and wash of the seas, but it never came.

"Dear God," Edward said. "We have successfully navigated over the top of the Goodwin Sands, in a storm, in this amazing boat."

Less than an hour later, they found the steamer, who gladly

towed the lifeboat home in the early evening. The steamer captain, relieved to hold his son, said they had been gone for over four hours.

On shore, the sleet was letting up, and though the street was icy and treacherous, many people had gathered to await the arrival of the men. Mrs. Gilmore emerged from a neighboring shop, leading a circle of praying women. She waved to her husband and then to Edward, and he nodded. She entered the pub.

The lifeboat men were greeted with blankets and ushered toward Cannon's. Edward held one of Lionel's arms and guided him through the well-wishers. He recruited Rev. Gilmore to take Lionel's other arm and Arthur to make way in front like a giant plow—in stocking feet.

Lionel reached the sidewalk of the pub, escorted on all sides. Though it was snowing hard, Mrs. Gilmore stepped out and beamed at him.

Lionel saw his coach in the street. "Pennington?"

Edward pulled Lionel under the protection of the awning in front of the pub entrance.

"Edward?" Lionel softly asked, his mind awhirl. "What is happening? How are you here?"

"Dear Lionel," Edward said, speaking slowly and clearly, "you saved me. I caught the ring you so desperately threw. For no small time I held on for hope of life. As God would have his way over a rebellious sea, I met with the changing tide somewhere northeast of the Sands. It sent me southward away from the fatal Goodwin. I went in the direction of Calais for a great distance, cold and exhausted. A large cutter came, a hoveller of a sort, almost alongside. They were kindhearted Belgians—kindhearted like you, my wonderful friend."

"Is Pennington here too?" Lionel said. "My coach was to be in Dover, and yet it is here. And you are here. I don't understand." Lionel saw tears streaming down Mrs. Gilmore's cheeks despite her happy smile.

"The Belgians did all they could to restore me," Edward continued, "and landed me, as they had done for others not long before, at Calais. I was taken to the hospital where I met a nurse whose story—I was shocked to discover—was not unlike my own." Edward choked. Tears rolled down his face.

The Reverend wept. He stood beside Edward.

Edward's voice became husky with emotion. "She did not know from where she had wrecked, and was more than a little confused. But I did know. She had such story to tell. Then we traveled together to Dover and found a most reputable coach, don't you know?"

Lionel shook, trying to comprehend Edward's tale.

Edward sobbed his next words more than spoke them. "Then I understood. 'Twas neither you nor anyone but God who blew me down the reach that I might finish the rescuing you had so earnestly begun. Not only upon the Goodwin, but alas, in the hearts of sailors who had grown cold but now so blazingly burn."

"I am not understanding you," Lionel said, his voice trembling.

"Dear Lionel," Edward said, grasping his friend's shoulders in a bracing grip, "brought here on a coach of your own making does this night come the answer to the ache of your broken heart."

He stepped aside and from inside the pub stepped a woman and a boy.

Alicia and Luke.

"My God! My God! My heart! My precious heart!"

"Daddy!" Luke yelled, running to his father's arms.

Lionel shook, his face flooding with tears.

Alicia drew close and embraced him tightly. "My heart," she whispered. They clung to each other and rocked, dropping down into a huddle in front of Cannon's pub, encircled by the people of Ramsgate.

Lionel sobbed, his body heaving mightily. For a length of time that he would not dare measure, he embraced his family, returned to him in a most miraculous way.

"My wife and my son," he said, his faced pressing against his wife's neck. He sobbed and laughed and kissed them, over and over again.

CHAPTER 20

Lionel received the news of his boots' being buried at the Goodwin as a sign to spend his later days more on land than on sea. He returned with his family to London and resumed his life and work.

But the invention of the lifeboat continued inspiring others beyond his lifetime. The idea spread along the coasts of dear old England in the form of many grand lifeboats and lifeboat stations. They appeared as morning lights that faithfully chased away the fears of night.

In Ramsgate, Reverend Gilmore often returned to the cliff where Lionel had liked to sit. He would take his journal with him and read aloud to the seagulls some of the words he had written, inspired by those earlier days.

There was one passage in particular he loved to read over and over again. He so loved it that even on some winter days he would venture out to the cliff to enjoy a fine view of the Goodwin Sands. He would recite from his journal there, as if he were speaking a sermon:

> I have often thought upon the question asked by
> Lionel atop the cliff that day. I still wonder the
> answer. What does it take to cause one to launch

his or her own vision of rescue in a world where so many are overrun by the various and troubled waters of life?

Rather than letting the lifeboats God has given to each of us to rot and canker upon the banks, while the cries of the despairing and the lost plead in vain from the dark storms and troubled waters at their feet, well would it be if more of us would stand watching the many who are in danger, overrun by the dark troubled waters of life—wrecked in poverty, in misery, in ignorance—wrecked for want of true teaching, true guidance, true sympathy, true love—well would it be if more stewards of God's loans might have the same noble conviction written in upon their hearts: that they have a call to save life! I wonder. Be there Storm Warriors out there?

etc.

bonus content includes:

- ▶ Reader's Guide

- ▶ Author's Note

- ▶ "The Wreckers"

- ▶ Maps

- ▶ A Conversation with Jon Nappa

- ▶ Coming Soon — Book Two in the Storm Warriors Series

READER'S GUIDE

1. What character qualities are necessary to compel a person to risk his or her life to save another?

2. Can personal tragedy change a person? For better or worse? Can you think of an example of each?

3. After fearing his family lost, what were Lionel's feelings toward his wife and son as compared to his feelings for strangers aboard other stranded vessels?

4. Is there a difference between what you're willing to do for your immediate family and what you'd do for a stranger? Why?

5. Besides tragedy, what kinds of experiences or revelations can change how a person lives? What was one such change in your life?

6. In John 13:34, Jesus says, "A new commandment I give you: Love one another. As I have loved you, so you must love one another." What's "new" about this command?

7. How do you know when the "new" kind of love that Jesus spoke about is present and in operation?

8. Why do we sometimes choose not to love?

9. How do we know when there is an absence of love?

10. Read 2 Timothy 1:6-8. What does it take to overcome timidity?

11. Do you know of a situation in which innocent people are suffering? What can be done to alleviate that suffering? How could you become part of that solution?

AUTHOR'S NOTE

Storm Warriors is a work of fiction and should not be viewed as a historically accurate chronology of events. However, like a parable told by Jesus, it is filled with truth.

Historically, it is true that the Reverend John Gilmore did write a wonderful nonfiction book entitled *Storm Warriors*, published in 1875. It chronicled the real-life exploits of the brave boatmen of Ramsgate on the perilous Goodwin Sands.

Although Lukin actually lived before Gilmore, the Reverend credited and admired Lionel Lukin as the true inventor of the lifeboat, especially the unique aspects that included airtight compartments and cork elements. In Gilmore's book, he wondered what might have motivated Lukin to invent the boat that ultimately inspired the designs of those who came after him.

The book you now hold is a tribute to Gilmore's heart and vision as revealed in his original telling. This volume seeks to explore the very question Gilmore asked, since it is a question worth asking ourselves.

Where possible, this fictional account does relate the rescues accurately as they occurred at certain points during Gilmore's lifetime. In some places, no effort was made to try to rephrase some of the much-used nautical expressions that Gilmore himself used, especially when desiring to remain true to certain aspects of historical rescues that actually occurred. Also, where appropriate, Gilmore's words were excerpted in his own voice as a device within the work.

In most places, I took much liberty in crafting a dramatic story that fills in many of the blanks. Timelines, lifetimes, and locations were of necessity merged and significantly condensed in service to the story. In all cases, this work is crafted with a hope and a prayer that the reader will be inspired by the truth it tells and challenged by the question it stirs:

What will it take to launch my lifeboat into the world?

The Reverend John Gilmore used to gather with the Ramsgate lifeboat men around a bowl of punch in his home. They would tell and retell stories of the rescues, and Gilmore would write them all down. He published many as magazine articles but went on to author a book entitled, *Storm Warriors; or Life-Boat Work on the Goodwin Sands.* It was published by MacMillan and Co., London, in 1875. Hereafter follows an excerpt in its original phrasing from his passionate work.

THE WRECKERS

Imagine a homeward-bound vessel some two hundred and fifty years ago, clumsy in build, awkward in rig, little fitted for battling with the gales of our stormy coast, but yet manned with strong stouthearted men, who made their sturdy courage compensate for deficiency of other means; think of many perils overcome, a long weary voyage nearly ended, the crew rejoicing in thoughts of home, of home-love and home-rest, the headlands of dear Old England, loved by her sons no less then, than now, lying a dark line upon the horizon, the night growing apace, the breeze freshening, ever freshening, adding each moment a hoarser swell to the deep murmurs of its swift-following blasts; the ship scudding on, breasting the sea with her bluff bows, rising and pitching with the running waves which cover her with foam!

Look on land! keen eyes have watched the signs of the coming storm, men more greedy than the foulest vulture, "more inhuman than mad dogs," have cast most cruel and wistful glances seaward! yes, their eyes light up with the very light of hell, as they see in the dim distance the white sail of a struggling ship making towards the land!

And now as the night falls, and the storm gathers, two or three ill-looking fellows drop in, say, to a low tavern standing in a by-lane that leads from the cliff to the beach, in some village on our south-western coast—soon muttered hints take form, and in low whispers the men talk over the chances of a wreck this wild night; they remember former gains, they talk over disappointments, when on similar nights of darkness, wildness, and storm, vessels discovered their danger too soon for them, and managed to weather the headlands of the bay.

The plot takes form; with many a deep and muttered curse, the murderous decision is taken, that if a vessel can be trapped to destruction, it shall be.

There is an old man of the party whose brow is furrowed with dread lines; he does not say much, but every now and then his eyes glare, and his features work as if convulsed; his comrades look at him, twice, and as a terrific squall shakes the house, a third time: silently he rises and leaves the inn; his mates now look away from him, as if quite unconscious as to what he is about; their stifled consciences cannot do much for them, but can give to each, just one faint half-realized sensation of shame. Now in the pitch darkness of the night, with bowed head, and faltering steps, battling against the storm, the old man leads a white horse along the edge of the cliff, to the top of the horse's tail a lantern is tied, and the light sways with the movement of the horse, and in its movements seems not unlike the mast-head light of a vessel rocked by the motion of the sea. A whisper has gone through the village, of a chance of something happening during the night, and most of the men and many of the women are on the alert, lurking in the caves beneath the cliff, or sheltered behind jutting pieces of rock.

The vessel makes in steadily for the land; the captain grows uneasy, and fears running into danger; he will put the vessel round, and try and battle his way out to sea.

The look-out man reports a dim light ahead; What kind? and Whither away? He can make out that it is a ship's light, for it is in motion. Yes, she must be a vessel standing on in the same course as that which they are on. It is all safe then, the captain will stand in a little longer; when suddenly in the lull of the storm a hoarse murmur is heard, surely the sound of the sea beating upon the rocks? yes! look, a white gleam upon the water! Breakers ahead! Breakers ahead! Oh! a very knell of doom; the cry rings through the ship, Down, down with the helm, round her to; too late! too late! a crash, a shudder from stem to stern of the stout ship; the shriek of many voices in their agony, green seas sweeping over the vessel, and soon, broken timbers, bales of cargo, and lifeless bodies scattered along the beach, while the shattered remnant of the hull is torn still further to pieces with each in-sweep of the mighty seas, as they roll it to, and fro, among the rocks.

Fearful and crafty the smile that darkened the face of the willing murderer, who was leading the horse with the false light, as he heard the crash of the vessel, and the shrieks of the drowning crew, fearful the smiles that darkened the faces of the men and women waiting on the beach, as they came out from their places, ready to struggle and fight among themselves for any spoil that might come ashore; a homeward-bound ship from the Indies—great good fortune, rich spoil—bale after bale is seized upon by the wreckers, and dragged high upon the beach out of the way of the surf—but see, a sailor clinging to a bit of broken mast, with his last conscious effort he gains a footing on the shore, staggers forward and falls. Is he alive? not now! Why did that fearful woman kneel upon his chest, and cover his mouth with her cloak? Dead men tell no tales! claims no property!

Have such things been possible?

They have, and have been done; traditions of such dread tragedies still linger on the Cornish coast, and it is a matter of history that all around our shores miscreants were to be found, who were ready to sacrifice to their blood-thirsty avarice those whom the rage of water had spared.

Yes, and still many sailors find their worst enemies ashore, and know no danger so great as that of falling into the hands of their fellow-men; but not now in the small harbours or fishing-villages of the coast—not now among the seafaring population of our shores, must wretches capable of such deeds be looked for, but among the degraded quarters of our large maritime towns—among the land-sharks, who haunt the docks, the crimp-houses, the dens of infamy, the low taverns—there Jack may still be wrecked, and drugged, and robbed, and perhaps murdered. But even there darkness has not got all its own way; for if there are many who are ready to ruin the reckless sailor, there are many others, thank God, who are ready to warn and aid him. Seamen's Churches, Bethels, Sailors' Homes, Sailors' Missionaries, and all sorts of benevolent institutions, seek to struggle with, and overcome, the bad effect of the many evils to which the sailor on shore is exposed.

And the sea-coasts where the Storm Warriors now gather tell a tale of hardihood, of courage, of endurance, and of skill, no less than the olden days could boast of. But now courage is glorified by mercy, and hardihood by sympathy, and endurance is sustained, and skill and enterprise are quickened into action by the noblest feelings, and readiness for self-sacrifice, which can move the heart of any man.

If our last pages have been gloomy in the picture they have given of what was frequently done not many generations ago, let us seek a contrast, which shall be as a light to darkness, and compare with those scenes of old, a picture of that which happens month after month, and in the winter season week after week, and sometimes, almost day after day, on our own coasts in the present time.

A homeward-bound ship is rushing along, skimming the green seas, seeming to rejoice in the pride of her beauty, strength, and speed; there is some fatal error or accident, and she comes suddenly to destruction. Many men are anxiously on the look-out; they have been watching her closely from the shore, and eagerly preparing for action at the moment of the shipwreck, which for some time they have feared must happen. And now guns fire, and rockets flash, and the signals quickly given are quickly answered, and the Storm Warriors rush into action; they are not now the Storm Pirates as was the case too often of old, they are the Storm Warriors; their flashing lights tell of coming rescue, and do not lure to destruction; for as the gallant life-boat men rush into all danger, make every effort, battling with mad waves and boiling surf, they fight under the noble banner of Mercy — THEIR MISSION IS TO SAVE.

269

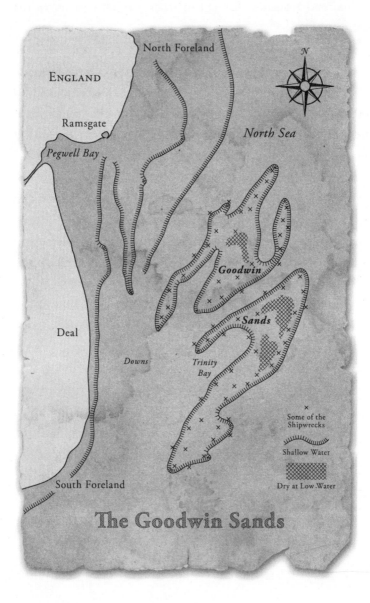

England

North Foreland

North Sea

N

Ramsgate

Pegwell Bay

Goodwin

Deal

Sands

Downs

Trinity
Bay

× Some of the
    Shipwrecks

Shallow Water

Dry at Low Water

South Foreland

The Goodwin Sands

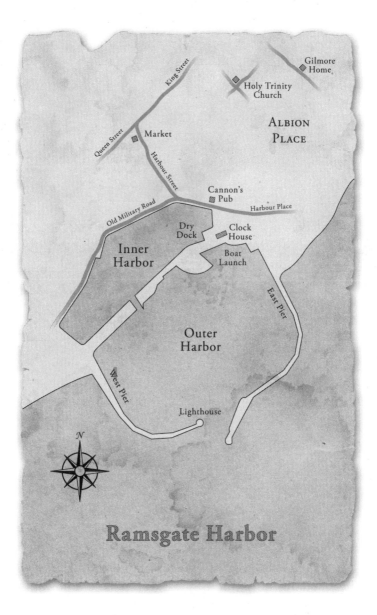

Ramsgate Harbor

A CONVERSATION WITH JON NAPPA

Q: Tell us a little about yourself. Who is Jon Nappa?
A: I've always been interested in story and character. When I was a kid, I used to make up stories with my G.I. Joes and film them with an old Bell & Howell spring-wound 8mm movie camera. Ultimately, this led to a career in writing for media.

As a result, my stories tend to be on the visual side, as I always imagine them from a cinematic perspective. I used to write screenplays for Todd Fisher and Debbie Reynolds and also was a studio manager in Hollywood. My work resulted in a personal invitation to meet with George Lucas at Skywalker Ranch, which was a high point for me.

Nevertheless, modern Hollywood proved unsatisfying to my soul. I longed for the opportunity to write stories that were more fulfilling and, hopefully, would help tip the planet a little bit in the right direction. For me, that meant trying to develop media projects and stories that inspired people toward faith and toward believing they could make a difference. I call it media with a mission.

Initially, this manifested in the form of an award-winning television series for kids, *Pappyland*, which aired for several years on The Learning Channel and many PBS stations.

I also created the *Super Snoopers* project, which was designed to inspire children to navigate the Scriptures on their own.

All of this has brought me to where I am today—focusing almost exclusively on writing adult books, both fiction and non-fiction, aimed straight for the heart. My purpose and prayer is that they will inspire genuine faith and good works. For more information see my website: www.believersjourneyproject.org.

Q: How did you get interested in this story?
A: I frequent old and rare bookstores. On one of those trips, I came across John Gilmore's 1875 book about incredible lifeboat rescues that took place in the nineteenth century off the coast of England.

Since it had been written during that time, it was not stripped down to the barest of words as so much of today's literature is. It was passionate, eloquent, wordy, and moving. Today, his style would be considered tedious and overwritten, but I found subtle distinctions in his rephrasings and parenthetical comments.

Beyond that, he had a most exciting story to tell: rough and ready men who braved the fiercest of elements to save people they'd never met. In light of the heroism of the 9/11 rescuers who lost their lives, such a story seemed important and timely.

I have always loved sailing too but never more than after I completed a media assignment that required sailing across the Atlantic Ocean aboard a 197-foot square-rigger in the middle of November. What an awesome experience! I will never forget it.

Q: How did you arrive at the idea of the historical/fictional hybrid you developed for *Storm Warriors*?
A: In today's world of terrorist acts justified in the name of

faith, it occurred to me how opposite the motives and actions were in the hearts and souls of these lifeboat men. Like the 9/11 rescuers, their faith and conviction led them to risk their own lives in pursuit of a long-shot hope of saving strangers in desperate need. If you take the time to think about that, the contrast is remarkable. Nothing could be more opposite.

Also, in his book, Gilmore wondered what might have motivated Lionel Lukin to invent the lifeboat despite his already prospering trade in land coaches. That question got me thinking: What does it take for any of us to cross the line from the instinct for self-preservation to the place of unconditional love and willingness to die in order to save another?

I chose to use the actual rescues as recorded by Gilmore as a background to explore that question. I wasn't so much interested in historical chronology as I was compelled to dig for the answer. Throughout the journey of writing this book, I believed I was taking the same approach that Jesus might have taken when sharing one of His many parables: telling an earthly story to teach a spiritual truth. I can only hope I came close.

Q: Are there any comparisons between your story and the recent movie hit *The Perfect Storm*?

A: That's an interesting question. I used to joke that *Storm Warriors* was a mix of *Twister* and *The Perfect Storm*. Of course, I was referring to the condition of the weather upon the sea. Both *Storm Warriors* and *The Perfect Storm* provide gripping drama upon wild seas.

However, there is a notable difference. In the movie, also based on a true story, the writers were well-informed about what took place on land during the storm—but they had to speculate about what had happened at sea. In my book, the opposite is true. Thanks to Gilmore having been so faithful in recording the real-life experiences of the rescuers shortly after each rescue was performed, we have a detailed record of what actually happened at sea — but I had to speculate about what happened on land.

Q: Are the Goodwin Sands still a hazard today?
A: Amazingly, they are. Despite being marked by at least three lightships and nearly twenty buoys, the Sands remain a credible threat. First, it is impossible to perfectly chart the Goodwin Sands because they shift. Second, the passage where they lie is the busiest shipping channel in the world.

When I visited Ramsgate while doing research for the book, a local fisherman gave me a ride out to the notorious Goodwin. He remarked that wrecks still occur today but are due to poor seamanship skills more than anything else. With today's advanced weather forecasting and GPS technology, it shouldn't happen, but it does. There are wreck charts from over the years that reveal thousands upon thousands of wrecks along the entire perimeter of the Goodwin Sands.

Q: Does the Goodwin really "give up" old wrecks from time to time?
A: In 1979, a storm stirred the Sands, and out popped a remarkably well-preserved 70-gun warship known as a man-of-war that had wrecked in a terrible storm in 1703. It's eerie. It really is a graveyard.

Q: What is Ramsgate like today?
A: It's a community in transition. It had various times of

prosperity and popularity and was, for a while, a favorite vacation spot in England. Today, with the Euro tunnel and affordable airfare, it has lost that distinction but is intent to rebound.

The older citizens feel a deep pride about their history and heritage while the younger folk long for departure to greater adventures. During one conversation I had with a young shop-keeper, he astounded me with his ignorance of the history of the Goodwin Sands. But the old-timers invited me for a tea and a chat while fetching their own notes and books on the subject.

The inner and outer harbors are still very similar to the way they appeared in Gilmore's time. The clock house is now a museum and contains many interesting items pertaining to the era of first lifeboats. There is a modern lifeboat station equipped with impressive high-speed boats that still apply basic insub-mergible properties first invented by Lukin.

Gilmore's house is gone and Albion Place isn't the land of vast farm fields any longer. Roads and rows of houses fill the surrounding area. But the church of flint still stands as impres-sively as when it was erected.

Q: Where might someone go to learn more about the life-boat cause, Ramsgate, and the rest?
A: These days there is one good answer: the Internet. The really motivated might venture to Canterbury and browse the archives. There are a few good books on the Goodwin Sands too, and you can still find Gilmore's book in fair condition from some rare booksellers.

Q: How familiar did you have to become with nautical terminology to write this book?

A: I have been to sea once and am an emerging fan—this will account to landsmen for my seeming acquaintance with nautical matters; I do not come of a sailor family and I've much to learn—this will explain to sailors the ignorance on such matters that they will not have much difficulty in detecting. Fortunately, this book is really about something more than just sailing or life boating. It's about courage to save.

Q: What's next for you as a writer?

A: Honestly, I'm very excited about my upcoming works. My project roster is full, and I can name the next several books as I hope to see them released. However, it's probably best to sit on most of that information for now.

I can say that there will be a second volume in the STORM WARRIORS series. It will focus on the work and mission of Sir William Hillary, who did much on land and sea to further the cause of helping the wrecked and unfortunate.

Okay, I'll let you peek but only a little. I have in the wings an exciting work on Longfellow that takes place in the same time period as *Storm Warriors*. It focuses more on the remarkable man than his deeply felt poetry. One other series I have in the works features much nautical adventure but in a C. S. Lewis-like fantasy setting. That's it—my lips are now sealed.

etc.

COMING SOON

BOOK TWO IN THE Storm Warriors
SERIES

In the next volume of the STORM WARRIOR series, real-life historical figure Sir William Hillary helps to reinvigorate the lifeboat cause after serious mishaps have stalled its progress.

In addition to personally leading boatmen to rescue the shipwrecked (more than three hundred sailors saved from efforts involving him), Hillary establishes the Royal National Institution for the Preservation of Life from Shipwreck. His rescues read with as much excitement as those you've seen in the first novel, but include much more than action at sea.

Sir William was an orator who advanced the lifeboat cause against heady opposition. His is a story about overcoming resistance and indifference and about the high cost of walking out a vision that offers no profit other than the fulfillment of the call to rescue those in need.

Check out these other great titles from the NavPress fiction line!

The Restorer's Journey

Sharon Hinck
ISBN-13: 978-1-60006-133-2
ISBN-10: 1-60006-133-8

Back in our world with her teenage son, Jake, in tow, suburban mom Susan Mitchell is ready for life as usual. But when a foreign threat invades their comfortable home, Susan and Jake soon find themselves drawn back through the portal to the world of the People of the Verses. Make sure you read the first two in the series, *The Restorer* and *The Restorer's Son*.

Every Good and Perfect Gift

Sharon K. Souza
ISBN-13: 978-1-60006-175-2
ISBN-10: 1-60006-175-3

Every Good and Perfect Gift shares a heartwarming story of friendship that overcomes all odds. Filled with laughter, tears, and everything in between, Gabby and DeeDee's journey will strike a chord with female readers of all ages.

The Reluctant Journey of David Connors

Don Locke
ISBN-13: 978-1-60006-152-3
ISBN-10: 1-60006-152-4

Family man David Connors is standing on the brink of suicide. One week before Christmas, he is burdened by a fractured marriage and a life disconnected from God and family. Yet in his darkest moment, he makes a surprising find: an old carpetbag buried under a snowy ledge. This is an extraordinary novel that features intriguing fantasy, lively dialogue, and a story of emotional power and unexpected humor.

To order copies, visit your local Christian bookstore, call NavPress at
1-800-366-7788, or log on to www.navpress.com.
To locate a Christian bookstore near you, call 1-800-991-7747.